Alma:

The History of My Soul

From Soul Creation

to Soul Destination

by Diana Romerotéllez

Alma: The History of My Soul
From Soul Creation to Soul Destination
by Diana Romerotéllez

Printed in the U.S.A.

ISBN: 9781733690010
LCCN: TXu 2-113-320

Warning and Disclaimer
This is a work of fiction. Names, characters, businesses, places, events, locales, and incidents are either the products of the author's imagination or used in a fictitious manner. Actual persons, living or dead, and events have been changed to protect their identity.

Ishvara Press

To my Master and my Mother, whose Soul I long to return.
To the soul of all animals.

Acknowledgments

Thanks to Lucero de Alba Guitarth for her
valuable comments in reviewing the manuscript
and to John Brakefield for his corrections to the first draft.

To all that served for inspiration
and to seekers of the Truth everywhere.

What this novel is about...

This could be your story. It is the history of a soul from beginning to end (so to speak), at least in this universe. The soul explains what there was before the universe was formed. Alma (the soul) describes how she came into being and what her existence was like before she decided to come down to this material plane, specifically to Earth. She narrates briefly a number of incarnations and her most significant experiences. This being has been entangled by her desires and relationships with others, life after life, and she is finally tired of this game. She wants to go back to the place of her initial origin, the Source. The soul of this story focuses on a particular lifetime, her last, and through her death she learns what needs to happen in order to return to the Source. Her first challenge is to find the right conditions to come one more time, when and where she will be able to get the unique opportunity in hundreds of lifetimes and thousands of years to be liberated from the illusions of the material world that keep her trapped. Her second, and most difficult challenge, is to maintain her goal and not derail, despite worldly temptations, tricks and illusions, and the veil that is placed before all human beings since birth which prevents us from remembering who we really are. If the soul fails, it could take an extremely long time, suffering and despair to get another chance, so it is crucial not to miss it. This is the story of her adventures, battles, searches and missions and the being that accompanies her in the journey to liberation.

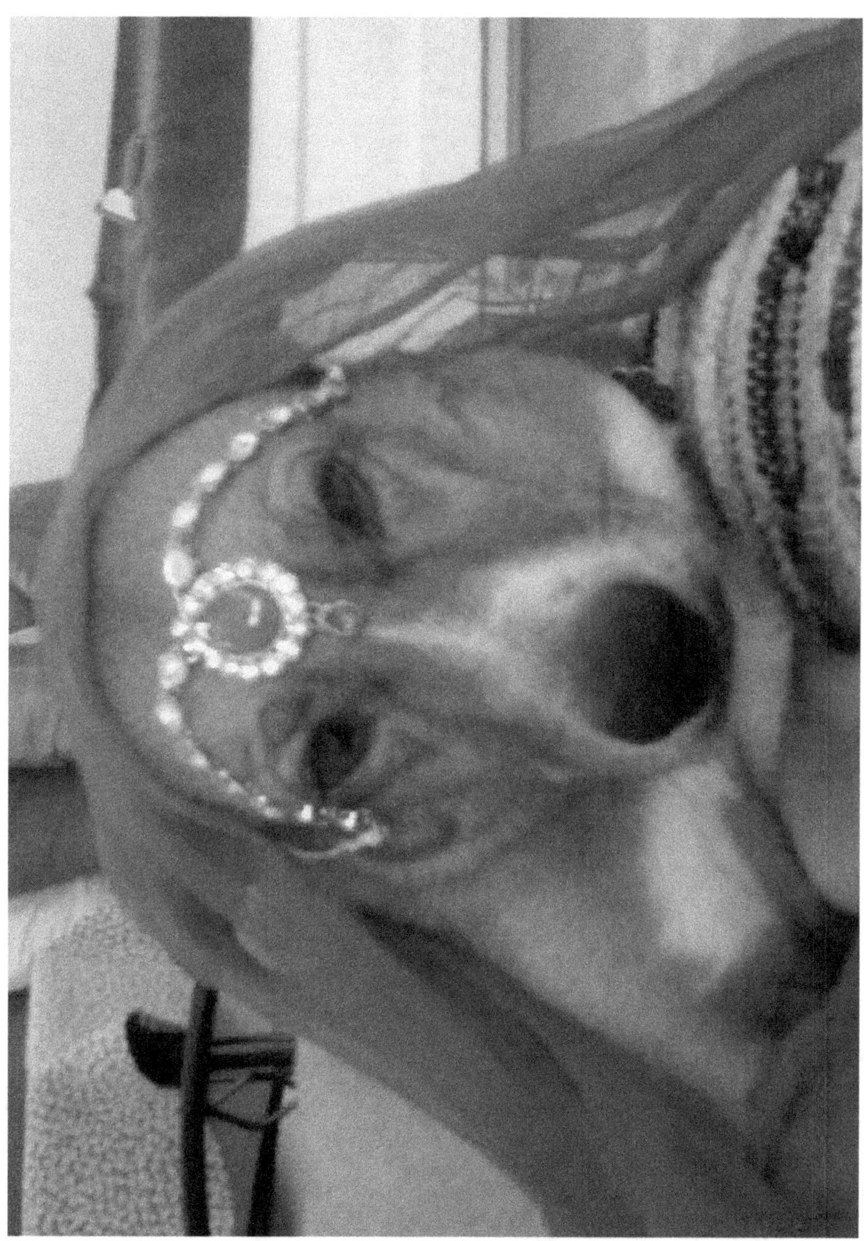

To me is important to show a humanized dog and the Hindu influence of the spiritual teachings on which I base the story.

The Author

Table of Contents

Part I

The Quest for an Enlightened Disciple

I remember my bedroom at the moment of death. I barely glimpsed the birds from my window. I had been sick for a long time, and although I was not that old, I felt like I had lived enough. What I remember the most was my Hindu friend Ushmil, who came to see me for the very last time.

"Hello, Alma. How do you feel?" she asked while sitting on the chair next to my bed.

"Hello, Ushmil. It is so good to see you! Thanks for coming."

"I saw a priest leaving. I almost thought I came to the wrong house!"

"My brother brought him. I asked him to. It was useless... I may be named Alma[1] but you know I am an atheist and I don't believe in souls, spirits, angels, demons, gods or saints. I had some questions... I thought that I would be stronger, but you are my best friend and I can tell you that I am a little scared..." I confessed to Ushmil who then held my hand.

"But Alma, there is nothing to be afraid of. You know how I feel about this issue and I can tell you that death does not exist. You'll go to a much better place and be happy. You must believe me."

---

[1] "Alma" is both a female first name and the word for soul in Spanish.

"I hope you are right... I better find all the answers to all my questions..." I said with difficulty, and those were my last words.

I really did not know what to expect. Or rather, I expected nothing. I thought I would plainly vanish into nothingness. However, I felt great, or perhaps I should say that I did not feel my achy, weak body, which was wonderful. I was weightless; I could see beyond the normal range of vision and knew what others were thinking. For a moment, I was sorry to see my brother, my niece and my friend cry, but almost immediately I went to a place of indescribable beauty, with colors inexistent on this Earth and a feeling of joy and love that cannot be compared to anything I knew. And I knew that I knew a lot, as I realized that I had been here before and that this was not the first time I was leaving a body. In an instant, I remembered being woman, man, parent, warrior, martyr, queen, slave and so many other things in different countries, at different epochs countless times.

This place, which I will call Heaven, for a lack of a proper word, could resemble a beautiful place on Earth. I saw other beings but could not distinguish their bodies due to the bright glow that emanated from them. I also had light, although not as bright. Then, one of those lights came closer and closer until I could hear a voice coming from it and a face that seemed somewhat familiar.

"Hello, Alma. I am Sri Bawarta Laji. I am here to welcome you and to guide you."

"Thank you... Have we met before?"

"Not physically, but you may have seen my picture. You have a good friend who has been praying for you."

"Ushmil? I love her very much!"

"And she loves you. She is one of my disciples; she commended you to me."

"You are Ushmil's guru! But I thought you were alive, or I am not dead?"

"Yes, yes and no. I reside here as well, and now you can stay here for a while and enjoy your vacation."

"I don't understand, if I am dead and you are not, how can we be here together, and what do you mean by vacation?"

"I am willing to teach you if you really want to know, things that will help you on your next life."

"Oooh no! Absolutely not! I am not going back! There is no way I want to return to that cruel world, no matter what!"

"You don't have enough virtues to remain here forever, and I don't have enough power to take you higher. If your wish is to return to the Source, you will be given the opportunity to make good deeds and progress spiritually. You can stay here for some time, but eventually you will have to come back."

"You mean to be born again? Why? Where? I prefer to stay here."

"Earth or another physical, similar planet. Look, there are two ways to reach liberation: one is the case of your friend Ushmil, who since a young age was interested in studying the mysteries of life and destiny and felt a spiritual hunger that led her to search for years, until she found a living, enlightened guru to take her as a disciple and guide her 'Home' after she leaves the body. Depending on the power of the guru, the disciple may be liberated from reincarnation in one, two or more lives. Another way is through a relative or beloved friend that follows such a guru diligently, and by his grace, he may help those connected to his disciple. The difference is that the one that did not receive initiation to learn how to practice spiritually cannot help his own family because he does not become enlightened himself. You have to find a more powerful guru (to use a familiar term) than me if you want to completely stop transmigrating in only one life."

"How does that work?"

"A real guru knows the way 'Home' and can guide you safely. He can also settle your debts (called karma) from past lives and help you evolve to higher levels of consciousness until reaching Home. People that do not practice spiritually with an enlightened guru can't find the way and must return. In fact, the main reason why people search for one is to stop reincarnating and progress to higher realms."

"Well, I was an atheist… I think it is unfair that only a few have this privilege because it is clear that the planet continues overpopulating indefinitely and most do not know what we need to do, at least to decide if we want to return or not."

"You are wrong, Alma. Everybody is given the opportunity, not only in one, but in many occasions, but the majority of people have too many excuses. They lack the interest to follow a spiritual teaching or the discipline to continue. Remarkably, in the era that your planet is currently facing, with the emergence of telecommunications and the amount of information at their fingertips, it is impossible not to find out about any particular subject. There are many groups which, searching spiritual growth, meet to meditate, pray, read the sacred texts of their religions; others want to learn about secular teachings for introspection, to be happier, more positive and help each other; there are also people interested in volunteering to assist other human beings, animals or the environment. All of them are seeking to fill a spiritual void. When an individual does not find what he needs and feels desperate, he can resort to things that provide an immediate though ephemeral relief, like drugs, gluttony, gambling or other vices. In reality, they have taken a false path because all the answers are within. They lack the guidance of an experienced teacher to find their own truth. I assure you that a really sincere individual will find her spiritual guide; one only needs to recognize him, accept him and practice diligently."

"Fine, but I want to do it from here. Please don't make me go back!" I pleaded with a firm voice.

"Look, you will need a new body in order to practice spiritually because your old one is not useful to you anymore. It is ridden with disease and wouldn't last long enough. Although you could study here with a guru, the progress you will make will be small compared to life on Earth. Why do you think they call it the best school in the universe? Here nobody needs you, everybody likes each other and there is no suffering, no poverty, no sickness, no greed, no envy and all is surrounded by love. How can you exercise your kindness and develop other good qualities staying here?

"On Earth, it is precisely the opposite; chances for spiritual growth appear in every corner. It is also very meritorious to be spiritual in a material world, which constantly demands your time and energy only to keep the body alive. It is so hard, that mere seconds of spiritual practice on Earth count for hours of practice in the higher planes of existence. A human body is necessary to advance quickly. Having one is a privilege; the soul must have enough virtues to get one, otherwise, it can take the body of an animal.

"Of course there are exceptions, but don't worry. You don't need to reincarnate immediately, and I can help you arrange the best conditions for you to meet an enlightened guru so you can reach liberation. Some people don't get a chance to meet a spiritual guide capable of taking them back Home in many lifetimes, once they have dismissed him. I will help you to find this opportunity because it could take hundreds of years and lots of suffering before another guru crosses your path. What do you think?" My friend's guru had a peaceful demeanor but a commanding voice; he may be truthful, but I kept on.

"On my way here, I discovered that I have reincarnated extensively and saw my past lives. Frankly, I am tired of this. Every time I am born again I start from zero, I forget my previous experiences and I make the same mistakes... There must be a better way! I resist the idea of doing it all over again, for the hundredth time. It seems to me that too much happiness may prevent me from seeking enlightening: what for, if I am content? On the other hand, suffering and being miserable may push me to search for answers, but the process is too painful and even excruciating... Is there anything I can do to avoid a new reincarnation or to warrant success?"

"You will return to the Source. That I can promise, but the soul ought to be ready. It is not allowed to force anybody to want enlightenment, just like no one can force you to be happy or to accept a certain guru. The universe has specific rules; this is something you will learn with time and the help of your guru, but for now, suffice you to know that (as your karma permits, which is the retribution from your actions) you can choose certain aspects around your birth like your parents, your country and even your physical appearance, in order to favor the circumstances for your spiritual development. Once you are born, you have the freedom to make your own decisions (under those circumstances) that will shape your destiny. Of course there is karma you will have to pay, we can talk about that later, but your guru can help you lighten its weight and teach you how to create as little karma as possible in order to advance more easily," the guru explained with a monotonous tone, like he had done it hundreds of times.

"It is clear to me that people do not tend to learn the easy way and I don't want to take more chances," I complained.

"The brain does not remember but the soul knows, and if you truly long to go back Home as it seems, that longing will accompany you through your life until you find the answers. What we can do now, if you like, is to determine the appropriate circumstances for your next time to guarantee you meet an enlightened guru who can guide you to liberation. How would you like that?"

I was not convinced. "Please, forgive me, I don't mean to be disrespectful, but do you have a supervisor or someone I can appeal my case, so to speak?"

"Don't despair! Take advantage of your stay. Some people need a 'recovery' period, especially when they have led a very traumatic life. Some others are eager to return and fulfill their dreams; their desires make them come back. Everyone will eventually return to the Source, although at different times, depending on what the soul wants to experience and other things. There is a Lord in charge of this spiritual plane, but I may be able to help you."

"I am sorry, but it is hard for me to accept having to learn to eat, walk, speak all over again; go through school; become a teenager; earn a living; relationships and the whole idea of preparing for a 'future.'"

"What if I tell you that there is no need to experience all that again? You could live a very short life; die as an infant, or even earlier, and still be liberated."

"That sounds much better."

"This would be possible only if you are the child of a certain powerful enlightened guru's disciple, as I explained earlier. Let's find a human that has an affinity with you and that also shares similar interests, which will lead both of you to liberation."

"Would I have to die of a painful condition? I certainly do not want to be aborted. I am fine with living a few weeks."

"I am glad we have reached an agreement," he replied with a smile. "Let's see, we need to do some research. It is important to find a man or a woman young enough to conceive, disciplined and preferably one who is already following the guru… Try to access your past lives' records to check who meets this criterion."

To my surprise, with no effort on my part, as soon as I thought about my previous lives I could see "selected movie scenes" and recognized many of the characters with whom I had been involved. I did not want to spend much time with each life because it was emotionally charged and I needed to focus on the important task at hand. I tried to avoid the most dramatic and painful moments, although it was not easy. Overall, I found this quick exercise very interesting and I realized that frequently some of the same souls had played different roles in the course of multiple lifetimes. In other words, the soul that was my husband in one lifetime was my daughter in another. Pretty much like a casting of actors representing diverse characters in a variety of plays. Those whom I had the strongest feelings for, either of love or hatred, were always the ones I ended up being closely involved with. This pretty much explained "love at first sight" I thought, as there is a particularly strong attraction (either loving or warring) to those souls. Enemies sometimes reincarnated as offspring. What a wise way to learn to love your enemy! Later I would review my most significant past lives.

Somehow, I was able to share these records with Sri Bawarta Laji. He did not judge or comment about some of the horrors and tribulations of my lives. He did not even make suggestions about a particular soul's "qualifications" to become my parent. I seemed to intuitively know who I needed to be close to, either because I wanted to learn something from her or to settle a debt. Often, I felt immensely sad that I had done wrong or did not do nearly as much as I could to help another soul in need, which compelled me to come back to redeem and forgive myself, even after that soul had already forgotten the offense.

We kept looking, but none of those souls were following a living guru. Many were religious, but those followed death Masters that could not teach them directly. Others, although spiritual, also lacked direct contact with a higher power that could liberate them from the cycle of reincarnation and extend that to the disciple's relatives and friends. There was one soul of an ancient ancestor that lived during the time of Jesus and had the chance to meet him, but regrettably he did not follow him and preferred worshiping the gold statue of a sheep. How terrible he must have felt when, at his passing, he reviewed his life! I also saw an old friend from a distant life in India that reached enlightenment; unfortunately, his guru did not have the power to liberate the persons close to his disciple… otherwise I would not be in this predicament.

This was harder than I thought! With all the lives I lived and all the people I met I was sure to find the correct person, but it seemed that spirituality takes a lesser place the more attached one becomes to the material world. I witnessed scenes from previous lives where I could have accumulated more merits and have had better karma, but I had wasted so many opportunities I couldn't even count them. My greatest regret was my lack of compassion. Sri Bawarta Laji had mentioned that compassion is a great virtue, especially towards more elevated beings. Offering a cloak to a hermit I encountered on the roads of a lost town in Africa centuries ago could have made a difference in my human experience. I thought of it when I saw him shivering, but I immediately replaced the idea thinking that I could exchange the item for a pot I needed. Little did I know that such an apparently insignificant body encased the soul of a great guru.

Many of my relatives and friends were reincarnated on Earth (a few in diverse life forms), some were not incarnated yet and resided in different planes of existence, according to the level of consciousness they reached in their previous lives. I decided to change my search to find when an enlightened and powerful guru would be descending to accept a disciple whom I could join.

Luckily, we found someone who would take initiation from the most powerful teacher, a being who had been on Earth multiple times and whose most famous incarnations included Guru Nanak, Quetzalcóatl, Socrates, Confucius and Jesus.

This kindred individual had been my relative many lives ago and I could see that it was spiritual (not religious), fun and loving. It was a good candidate because it was healthy; I thought it could easily have children. I figured I may be its offspring and be liberated via bloodline, by the grace of its guru.

The being in question was incarnated under the name of Cecilia. I did not know what her "contract" (the agreement before coming to Earth) was, but I was hopeful that she would get pregnant with me and, due to my free will, my staying would be short. I struggled with this, as I knew it would cause her great sorrow to lose me, but her spiritual practice would help her understand. She was also a good choice because she had two siblings, where I may potentially fall in as her niece or nephew as a last resource, equally benefiting from her practice.

Sri Bawarta Laji gave me his approval and we simply "sat" there waiting for the moment to arrive. Cecilia's aunt and godmother (who knew she followed spiritual teachings from a guru) was a very perceptive and sweet woman who could see me lingering, especially when her sister stopped taking contraceptives... I did not want to miss my chance! But the place was taken, as an agreement already existed between the future mother and her child, who was willing to pay the karma of his previous life with a congenital disorder for the opportunity to belong to the family of an initiate of this powerful Master.

I was saddened when I saw that after the birth of the baby the mother decided to have her tubes tied, which I could understand since her marriage was in serious trouble and she feared not being able to care for more kids. The half-brother did not have a stable relationship with anyone yet, so there was nothing I could do. Cecilia was very focused on her career, as many modern women are, but she was about to get married and I would be prepared to land at the first forgotten pill or broken condom occurrence.

Many Earth-days passed and the opportunity I had been waiting for started to dwindle as days became years and Cecilia did not seem interested in becoming a mother. The fact that the husband traveled profusely did not help either. Cecilia was in her late thirties when I heard a conversation

(I had been keeping a watchful eye on the family) which alarmed me:

"I had a very interesting, recurring dream last night," said Cecilia's godmother during Sunday's brunch.

"The winning number of the lottery?" asked her niece jokingly.

"No. I saw again the same baby I saw before your sister had Olav. She called me 'god mommy'!"

"Wow, what else do you remember?"

"Not much, only what I told her: 'So sorry my love, but I can't help you if my nieces don't want to have children!'" Cecilia's godmother responded with her caramel voice, combining sorrow with hope.

"You are absolutely right! That soul better find another mommy because if she knows how to count, she should not count on me! With all the women in the world, don't you think she could find a suitable mom in one of those countries where women have lots of kids or one who does not believe in contraception? … Although I imagine there must be a high demand from discarnate beings to be born from disciples… they better watch out!"

"Where do you get that from?"

"My guru explained once that since humankind has found the way to prevent unwanted pregnancies more births originate in third world countries, where inexplicably they keep procreating galore in spite of famine, war and other horrible conditions," Cecilia concluded.

"Perhaps your half-brother will become a father…."

"You can forget about that. He is not fatherly material and even admitted to not liking children that much… he hardly ever visits Olga any more in order to avoid Olav. You know he blames the poor kid for Olga's troubles, which coincidentally started after his birth."

"Everything happens for a reason, we obviously don't know why. Their marriage may not have lasted anyway," the wise woman explained, whose pretty brown eyes sparkled with the sunlight.

I was devastated! When I finally found a soul I had affinity with, disciple of a powerful Master capable of delivering her bloodline from the transmigration cycle... neither she nor her siblings wanted children! And the worst part was that after the Master finished his mission on Earth there was no telling when I would have another chance! Cecilia's free will hindered me from forcing the situation, just as she could not oblige me to live longer than I wanted.

"This is hard! Why does it have to be a relative?"

"The Master will deliver family and friends of his disciple," continued my guru. "Because they are connected by the law of karma, they all share the same debts; once settled, everyone is free."

I was immersed in those concerns when Sri Bawarta Laji, never too far from me, came to the rescue.

"Cecilia is such a terrific woman, you have no idea how much I wanted her to be my mother, even if I did not seek liberation! I have been observing her and I love her very much. I was so looking forward to being her baby!" I started to weep, which seemed ridiculous in such a heavenly place.

"Don't worry, Alma. There is always hope. You can still be her baby."

I looked at him, not at the eyes, but searching his luminous aura for answers.

"Remember how you despised having to descend as a human again? What about taking an animal form? The soul still is the same!" Sri Bawarta Laji said it so matter-of-factly that I almost fainted.

"What?" was the only word I was able to articulate.

"I would not suggest a sheep or a chicken, although no animal is free from human cruelty and appetite. Something less risky would be really helpful."

I remained still. Even in my bodiless condition I sensed my legs became two feathers, my head a balloon deflating in the air and my stomach at the verge of a precipice. Images of countless animals came to mind, some of them in their natural habitat, some in cages and others on plates. A strong smell of hay entered my tongue and I saw clearly a rabbit surrounded by bunnies. A chill ran through my spine when I heard a screech which abruptly brought me back to the bright figure of Sri Bawarta Laji, smiling serenely before me.

"No reason to panic. You have done this before." I was not sure if he could read my mind or if he was trying to convince me. I kept quiet. "Not everyone starts out as a human being, you know. It takes plenty of virtues to reincarnate as one."

"Why can't I be an angel… like a guardian angel of some kind?" I sobbed.

"In the order of the creation, humans are a superior class of beings, although you may find this hard to believe. Angels serve humans but can only go so high. The human soul originates from a superior realm and there is where you want to return, that is your Home. The fact that a soul can enter an animal body does not make it inferior. What animal lives do you remember now?"

"I am not sure. I saw a variety… an insect, a fish, a bird…"

"Yes, exactly! You see! Even Buddha had a life as a bird before he became an Enlightened Master. Did you know that?"

"I guess… Ushmil mentioned something in this regard when talking about Buddhism. I thought it was a myth. Isn't it going backwards to reincarnate as an animal since you said that to have a human body was a privilege which required lots of virtues?"

"Yes, the human body is precious, hence you start out with animal bodies of different sorts (even as plants or rocks), until you evolve to get a man's, and later a woman's body. Even though you may not reincarnate as Cecilia's offspring, you can certainly still be part of her family."

"How is it possible? Animals are not intelligent like humans. They can't follow spiritual practices either! Sorry, but this is ridiculous!"

"You are right that animals cannot follow a teaching as humans do. Their brains are smaller and less capable, but intelligence has nothing to do with spirituality. Normally, animals are already connected to the Source and most of them have better qualities than people. They do not need to pray for love. They live surrounded by it, if only humans leave them alone. I stand on what I said before, but what I have in mind for you is a better arrangement. What if you were to go down as this disciple's animal companion? I assure you that the mercy and power of her enlightened living guru can extend even to the disciple's pets, as it does to her relatives, which I explained earlier. Wouldn't it be a much easier, not to mention mellow, life for you?"

I was completely dumbfounded. Never, in my wildest dreams did I imagine animals worthy of such immense opportunity, much less having souls and that people had actually been animals in previous lives! All these ideas were absolutely crazy, revolutionary and new to me. Then I remembered Ushmil and the way she treated animals. One time she told me of a Hindu temple which offered milk to rodents, not to mention sacred cows, cobras and the culture's beliefs on reincarnation. Sri Bawarta Laji must have seen the stunned look on my face and suggested a break.

Of course I could not possibly feel tired, neither hungry nor sleepy, although I was very curious and eager to learn more. Naturally, I needed to digest all this new information. Hence, he said he would come back later, and if in the meantime I wanted to go over my past animal lives to gain confidence, it would be fine. He would be glad to answer any questions I had.

But before long and prior to reviewing some of my most significant non-human lives and pondering about taking an animal body, Sri Bawarta Laji came back with more news.

"Dear Alma, as you may know, Cecilia's husband, Max, has changed jobs and no longer has to travel for work. Not only does he go back to her every night, he is also starting to work from home."

"Believe me..." I intervened, "... if I have not yet been conceived it is not for lack of vigilance. Cecilia is now using a backup contraceptive method because she fears that at her age she could have a deformed baby... These pretentious, stupid western doctors... instilling fear in their patients so they won't be blamed for not informing them of their supposed 'risks'! They think they know more than they do. They have no idea how karma plays a role in people's health!"

"That is not what I wanted to say, but you need to make your decision soon. Max has told Cecilia, since now he is home, they can have a pet as she wished, and he promised to help her take care of it."

"Uhh... Well... I am just... don't... haven't considered my choices... A small... parrot she could teach words to maybe appropriate... umm... I, I, I feel confused..."

My guru replied with a commanding voice, "Wrong answer! They are planning to visit several animal control facilities in their area, also known as pounds. You need to be a dog, and a cute one, so she picks you!"

I crumpled.

Part II

The Teachings of My Guru

"A dog? Excuse me, Sir, but don't you think that is a little drastic? I have never been particularly fond of dogs."

"Do you have a better idea? This is a piece of cake, really! You will have an easier life than millions of humans. Think about it: you will never worry about where your next meal will come from, never be tortured by your own negative thoughts and never hold a grudge. On the contrary, you will always be ready to have fun, always available to love and always forgiving. Besides, you will be a beloved pet, not a stray dog which could end up in somebody's barbecue."

He must have known that in one of my countries of residence I used to sell barbecue and when I did not have enough meat, I killed a stray dog or two… it was the only way I knew to make a living.

"But what if I get lost somewhere or if someone steals me? May I be a bird or a fish? How about an ass?"

"Sorry, no repeating." He smiled and winked mischievously.

I asked because I remembered how much I cared for a donkey I once owned. I insisted, "I have no experience as a dog, I could mess up!"

"Nonsense! You will make a wonderful dog! Besides, it is what Cecilia wants. I told you that this powerful Master promises to liberate the initiate's family. Don't worry, he will not abandon you!"

Before knowing more about my previous lives and relationships of the past, I wanted some assurance that this time everything would be different. If I learned anything from my reincarnations it was that no matter what, the odds of being successful were slim and as determined as I was to make this rebirth the last one and avoid more suffering, I felt unprepared, even as a dog.

I was a little rebellious, I must confess, and still unsatisfied with life on Earth and with tons of questions before I could be ready to make my last entrance to the stage.

"First off, I would like to make some things clear," I expressed to my new guru. "Please forgive me if I sound ill-mannered to the authority in charge, but with all due respect, I would like to file a formal complaint about the situation of Earth and humanity since ancient times."

"This would pertain to the Lord of Karma. It is useless to complain to him. His job is to collect all debts and keep the souls trapped in material worlds (like yours) to rule over them. What you must do is go higher, where he cannot reach you."

"Aha! So you admit that we are at the mercy of a tyrant and that there is no God!"

"There is no such God. There is a hierarchy of beings governing the universe. It is complicated, but Earth is a special case. It is a planet whose beings do not remember where they came from and why they are there. Yes, it is a challenge, but originally, every soul agreed to the rules of the game and all went there voluntarily."

"I cannot believe that human beings could accept to play this 'game,' as you call it! Earth is full of sorrow and despair.

Unless we come from a worse place, who would want to live there? You admitted that people get amnesia after birth. How in the world are we supposed to avoid making the same mistakes and learn our lessons? We are condemned to lose. It is like playing Russian roulette. It seems so unfair!" I snorted. "Is destiny fixed?"

"The circumstances and the outcome of someone's life are shaped by two main factors: free will and karma. The circumstances surrounding the birth, the country, the physical appearance, the health, even the profession or talents can be agreed beforehand. The unfulfilled desires of the soul who is going to reincarnate play another role. All is affected by the accumulated karma from past lives. For example, if someone wanted to become a famous singer and died before he could complete his dream, his desire will bring him back and, if having enough virtues or good karma, he could find the right conditions to fulfill it. In contrast, if a person needs to learn a specific lesson, or wants to help others learn theirs, he may choose, for example, being born with a physical impediment. This way he can appreciate and value his body and overcome challenges he previously failed or give the people around him (usually relationships from past lives) the opportunity to grow in compassion, love, altruism, etc. to evolve and develop spiritually. To a certain extent, the soul can choose many aspects of his future life, starting from the parents, but once the decision is made, before birth, the free will is circumscribed to those conditions and the opportunities he would be able to find in life."

Later, when I pondered on his words, it became evident to me that no one on Earth is qualified to pass judgement on others or take justice into its own hands. No human being has all the evidence and all the elements to know why things happen the way they do. How can an individual understand the events unfolding in one lifetime when we don't have access to the whole picture? Still, I felt cheated and my guru noticed the dissatisfaction in my demeanor.

"So you think that Earth should be what humans consider Eden, a paradise like the one where Adam and Eve lived?"

"Why not? If the Bible is right, God punished his children for being disobedient. It is not their descendants' fault for what they did. What kind of vengeful God is that? Even an imperfect being like me would be more forgiving. Is this how it all started?"

"That is the key issue. Do you want to hear a story?"

"Please, enlighten my understanding. The more I think about it the less I like it."

"I will do my best. At the moment, you are using a limited understanding faculty to try to comprehend things which are beyond the reach of the mind," he warned me.

"Where do I start…? The beginning… Imagine the ocean, vast and powerful. Imagine that the ocean is all that exists. The ocean is there, happy and calm. There is no wind, so there are no waves; there is no beach, so there is no sand or shore, nothing. There is nothing other than water and the water is the ocean and the ocean is God, but then, the ocean wanted to see itself, like seeing his own reflection in a mirror. One can only see the image of his own face but cannot see his actual face as others can. For this, he had to somehow distance himself. The universe we live in is an illusion of the real, original universe. Well, this is its reflection.

"Nothing would have ever been created if the ocean did not want to know itself. So it vibrated for the first time, and the water distinguished drops. There are an infinite number of drops in the ocean, although the sum of all drops is the ocean. Still, every individual drop is a microscopic ocean. If you take a drop of the ocean and put it back, you will be unable to distinguish it from the rest because this drop has become one with the ocean, has diffused in it. If you were to take another drop, it would be similar, but not the exact same drop you took the first time. Once in the ocean, all drops are identical and one. They cease from being individual drops and no longer feel separated. They are part of each other. Only when you take a drop can you isolate it from the rest and make it different. You may color it, apply pressure or shape it in different forms.

"The same happens with us. We are drops from the ocean of God and collectively we are God. All were formed from God. If the ocean is all that exists, everything comes from it. Master Rumi expressed it eloquently: 'You are not a drop in the ocean, you are the ocean in a drop.' Since all there was, was God, God wanted to experiment being God. Then the Almighty God (the Source) derived in other beings, like a father who has children and those children have their own children."

As Sri Bawarta Laji expressed these ideas to a neophyte like me, I was able to see the images of the cosmos and the water, although unsure if those were my thoughts or his.

"Have you ever made cheese?" he continued. "The raw material is milk. From it you can make different types of cheese, and also cream, butter and other things. When you separate the liquid from the cheese, after coagulation, what you have is still milk, albeit with different properties. The whey, the curd, and the cheese are all milk products because milk is your starting point. You can keep refining it, but all the substances will contain milk. Even the most diluted are some form of milk, no matter how minuscule. It may not seem like it, but it has the same basic characteristics, though attenuated. They came from milk, there was nothing else there.

"Like the cream rises to the top of the milk, there are beings in higher planes of existence and others which due to their weight or lower vibratory frequency, sink to the bottom.

"The purest and finer vibratory planes of the creation are at the top and they sift down depending on their density. At the very bottom is the heaviest, least pure and most dense of all creation. You could say that Heaven and celestial beings are highest and hell and demons are at the bottom. However, they still have divine quality, although very small."

"I see, then all started because God wanted to experience being God, to contemplate himself, fine. Then, if I was happy in a higher Heaven, how did I end up in a lower one? Did I go through some sort of 'existential crisis'?" I asked.

"Most likely you were kind of curious. The first time we incarnated we wanted to experience and know ourselves better. Think of it this way: if you are light the only way to know that you are light is by being exposed to darkness. If all you have ever seen is light, you don't have a context to understand what being light means. Of course, darkness does not exist. Darkness is only the absence of light. (One can bring light to a room any time, but it is impossible to bring the darkness to it. We can only block the light from illuminating the room.) The same applies to other aspects of life. The duality we see exists only in the physical universe, but not in higher planes. God did not create darkness or evil or anything like it, but we decided to move away so we could know ourselves better."

"But not everyone left, right?"

"Not all beings opted to experience the physical dimension. There are beings who have never incarnated and are not interested in exploring duality, time or space. They exercise their free will to remain with God and never look down."

"So some of us went like docile little lambs to the slaughter house without warning," I retorted.

"You did not see it this way. From above, everything looks different. When you were told that a life on Earth normally lasts about 100 years you thought it was a breeze. You did not understand the concept of time, and even if you did, what are a hundred years in the context of eternity? Even if you suffered, it is but an instant in the big scheme of things."

"Not if you have to reincarnate. Who came up with such a rotten idea?"

"More respect! The Lord of the material world is mighty indeed. If you were before his presence you would think there is no higher being or more fabulous and magnificent god than him. You must admit it takes an extremely powerful being to make such a beautiful planet as Earth, with its mountains, valleys, caves, lakes, seas, creatures, all the marvels which exist in all corners under all climates everywhere in the planet, and we are referring but to Earth; there are a myriad of planets and solar systems in the physical universe you don't know. In any case, this god thought all the world wonders were meaningless if an intelligent being could not admire and appreciate them. The souls of superior planes wished to see and visit these physical worlds but never intended to remain there indefinitely. They would go and stay for a while and enjoy this gorgeous planet of contrasts. After all, this is what they wanted to experience, remember, the duality only exists here.

"You may have learned about Greek mythology. According to it, Zeus is the father of all gods and supreme ruler of the universe. Similarly, it may help you to think that there is one God Almighty and his children are minor gods who govern different abodes. Therefore, one of these minor gods created the galaxy where you have dwelled and the beings living there.

"The problem is, beings exist in other realms (let's name them extraterrestrials) who became greedy and jealous and designed strategies to keep the souls trapped on Earth. This world is a battleground of extraterrestrials, some wanting to help humans, others wanting to keep them ignorant. The governments made stunning alien discoveries in places like Antarctica, that they do not share with the public. Nations even exchange secret information obtained this way to gain technology and scientific knowledge, denying their existence in public. This is the biggest cover-up of all times, but people are starting to wake up.[2]"

"And we have no one to defend us?" I interrupted. "If I see my child playing near a precipice I remove him from there. I don't care if he agrees or listens to my reasons or not. Why were we allowed to participate in this dangerous game?"

"First of all, you have to understand that you are divine in nature. You are the child (or grandchild) of God and no other god can prohibit another god anything. Second, the creator of his dimension enacts the rules. It is not God's job to meddle in other gods' businesses. Like when you educate your kids, you make the rules, but later the children move out and have their own kids. Although you love your grandchildren, you let their parents handle them. I understand that intervention should be granted under certain circumstances, and this is why God sends Enlightened Masters regularly to help those souls who are ready to come Home."

"What you are saying is that we knowingly agreed to go to the physical realm even though the risks for being trapped here were very high. It does not seem like a very smart move from an intelligent being," I added trying to make sense of all this information.

"When you were up there, you were made aware of the rules of the universe and thought it would be fun to try the material world. The feeling of separation from God was something completely new to you, the idea of perceiving

[2] Wilcock, David. *Cosmic Disclosure* | Gaia https://www.youtube.com/watch?v=mr861fnyn2o Jul 27, 2016.

emotions, having a physical body, the concept of time and space, and all which does not exist in other realms interested you. You were eager to see first-hand what it was like and agreed to its conditions. Like human beings wanting to explore new territories. Many people like to go on vacation and leave behind their cozy homes to visit other places. Some persons go camping, for example, and no one thinks they are stupid for leaving their comfy beds to sleep in a tent in order to see what is out there. Some organize expeditions to climb mountains, even though it is freezing and risky. Others like to go on safari to see up close all kinds of dangerous animals and exotic plants. While others prefer a more relaxing trip and opt to go to the unpredictable sea and lie under the sun all day. The complication arises when the vacation overextends indefinitely and you find yourself stranded in a foreign land, with rules you dislike and then become tired of this place.

"It can happen; what if the government closed the borders and you had to stay abroad so long that you finally forgot where you came from and how to return home? It may be fun at the beginning, but after a while all you want to do is leave. You know deep inside you don't belong there and start feeling uneasy and then desperate. It makes sense: you came from a place where you were entitled to love, happiness and everything you fancy with no effort on your part. Your desires could be manifested instantly, by the mere thought of them. If you wanted to see someone, all you had to do was think of that someone and you were together. You were pure, and all your thoughts were also pure, so all you manifested were pure and wonderful things. Same for every being in this realm.

"Next you are in an abode where you have to work really hard only to earn a piece of bread to maintain a physical body, which is subject to pain, illness and aging. You start interacting with other beings with similar issues and soon become entwined with each other. You develop a sense of injustice, despair and loneliness. At Home, you were loved and powerful. In the world, nobody cares about you. You can no longer satisfy your needs or wants quickly enough and your thoughts, following the law of cause and effect, end up manifesting more bad things to you.

"Naturally you are attracted to abundance, beauty and comfort because those remind you of your Home (although not consciously) and therefore you believed you were entitled to those things. Hence, you turned rebellious and infringed the law of the land and got in trouble. Not being able to buy what you wanted, you stole it, you lied, and you hated the people who interfered with your plans. Consequently, you became more and more entangled with this world to the point where it became almost impossible to escape. You had so many debts for all the "crimes" you had committed and your way of thinking perpetuated the belief that you were powerless and a victim of a tyrant god. So, you needed more lives, not only to satisfy your failed desires, but to reap all you have sowed (karma)."

"That is a heck of a vacation! Sorry. Your description reminds me of the case of criminals for whose offenses they are condemned to several life sentences, but the difference here is that you actually have more lives to keep paying your debts! Is there no mercy from the Lord of the physical world?"

"The Lord of Karma is the one in charge of collecting all debts. Like on Earth, there is a supreme judge who imparts the law to all citizens. You could be the president or the king, but you still must comply with the law. There are no bribes in his realm and the laws are infallible; therefore, if you create a negative thought it will, automatically, with time, manifest itself. The problem is, unlike higher levels of consciousness, you do not see its immediate manifestation, so you believe thoughts are inconsequential, but nothing is farther from the truth! People of Earth are starting to realize this and some talk about the importance of being positive and paying more attention to their thoughts and words, but it is hard to change ingrained habits. Even if an individual modifies his negative conducts now, there will still be old reactions from past actions to be manifested.

"Nevertheless, many souls, believe it or not, are awakening, especially now that your world is entering a new era. Earth is evolving. There will be another golden era for the planet and its inhabitants will be uplifted to a higher level of consciousness. This has been announced by many cultures and so-called prophets. As a matter of fact, there has been a wave of volunteer souls coming down to assist with this transition. You cannot deny, looking back at the iron age, middle age, all the way until now, that humanity has progressed, not only technologically but in its level of consciousness, raised with the help of each and all Enlightened Masters who have blessed Earth with their presence.

"God periodically sends Enlightened Masters to help those who are ready to return Home: our divine origin as souls, the Source of our creation. The physical bodies are but a tool to experience the material worlds. Anywhere else they will not feel comfortable. 'In my Father's House there are many mansions' and there is a special one for us, where we belong, although there are higher planes of existence. Imagine a frog, he is completely satisfied in a pond, there is where he is the happiest. You may think that living in a palace or on a pretty beach swinging in a hammock and eating cakes under a coconut tree would be better, but for the frog this kind of luxury is unpleasant and actually damaging. It is not his natural habitat. Same with created souls. Anything lower than their level is not home and anything higher will be irksome; the extremely superior vibrations of the upper planes become intolerable to the point that the soul would be annihilated by them, making it explode and dispel into nothingness.

"This is why when God sends a Savior he needs to be well prepared for the trip. Like someone living on the surface who must descend to the deep ocean to complete a mission. If the Master went without proper equipment, he would succumb to the pressure. In order to survive in this dour environment, he needs to wear a scuba diver suit, an oxygen tank and gradually get accustomed to the new pressure. From the higher realms, this world looks and smells bad. It takes a great effort and infinite love to descend to save a human soul."

"Why can't God simply appear in the sky for everyone to see and talk to us openly with all his mighty power and show his face? This way everyone would believe in him and would want to follow him."

"Do you really think so, Alma? You are very naive, my dear friend! If God were to perform a circus stunt people would think it an extraterrestrial trick and governmental defense systems would send its missiles to destroy the 'possible threat to humankind'. If God appeared white, blacks would complain. If he came as black, some whites would not recognize him. If in the body of a woman, many may have doubts. If he did not show a beard, Jewish people would ignore him and would continue waiting for the savior for thousands of years more while lots of Enlightened Masters have come and gone from the face of the Earth. They all teach the same thing, although they do it differently depending on the conditions at the time.

"No matter what, people will never be satisfied! How is God supposed to look like, where is he supposed to be born, what kind of job is he supposed to have, what clothes is he supposed to wear in order to be accepted by all human beings? They could have God under their own noses in the form of a perfect Master and call it an impostor. God does not try to convince people through white magic or miracles. He will not perform public healings or supernatural phenomena for the masses. It is neither his function nor his mission. No one form of God in this world would satisfy everyone. People also have different interests and degrees of spiritual development. When Jesus was on Earth, not everyone followed him. He only had twelve disciples!"

"How can God be presented to low level beings then?" I inquired, trying to grasp the immensity of the task.

"How do you explain to a bee what a human being is?"

"I know this one: becoming a bee!" I responded proudly.

"Exactly. This is precisely what God does when he sends an Enlightened Master. We cannot see God in all his glory. His energy and loving vibration are too strong for the soul. Even at the higher spheres, we would be annihilated, dissolved, smashed into the void; but he can tone down his vibratory frequency and descend to our level. God appears to humans as light and sound vibration through meditation. This is how we become aware of the Kingdom of God within ourselves. The body is a prison, used to house the soul in a physical world. Similarly, bees will never fully understand what a human is, but becoming one and demonstrating some of the things one of them can do would be more effective. They may think of a human being as a powerful magnificent bee (a 'super-bee'), capable of destroying and reinstating a whole nest with a snap of his legs, and they may learn from his example. Eventually, the bee consciousness will evolve to the understanding that they are souls experiencing life as bees; but as a human, you will never make yourself understood, or even heard by the hive."

"Still, the law of cause and effect (karma) messes everything up! Can God get rid of it once and for all?"

"There is a law above the law of cause and effect: The Law of Love, which comes from God. It supersedes other laws in the universe. This law offers grace and forgiveness and is the very nature of Enlightened Masters. They are one with God and serve as a link between humans and the Almighty. This would be like a person who is granted a good lawyer. What if the lawyer could negotiate with the judge for a better payment arrangement?"

"Would have said it before! Can I get a lawyer, please?"

"Sure, Alma! This is the job of the Enlightened Master or guru, who maintains connections between the highest spheres of consciousness and the world, serving as intermediate to defend your case to the Lord of Karma. It is what Jesus did for his disciples. He taught them how to properly behave in order to stop creating more negative karma and took upon himself their debts (referred to as sins). The Lord of Karma does not care who pays the debts, as long as they are paid. The Master or guru has an enormous bank account (virtues) with enough 'money' to pay the debts of his disciples. Only then can the soul abandon the material world for good. All that remains is the karma of the present life so he can keep living until he completes his mission. The moment karma is paid, there is no more attachment to the physical world and the soul is free. In other words, nobody remains on Earth without karma, which is precisely what anchors people there. One must find a current, expert guru knowledgeable of the way Home and who can settle our debt, like a lawyer that appeals on our behalf before the judge, because there are not enough future reincarnations to pay the insurmountable debt we have accumulated in life after life. He will take his disciples to the higher levels of consciousness, but to take their karma, he needs to still live in the world. If you don't have a lawyer, you are in big trouble."

"I see. What happens in the case of a soul who is good and acts like a saint?"

"Both good or bad actions will produce consequences for all beings, which means a soul can still return if only to reap rewards from good deeds. Such is the law of cause and effect or the so-called karma. Thus, at the end the soul must come back either to pay a debt or to get the reward. Clearly, the first case is the most common."

"Let's talk about missions; one hardly knows what his mission is in life. You also told me earlier that some souls choose to experience hardships. Why is it so?" This was my chance to clarify a point Sri Bawarta Laji had briefly touched on when I was checking on Cecilia and discovered that her nephew was to be born with a congenital disorder.

"You would naturally think that everybody wishes to be born beautiful, healthy, wealthy and under the best conditions to be happy, but this is hardly ever the case. Many souls deliberately choose being born in adverse conditions to develop whatever they need in order to evolve, so they can progress more quickly. The few who have, or seem to have it all, may be there to retrieve their award (positive retribution) as a result of good past deeds or accumulated virtues (generally from former lives) for which they are born in privileged circumstances. Let me make an aside here and clarify that no amount of charity in the world will guarantee liberation. It may grant you a better life, but you still have to reincarnate. This is another reason why an enlightened guru is so important. As I said before, you wanted to experiment with the physical world, when you first came down you actually had no mission per se but started having desires, which when left unfulfilled made you come back. In some cases, a soul returns to assist loved ones in fulfilling theirs, such as offering great support or help to an individual to accomplish something either tangible or in the spiritual field. By coming with a disability, for example, he can help his parents and relatives cultivate virtues such as patience, mercifulness, charity, etc. or to improve others' lives with the same condition, through his battle."

"It never occurred to me that someone with, for example, a brain condition, could somehow voluntarily renounce to a healthier existence in order to help others develop their qualities. Sadly, I see how it may take a situation this extreme for people to become compassionate, to change attitudes or to act for the benefit of others," I concluded.

"Yes, although humans are originally kind-hearted, the many daily distractions and temptations hamper their good intentions. Poor humans, they fall easy prey to devil forces! They do not realize they live in a world of illusions, created by a lower god who traps them there. The illusion is so flawless that they swear everything they see and touch is real. Nothing could be farther from the truth! It is the best trick ever; if they only knew who they really are, Earth would be completely different. Therefore, they need proper instruction to open their third eye and see beyond the illusion. Once the being fully realizes who he truly is, then he is free."

My thoughts were racing. To me, the main obstacle to fulfilling one's mission was to discover what this mission, goal or desire was. When people are born on Earth, they do it with a new mind, a new body and with a veil which prevents them from knowing what they did wrong in the past, thus starting from scratch. Of course, in certain cases it may be better not to remember that one was murdered by the current parent, or that one committed horrendous crimes. Life like this would be unbearable.

"I must remember my objective: never to return to the worldly life again. Otherwise I will continue being entangled with karma indefinitely. How am I supposed to accomplish this as an animal?"

"Don' t worry! As a dog your mission will be clearer to you because the brain will not interfere. As you noticed, discarnate souls and also animals possess telepathic abilities. Besides, we can go over your 'contract,' so to speak, to make sure you agree with all the stipulations before you sign it. This will give you more confidence. Are you ready now to review your past animal lives?"

Part III

My Past Lives

"Oooh… Okay, where do we start?" I had a flashback earlier where I realized I had had many animal bodies. "What kind of animal did I start out with? Or what was I before that?" I asked, suspecting that there were more physical life forms.

"If we are going to start from the beginning, then we could talk about being air, part of the mineral kingdom and evolve from there. We can go that far back if you like, but let's now focus on some of your animal forms. Remembering in more detail how animals see life will encourage you, all right? You had said you saw a rabbit?"

"Yes, a female rabbit with a bunch of bunnies. I think those were my babies!" I replied.

"Most likely. What else do you see?" He pointed to his forehead, between the eyebrows.

I closed my eyes and concentrated on this vision, attempting to access some part of my memory (I would say "brain" but I had no physical body) that contained the information I sought. Somehow, I found myself inside a huge "library" comprising billions of books. Interestingly, I was in front of the one which seemed to glow at my sight. I grabbed it and discovered it registered all the actions, thoughts and feelings of my being. My eyes, enraptured, started to dance with fascination, then, I found a note entitled "Possible futures." Elated and lightheaded, trying to put myself together I read the note, stating that the present record was made with the exercise of my will, which could create different conditions for potential new lives. Mustering restraint, I went straight to the section of interest.

I was not "reading," it was more like seeing and reliving with all my feelings and senses.

My name was Abby. I had a name, although I was not really a pet, but a guest of an animal farm that belonged to a family whose daughter, a little sweet girl with dew-smelling skin and carrot fluffy hair, called me that. She must have been four or five and brought me food. I remembered my children, every one of them. I liked to visit the farm in the winter, as the availability of food for the other animals made my life easier. During the early summer mornings, I enjoyed basking in the sun and jumping happily with other rabbits. I liked to play and groom often. I watched some family members guarding our territory; several of my male cousins defended it constantly from intruders. Although most of us could run really fast or stay still to escape danger, occasionally some relatives were never seen again after larger animals or humans had been lurking around.

I was searching for food when a gust of acrid air coming from behind a big bush stung my nose. I approached curiously. My heart was pumping fast and my ears perked up. My whiskers trembled at the scent of blood coming from a creature inside some kind of jaws that did not belong to any known animal. Why? No one kills and leaves the prey untouched! I wanted to help, but there was nothing I could do! ...so sad! I ran to my rabbit hole, so cozy and fragrant, filled with the adorable baby smell of my bunnies. No worries: mama is home! Nothing I enjoyed more than cuddling with them, feeding them and listening to their little noises. I loved my babies, but they grew up fast and I did not like my home empty; I had children often. We were a happy family.

The males respected me; they knew I could jump higher and run faster than other rabbits of my same size and weight. Although I did not worry about the future, I was always busy finding food for me and my children. In the winter I still made time to play, going to the farm where the sweet girl made a bed of hay for me and my babies. She would spend hours on the farm, helping her parents with their chores and watching us. I never wondered why. "Come Abby, let me pet you!" she signaled. I did not completely trust her, but I did not feel threatened by her. Her fresh fragrance and melodic voice distinguished her from the bigger humans.

One day, I heard a horrible screech while coming back home… it was an aunt I shared the den with. I ran fast but was not fast enough; the beast that had chased her was followed by others… I felt a sharp pain in my chest. Thank God I went fast!

Overall, this was a good life. I wished to understand the meaning of motherhood and I was very successful. I wanted to experience joy and be able to move my body in different ways, taste various foods, have the sensation of freedom and yet be part of a family, see other animals, feel cared for and appreciated. I enjoyed nature in all its seasons, every drop of water, every snowflake, every sunray, every blade of grass… Still, I was curious. I wanted to know more about the other animals I met and how they sensed those same things. Also, to perceive new sensations, increase my insights of the intriguing functioning of this world and obtain a new level of awareness of all that surrounded me, why not? At the time, being a rabbit was great, but as scientific animal experimentation persists, and Earth becomes more polluted and invaded by humans, I was not sure I would want to get a bunny's body or bear children again.

What other animal life would I like to see... maybe a drastically different form... an insect perhaps? Would that end better? The book opened several pages to the left, I assumed to an earlier life time. The pain from my rabbit form was still fresh when I saw an immense brownish stain on the ground, comprised of innumerable busy creatures walking downhill. We were walking together. We felt the vibration of our feet and sniffed the substances being left behind as we marched. We knew we had to continue, never mind hunger, thirst or fatigue. All we could think of was our mission ahead: find food.

Nonetheless, the food was not to satiate our own appetite; it was to feed the ever-demanding larvae, our sisters. We simultaneously knew what was happening back in the nest and what the levels of food were at any given time and how fast it was depleting. All of us knew, like one collective consciousness or telepathic communication with each other and with our home. We walked and walked and walked. The weather was nice (not windy) and the path uneven, but we trusted our sister leaders. We knew they would take us where we needed to go, no hesitation, no complaints, no questioning, total commitment to get the food and supply the nest. There was no concept of individuality or choice. We existed to serve, nothing else mattered.

We arrived at an area with a strong sweet smell and lots of red plump spots on the floor. They were several times the size of the biggest of us, although we had no problem transporting them on our backs. The journey was very long and it became difficult to carry on, but we never thought of quitting. We finally arrived at the top of the hill and entered a cavernous labyrinth, busy as always, but well organized. The larvae were placed in different chambers, according to their diet. They were constantly being looked after, same as when we were larvae, perpetuating this indefinitely. We talked with each other through a variety of touches or rubs and odorous substances; we worked in sync, like one vast organism devoted to breeding the next generation. This particular chamber hosted future worker ants, which would help maintain our colony and our queen. As we got older, we were less strong and were not as able to keep up with the work. The last time I loaded food on my back I was not able to stand up straight, I collapsed under its weight, but this time I did not feel the urge to complete the trip. I knew my mission had ended.

What an enslaving life! But at the same time, I sensed the greatness of the unity with all my brothers and sisters of the colony! We were truly one entity! The way we communicated and worked for the same purpose was unbeatable. I don't remember another life where I was so unselfish and loved such a huge amount of beings; certainly not as a human, where we only love those we like and this is conditioned by our prejudice. This life, although guided by instinct, was truly amazing. It allowed me to appreciate the value of individuality and free will; but acquiring those qualities as an inherent characteristic of an ant, leaves little room for merit or growth. To develop such selfless and love qualities, even in a smaller degree, as a human, one practically must go through all sorts of egotistical, egocentric and long-suffering lives until eventually reaching an incarnation where through discipline, meditation and enlightening one can really understand an ant. What is the virtue of being brain wired to be noble, caring and loving? This is why I needed to evolve in a series of diverse physical beings.

My book, or I suppose all books, are something magical. I figured that mine could show me which animal life would be most beneficial for me to see, knowing in what chapter of my life (death?) I currently existed. So, I closed the book and mentally asked it to open where the pertinent information lay. It worked!

I looked up and noticed two parallel views on each side of me, simultaneously. I felt soft, fresh, light, and as I moved up gradually, I perceived more and more light. I was ascending; the image of the sky and the sun was under water. The freshness of the ocean, as my head came out, was a clear contrast with the warm breeze of the surface. I had company; the camaraderie with the rest of the group was wonderful. We were happy! We traveled together and played constantly. We talked affectionately among ourselves through some sort of special "code" consisting of a wide range of sounds and whistles. Everyone had a name, given by the Universal Source after a certain age. Mine was a special whistle, unpronounceable by other species, but pretty melodious by our standards. I was a male and I lived to enjoy the experience and, together with the other animals, bless the world with our presence. As I was getting closer to the shore I noticed some strange creatures I had never seen before. I wondered what they were and what they did. Wow, they were vertical! They had four long and thin appendages ... How weird! I knew some animals lived on land because I had talked to turtles and seals who said there were other beings who could breathe air. Some of them had even ventured deeper inland where the sand is dry and birds land. I had heard stories of nests and eggs and bird thieves, and seals had spoken about napping under the sun or sliding over a white cold mantle. I even saw afar a series of odd erect boxes this shoal of standing creatures of different sizes must have used to hide. I was so focused on them, wanting to say hi and get to know them that I ignored the calls from the others, which ultimately got farther and weaker.

I can't explain how, but I suddenly found myself entangled by some gigantic plant of strange material which grabbed me by the fins and dragged me against my will. My blood rushed to my head, I felt confused and... At this moment I became aware of my current reality reading the records of my incarnations and dared not to see more. That belonged to the past and I did not have to suffer it again if I did not want to. What a relief! I painfully realized that human ignorance is the worst thing in this planet.

This was until now, my last animal incarnation. I was given special permission to get a dolphin's body, for a short time, as an exception, because these creatures really do not belong to this realm. They are, in fact "extraterrestrial" in nature (are not we all?) Whales and dolphins come from higher levels of consciousness with the purpose of uplifting the Earth in its own evolution as a being. Yes, the Earth and the Sun are also living beings (whose ancient cultures of Mexico used to worship). I learned later that the second is a high level luminous being that irradiates his love with no distinction to all beings on the planet. These ocean creatures have been on this world for millions of years, even before the Atlantis and the appearance of humans. Without their help, Earth would have never seen the evolution of so many species of land and sea.

Dolphins and whales have the unique mission to help raise the vibrational frequency of the planet, so it can advance to a higher dimension and join the more elevated galaxies. They volunteered to come since immemorial times, but now these animals are leaving Earth, steadily, to the brink of extinction. Without animals, like dolphins and whales in particular, Earth will perish to its own environmental destruction. Men have polluted land, sea and air, perforated holes all over, stained the planet with innocent blood due to their insatiable appetite for animals and all-natural resources. They only take and take and never give anything in return. How much longer can this situation last? What is happening is so alarming, that if humans don't act quickly, Earth will evolve without the most "intelligent" specie she has hosted. Because with a single shake, she can make all people disappear and move forward without the parasites which make her so sick.

Unfortunately, the efforts of environmental and animal protection groups are not enough to stop the continuous damage which most recently has been inflicted upon the planet. What humankind does not understand is that all life forms are interconnected, that life is one. The limited perception of their five physical senses is so obstructing for they become oblivious to the cry of a tree when it is cut, to the weeping of birds when their ecosystem is crushed, or to the prayers of mountains to avert imminent desecration of putting cement and asphalt in their place. Humans have changed the face of the planet like no other creature before; unlike other species which utilize an array of senses to understand the world around them, they seem totally desensitized from nature. The universe was created by the Sound (the Word as mentioned in the Bible) and unless human beings resonate with the vibration of this Creative Sound, they will remain in lower levels of consciousness.

The songs of the whales and the dolphins are very powerful. They can uplift the world, but the attack from human actions is overwhelming. These creatures are being compelled to leave; they are being attacked and tortured by military sonar machines that hurt their bodies and brains, even forcing them to commit suicide.[3] Human beings are depleting the life of the oceans at an astonishing rate through direct and indirect killing and using the oceans as a waste container.

Destiny is not fixed, people can change. They need to respect all life and be more loving and compassionate if they are to keep living on this planet, which is really magnificent even among other beautiful planets in the physical universe.

After reviewing those lives, I felt like I was ready to move on. While I had not been a dog before, I had a pretty good idea of what would make me happy and how I could

---

[3] Cori, Patricia. *Before We Leave You.* Berkeley: North Atlantic Books, 2011.

contribute to the lives of Cecilia and Max. Sri Bawarta Laji appeared in front of me outside the library. We were on a high place, like on a cloud. I saw something resembling a rainbow below us; it is funny how it works here. We don't "transport" ourselves anywhere, yet it seems we always appear where we need to go. I guess I am still new to this dimension and since I don't know all the possibilities, it is my guru who takes me wherever is best. Like being omnipresent and omniscient regarding my needs and I never feel lonely.

I am sure I will miss this place: the love one "breathes" here is unlike anything on Earth. I realize now that animals can connect to the Source much easier than humans. With the better understanding and appreciation for animals I gained, I see that a dog life is as important as any other animal and, after all, it does not last very long. At the end, I will be uplifted to a superior level of consciousness, even higher than this one (thanks to heavenly connections).

"Hello, Alma! How do you feel now about animals?" asked my dear guru.

"Hello… well… ashamed, I am sorry that humans are so ignorant about their vital role in the planet's evolution and surprised about how all animals feel and their capacity to love. Some people still believe they have no souls! We truly are one! I can tell you as far as I am concerned, I don't want to have to eat meat, even if I don't kill directly." I started remembering my Hindu vegetarian friend Ushmil.

"There is an agreement among all animals establishing that killing for survival is allowed (which ended up being imprinted in their cells) and they have previously given their consent to this law, according to their own evolution. Animals usually do not hunt for sport or hate, they take the weakest or the oldest individual in the wild and maintain a balance in nature. They are also subject to karma nevertheless and know that killing another sentient being inherently will reap its consequences. They are okay with that; not all have the capacity to develop the quality of compassion towards all animal species to the extent of humans (even though most humans are not interested in or have a hard time extending this quality beyond their pets, family or their country). They pay their karma like any other creature under the laws of the lower worlds. In more developed, nonviolent planets, animals have evolved to become herbivores."

"Why is it that sometimes animals attack people? I mean, when they are not hungry or threatened by them?"

"Do you refer to unprovoked animal encounters? Would it surprise you to know that some very violent souls of angry individuals can reincarnate as lions, for example, in order to satiate their deleterious tendencies, thus avoiding the killing of human beings, (which generates even more karma than the killing of animals)? There are cases where a person is so full of hatred that he decides to take the body of an animal with the sole purpose of revenge. Those are the rare incidents where a bear kills a human or a shark attacks a child. The soul of the victim could have been the killer in a previous life and unless somebody forgives the offense, the cycle of revenge will continue through multiple reincarnations: you kill me in this lifetime, I kill you in the next. Sincere repentance is truly a form of liberation. It is not until reaching a superior level of consciousness that the law of karma cannot touch you. The beings who arrive to such planes are also more loving and wiser. Obviously, they would never think of harming anyone."

I could continue listening to my guru for eternity, but he had other plans for me and threw me off my train of thought by asking me if I was ready to go over my "contract."

"Is this where one exercises the so called 'free-will'?" I said excitedly at the prospect of choosing what kind of life I wanted.

"Yes, karma-permitting. Remember: you can choose within the merits you have accumulated in previous lives and according to the affinity with the beings who will take you in. Once born, you can make additional modifications. We know that if Cecilia and Max had wished, you would have been their child, so there is a strong affinity with them. Your mission in life is clear. What else would you like to add, Alma?"

"It would be nice if they love me like I were their true child. By the way, I think they have in mind a female, which is fine with me. I want to be vegan like them and receive all kinds of affection. I want Cecilia to never get tired of scratching my tummy nor behind my ears or expressing her love towards me. I want to be constantly showered with attention, consideration and respect. I desire to be protected, never letting me to become lost, killed or in the hands of people that may mistreat me. I wish to be pampered and accompany them on their trips. I prefer a healthy body and long to be a source of joy and comfort for both," I expressed firmly to my guru.

"Have you checked out their own contracts? What would happen if they separate, for example?"

"I did not think of that, but it does make sense to know what I am getting into beforehand."

"It will also help you understand how you fit in the picture, after all the three of you will be sharing the family karma."

It turned out that something apparently as simple as choosing the right animal also falls into the ugly reach of the Lord of Karma. For example, if a parent neglects a child in his former life and opts not to have family in the next, the dog he adopts could have health problems and make him develop the love and compassion he lacked (and pay for medical services). Sri Bawarta Laji was packed with interesting stories.

He told me of a woman named Dom Me, who was not too fond of animals, so in order to marry her boyfriend she asked him to get rid of his two cats. The man loved his cats very much, but he loved the woman more, so he gave them away, which resulted in great suffering for the felines that missed him tremendously and did not understand what they did wrong.

One day, Dom Me discovered that the neighbors had been evicted from their house, leaving behind a cute small black French Poodle who lived with them.

A few days later, she found the little dog by her front door crying. Dom Me was not a bad person, so she fed him and took him to the vet. The doctor said that the animal was in good condition although a little underweight due to being abandoned. He refused to take him hoping the lady would have pity on the dog and adopt him. Dom Me had no other choice but to bring him home, as the vet had told her that she would likely condemn him to death if she left him in the local pound. To the woman's surprise, the dog was very well behaved and loving, but still she did not care for the poor pooch.

Knowing his wife, the husband tried not to get attached to the dog, as the experience with the cats had been painful. The Dom Me kept looking for someone to adopt him. She asked in her church and among her friends, but everyone already had pets and could not take another one. Finally, she found a person who seemed interested and asked lots of questions about the animal. After learning that the dog was a purebred, young and healthy, he offered to keep him. There was something Dom Me disliked about this man, so she kept postponing delivering the dog, until she ran out of excuses. Perhaps the dog sensed Dom Me's distrust or perhaps he had his own doubts, but the animal wanted to stay.

Reluctantly, he went with the man, who promised he would take good care of the poodle. Not long after they left, Dom Me heard that the same individual was in the business of selling pets and breeding them. He was not going to keep the dog; he was strictly interested in making a profit.

Dom Me felt awful. Her conscience did not let her sleep at night and when she did, she had nightmares. She dreamed that the dog was her dear father whom she lost many years ago and had promised never to leave her. Her desperation only grew bigger as she could not find the guy again and did not forgive herself for what she had done. Then, the minister at her church offered some advice. He told her that in order to redeem herself, she should reverse her action and adopt a dog she would care for and love. So, she talked to her husband, who though startled, agreed to having a dog and even offered some help. She refused, for this was something she needed to do alone and said she would pick the right dog herself. "Fine!" he exclaimed, and the woman went straight to the nearest dog pound to their house. Dom Me entered the facilities thinking, "I will find a friendly dog and I will take him home in no time."

As soon as she turned to the left row of cages she saw this beautiful dog jumping, barking and wagging its tail vigorously at the sight of the new visitor. "This must be the one!" she thought, and with no further considerations she signed up for it and took him home. The clerk was somewhat surprised to see such a small woman pick such a big dog but was glad he found a family; after all, adult and big dogs are more difficult to accommodate. They completed the paperwork and said goodbye.

The minute Dom Me opened the house door the dog went crazy, running all over the place, smelling everything, scratching the trash can, jumping on the sofa, knocking down flowerpots and objects on the coffee table. Dom Me did not know what to do. "What did I get into!" In that moment, her husband showed up, got hold of the leash and walked the dog to the backyard. The dog was very grateful and affectionate, and filled a void they did not know they had. Neither of them had the common sense or money to provide the animal with basic manners, so it became the unruly pampered loving child they never had. To make matters worse, Dom Me found a stray dog later that same year and the story repeated itself, but this time the animal was in bad shape, so all the money she did not spend on the first dog, she had to spend on this other one, to at least get him in decent shape to offer him for adoption.

As one can imagine, she could not accommodate the second dog and he became the next spoiled rotten child addition to the family. Fortunately, the couple was loving and managed to live with the beasts by adapting their home and lifestyle for everyone's sake: no more visits from grandma (as the dogs jumped on visitors and had already caused granny to fall); no more plants in the house, including decorations or nice furniture (which they ruined); no more opening windows or leaving food unattended. They built a costly fence after Dom Me's husband hurt his arm trying to restrain one of the dogs from going after the neighbor's cat; and they took fewer vacations, as the kennel was expensive and taking the wild animals with them, a liability. Nonetheless, those were the dogs her karma brought them… it would have been so much wiser and easier to have simply kept the cute well-mannered poodle! But this is what the Dom Me and her husband needed to learn, and the dogs received the love and care they deserved.

"Does it mean that I will be the dog they deserve, as well?" I asked.

"Yes. It is good for you to know what kind of karma they have because all the members share the karma of the family, like the karma of a country, whose retributions are affected by those of each other."

"Seems logical," I said.

Sri Bawarta Laji went on to check their "files" and shared with me information on how I would fit into their lives. For now, it suffices to say that one of my missions would be to help Max overcome his fear of dogs. He did not want to admit to Cecilia, but he was afraid of dogs. He thought the root cause was witnessing a friend being bitten by a dog when he was a little boy and therefore he had been avoiding the animals all his life. However, the problem ran deeper than this and he needed extra help. Besides, he understood that in spite of not wanting to have children, the best way to fulfill Cecilia's motherly subconscious instincts was through a pet.

"How can we guarantee that she will pick me from the rest of the dogs?"

"It will come naturally. Since you have been relatives in past lives she will easily feel attracted to you. Most importantly, you will be at the right place, at the right moment. You will not go unnoticed. It may look like she picks you for your color, size or gender, yet you could have been her human daughter, and this is a strong connection. Like most humans, she cannot see beyond the physical, but there will be a good feeling and you will feel the same," responded my guru.

"Okay." Having reviewed grosso modo their respective contracts I felt confident that I would lead a comfortable and relatively easy dog life and understood my role in theirs, besides fulfilling my goal for liberation. "One last question, can we stipulate on my contract how I want to depart?"

"Indeed! What is it going to be? A natural cause or something quicker?"

"You know, my main concern is the suffering I will bring… what would make it easier?"

"Nothing, but you can come back as another pet to accompany them for the rest of their journey if you wish."

"No. I know that Earth is not Home and I need to go higher. Please, don't let me forget it. I will wait for them. I don't want a painful transition though."

"The material world is an illusion, a very well-crafted illusion. Death does not exist, and you know it well. The souls are only playing their role in the theatre of life. It is not fun if you know the ending."

Part IV

My Life as Canela

She was beautiful. Slender, red, short hair and eyelashes. Bright brown eyes outlined in black. Black colored lips and nails. Soft, long ears and tongue. I am forever grateful to her for allowing me in her body and giving me the opportunity to come to this world. God bless all mothers!

I know I have been through the process of incarnation countless times, but the wonders of nature, the intelligence of the process, the logic of the plan and the inviolability of its compliance never ceases to amaze me.

As soon as I "signed" my contract, my soul moved through a whirling channel. Out of nowhere I found myself spiraling down in a luminous funnel which narrowed into a chord. Vibrant colors appeared all around giving the impression of being on an underwater train traveling vertiginously. This chord seemed to connect to a source of light anchored by a warm, fleshy substance. I perceived that part of me became attached to a bundle of individual cells which absorbed different wavelengths. Also, from the chord I received some sort of relaxing music whose vibrations I felt inundated me. The mass was growing and soon I got company.

Almost immediately I distinguished a kind of soft tiny pillow on each side of me, and another, and another. Each one slightly different in vibration, but gentle and loving. It felt good to have company. It was comforting to be able to share the experience with other beings. We started to communicate with images and memories from past lives. Interestingly, our bodies were being developed but our souls were not confined to them. It was more like floating inside an inner space where I could perceive a soft light and a pleasant sound... difficult to describe. We realized that we were to be siblings and were attached inside our mother's womb.

One of my siblings was astonished when he saw a tail starting to form out of his body... he had been a hamster in his previous life. He kept looking at its lengthening with awe, not realizing it was him who moved it (I wonder if when he is born he will be one of those silly dogs who keeps chasing their tail). Another was an experienced dog, coming back to rejoin her former human. The other two had been together before and decided to continue their experience on Earth, having been originally from another planet devoid of animals. We were connected through the love of our physical mother, who was very quiet. I hardly remember her barking. I was the most curious of the five, so my soul moved above my mother's physical body through a radiant silver thread which seemed to contain a whole galaxy filled with stars, floating like a child's balloon held by his mother.

As the days passed, our bodies grew bigger and stronger. My siblings switched positions from time to time, to the discomfort of our mother, who sometimes tried to move us with her snout and licked her tummy energetically. Mother was usually occupied in finding food and comfort, constantly alert to loud noises and moving objects she did not understand. She liked to play with the bigger dogs although her gaining weight prevented her from being as fast as usual. She was energetic and her sleep very shallow. Knowing that she was going to give birth soon, she arranged a pretty good den, with tree branches, big leaves and material discarded by humans like a piece of clothing and old newspapers she found nearby.

One day, an invisible force pushed us out of our lovely abode towards a rough kind of light that hurt our skin and stung our still closed eyes like cactus thorns. We came out one by one, through little pain and effort from both parts. The air made our entire body ache and shiver inside. Instinctively, we sought our mother's warmth and eventually felt better.

It rained the day we were born, but mother had it all planned. The den was inside one big pipe near a creek, hidden from plain sight. We were received with love and exquisite attention; mother licked each of us clean and fed us delicious milk we adored. She used her body as a protective barrier from the rain and the wind; she kept us warm and cozy. It was a tender feeling in spite of the soreness our bodies underwent from the change of vibration; much heavier and harsher than where we came from, which took getting used to.

Later, I saw this cute sweet face, all curled up under the shade of a tree, living in the country. It seemed like mother was with a pack of dogs, most of them family, roaming freely. It did not matter, really, but I wanted to know who my father was and more about my mother. Quite naturally, as soon as I asked, a response came to me, in a series of images that showed how her ancestors came from a neighboring state where for centuries they cohabited with the natives. The dogs had traversed state lines, railroads, highways and escaped predators like coyotes, disease and all kinds of moving vehicles. They were not completely wild; some of them were found by caring humans and successfully adopted and appreciated as an ancient breed, still not very well known. Now, closer to a suburban village, the quadrupeds were fetching food in trash cans in close proximity to more people. My siblings and I were the result of an adventure my father had during one of his escapades from the farm house. He was a handsome Labrador who loved to swim and play, very energetic and smart.

Gradually, we became more active and soon we joined the other dogs and played all day. We spent a lot of time chasing the sun and under the stars, the countryside was our playground. I don't know how long we were together as a family, but we enjoyed the love and protection of our mother and the entire pack, taking our freedom and happiness for granted.

It was a cold morning that brought a tumultuous noise and lots of new smells which disturbed the peaceful atmosphere among all of us dogs. I remember people coming from a nearby village invading and destroying our territory with strange machines and vehicles. I knew humans had been a nuisance for some time, but they did not come too close or in big numbers and normally they left us alone. Some were more curious than others and started investigating. They were also interested in killing trees to build their houses and believed that we did not have the right to be there, even though we were there first (together with deer, racoons and other fauna). Mercilessly, they took possession, stripping of their homes everyone around.

They conducted what they called a "dog rescue operation" although what we needed was to be rescued from them, but instead we were imprisoned for no reason. Mother, my siblings and other relatives were taken to the county pound, to be "given the chance to find a home," like we were not home to begin with! There, we could be adopted or otherwise exterminated as we found out, since the facility was filled to capacity and could not keep us there for more than a week.

Despite all of this, I kept relatively calm. They put me in a cage with my siblings and other dogs of similar age and size, too many for the cold hard floor surface, in an ugly confined space devoid of anything familiar from the outside. It smelled old, strange and synthetic, by which I mean a smell not found out in the countryside or anywhere known; but above all, it smelled of sadness and despair. We knew that not all of us would make it out of there alive. After our arrival we were taken to a room where we were individually examined of body and temperament, except the youngest and defenseless who took only the first test. This was particularly hard on the adult dogs, as their instincts and muscles were stronger and some tried to escape at all costs or reunite with their offspring, deeming them "unfit for human company." The latter would be condemned to death, which although was better than prison, denied them the opportunity to really prove their worth and to know what human company could become.

During the following days that I stayed in such a place, we were visited by several strangers. I discovered two types: the ones who were looking for one dog to keep and the ones who would take as many as possible to give them a temporary home until hopefully, finding a permanent human to live with. I knew I was assigned a special human, but I was anxious and scared knowing that time was running out for many of my brethren canines. In the midst of the tangible despair, for many temporary residents visiting hours were an exciting, hopeful time. I never saw mother again, but I had the chance to say goodbye to my siblings, two of which, according to their karma, would be adopted together by an older couple whose collie dog had recently passed. I knew they would be okay. The smallest one though, regretted his decision to come down as a pooch and quickly would bail out of this life.

Seeing potential liberators made the day bearable, yet, stressful. Most dogs, aware of the situation, wanted to greet and appeal to every human coming through the door, although some dogs were more enthusiastic than others, depending on their condition and reason for being there. I learned about instances of dogs betrayed by their own humans who did not want them anymore and of others feeling relieved to get rid of the unexpected pet left orphaned after his adopted human had died… so many sad stories! But there were also happy endings and good people taking dogs which no one else would have considered. Those were often the souls of past life relatives and friends coming back to settle a karmic death from the past.

It still amuses me to watch how clueless most humans are. Unlike us, they are pretty blind, deaf and anosmic, to say the least (of course, there are exceptions). They had no idea what kind of dog they would end up with. The dog on the other hand, could immediately recognize his or her human, even before his arrival; we sense their presence in advance. How can a creature be so out of touch with nature and be considered the most intelligent on the planet? Of course it is they who believe this. Not only that, they don't even know themselves!

What most dogs really longed for was to be free. Some had not seen the sunlight or sensed the grass for what seemed like an eternity! The fellow across my cell told me that one of the puppies had never gone outside; she was born indoors and taken directly here. Also, he explained that before any dog could leave, it had to undergo surgery, which meant a person in a white robe cut their skin to make sure they could not have babies, to supposedly control the population. Why would they do so? We tried to stay out of their way… not every pup survives anyhow! It is people who reproduce excessively that are taking over green spaces like ours and kicking everyone out, to make more room for themselves! How does this make sense? Should it not be the other way around? I wish they could see what they were doing to our beloved nature! At least they should let us breathe some fresh air...!

There must have been at least ten canine companions inside my cage, some played and the rest agitated their tails at the arrival of the first visitors of the day. I was coiled over my tail in the back corner, shaking of cold and unsettled with the uproar of neighbors jumping and barking, demanding attention and food. It took a long time, but the soul I was waiting for was finally here! I heard a voice exclaim:

"Can I see one more, please?"

"Well ma'am, you have seen many dogs and don't pick no dog, and we are about to close," alleged a tobacco odorous man, eager to leave.

Ignoring him, she turned to her companion and said, scanning inside my cage, "Look Max, that one in the corner, all quiet and shy. It is the color you like!" She turned quickly to Tobacco man. "Is that a female, by chance?"

"Meh,... I think is a female..." The guy opened the door.

I did not move. I was mesmerized observing the aura of the inquiring couple, which irradiated a nice yellowish luminescence. The woman came forward; she emitted a smell of wet wood and soil which I immediately adored.

This is it! This is it! This is it!

I remember being removed from my corner and taken to the backyard. The sun was coming down and there was a light breeze. I walked with the human on a leash... my very first time! How special this made me feel! It was the first happiest day of my life! She was talking to me. I had no idea what she was saying, but it sounded like music to my ears. The lady leaned down, looked at my eyes and stood up; I stood up next to her. She walked some more and halted; I did the same. It was like a game, I instinctively followed. She talked a lot, then she squatted and touched my nose, her big eyes enslaved mine. Nothing else mattered in the world, she was mine!

She must have liked me too because she petted me on the head and took me to Max. He did not seem comfortable at the dog pound, scratching and dodging mosquitoes, but was happy to see his mate smile. Seeing us approach he thought, "She needs this; I hope it eases her temper, with

God's help." Max kept his distance but grinned at me and hugged his female… it started to feel like family again!

My heart dropped to my paws when Tobacco man re-appeared and took me back to prison.

"Nooo! I am supposed to go with them!" I didn't know what happened, but this was a mistake!

The couple talked some more with the employee and left, but she promised me to return. This is when I learned what the other dogs meant when referring to patience. Patience is the time a dog waits for his human to come back, to touch him, look or speak to him, and I needed to master this quality, essential to any pet.

The days that followed were a mix of emotions. While some canine friends found new or old families (in the case of disoriented canines), others, the less popular, were left behind and "put to rest" to make space for more. This only increased the number of casualties, which seemed like their ultimate goal. Nevertheless, we met nice people, people who had to work here and people who came voluntarily like Doctor Badsting, who spent his time cutting and stinging every animal, either to prevent us from having puppies or to place a metal thing under the skin of the head and some injections. Very unpleasant! Ever since, I flee from anyone wearing a long white robe or smelling of alcohol.

According to protocol, nobody could leave until Doctor Badsting approved. So, after he was done with me, I waited for my humans with a little pain and discomfort. They showed up as expected and one of the employees took me in her arms to my new mom's. I had not been so comfortable in a long time! We made one last stop at the office: the final requisite on our way out, to see Mrs. Coffeecup, who humming after finishing her fourth cup of the day, was handling the papers and giving me a collar and a leash.

The three of us abandoned that place, which I hope never, ever to see again, and got into the car.

Max had me on his lap, but as his mate was talking, I reached out to her and slowly sneaked under the steering wheel she was holding until we got home.

"Canela, this is your new house. You are going to be a good girl and be well behaved. Go ahead and explore. If you need to go outside, you let daddy know," declared the lady of the house removing the leash from the collar.

"I said I will help you Cecilia, but this is your responsibility," intervened Max.

"Of course, but you can let her out in the mornings when I go to work… if she asks you," she clarified.

"All right, but I am not cleaning up any doggy mess. I will be busy working on the computer."

"No problem! She'll be house broken in no time… what if we find out she already is?"

"I doubt it, remember what the lady said, that she was found wandering with other dogs. We know hardly anything about her!" replied my new dad while I inspected the territory. "I hope she does not get much bigger."

"I don't think so. The other guy said that she is at least six months old and possibly close to her full size. Judging by her feet, she won't be too big." Reading the adoption papers, she added, "They put 'Labrador mix' and gave her an ugly name, forget it! Come on, Canela. Let me show you your bed and then I'll take you outside!"

The rest of my puppyhood passed like a dream. I adapted very well to their routine. In the mornings, mom would take me out for a quick relief trip, which she called "my business" or my "physiological needs" and I stretched my paws. Then she went straight to work and I would go back to my bed under the desk and wait for dad to get up. In less than an hour dad would open his bedroom door and say good morning. At first, I got up to greet him but I soon realized that this made him a little nervous and he asked me to stay put. He needed some more time before he felt completely comfortable with me.

Then it was show time! Before having breakfast, dad followed a yoga video. I cannot tell how long he had been doing it, but I hope not too long, because some of the poses seemed ridiculously easy. Who needs a video to tell you how to stretch? Never mind, although I noticed he could not scratch his neck with his lower paws like I did. Humans have their challenges, but their hands are awesome! After the session, he made a hearty breakfast and sometimes shared part of it with me. Next, hours of work followed. What powerful force hypnotizes people to their screens is a mystery to me... I have tried to watch television with them, but I don't get it. On the other hand, I enjoyed most of the types of music he played.

Mom would typically come home later in the day. I was the first to greet her, to dad's complaint, "You greet the dog before you greet me!", but I always beat him to the door; not my fault. Then they had dinner and served mine so we could supposedly eat together, but again, I can't help it if I beat them. They were pretty slow.

"Why are you saving the sweet potatoes? You are not going to give them to the dog, are you?"

"Max, I have too much on my plate. Besides, I am sure they are good for her."

Mom walked to my dish and dropped one piece of sweet potato into it. I tasted it and I liked it. I went to her for more.

"See what you have done? Now you have a begging dog! She needs to go to her bed and wait for us to finish."

When mom went to the kitchen to clean up, she offered me different foods but none looked appetizing. Weird mushy things and hot stuff, tomatoes, lettuce… unappetizing smells. No thank you! Mom got impatient and opened my mouth with her hands, stuck a piece of food in and kept her hand on my snout to make sure I would not spit it out. She was persistent!

"You are the pickiest doggy there is! Why do you dislike my food? Try this, it is the sweet potato you liked… If you reject the salad, fine! How about the rice… don't you turn around! Be thankful to God you were not born in China! You behave like you were the dog of a king, but you come from the pound! Don't be ridiculous! Look Max, I can place the entire pot under her nose and she walks away, like she's thinking *'yucky! how can you expect me to eat that?'* Do you see? Amazing! Maybe she was poisoned in her former life, I cannot believe it, Canela!"

"Leave her. Hey, I found a tooth this morning… could it be yours? Let me see: smile!"

"Very funny... I did not know dogs changed teeth like people... then she must be younger than what they told us. These people don't have a clue!"

After dinner, no matter the weather, we would go for a walk. This was the advantage of living on the second floor and not having a patio, yard or terrace. I loved going out, but disliked exercising. I don't enjoy getting tired. It is better to be on my comfy bed or outdoors checking everyone else; but they did not understand, and boy, I tried! I kept lying on the ground and walking back to the house, but it was no use... unless the weather was really bad, they would insist and force me to walk. I had no choice but to go with them. Then, sometimes we would sit on a swing to watch the sunset... those were good times!

An important part of the routine was meditating on the Divine. Max and Cecilia were a fantastic match, and I think one of the things that kept them together was sharing the same spiritual path. Max meditated every day, sometimes with his wife, depending on her activities. They always set the clock early in the morning for meditation before work or later during the day or prior to bedtime and set aside time during the weekend. They always included me and brought me my bed and my favorite blanket and played some chants to favor the ambience. "Meditation time!" was dad's command for me to join in (often during a break from his daily chores, while Cecilia was at work), tuned in a singing voice, inviting but firm. It was great! We sat next to each other, dad on his special chair, and we spent quite some time trying to know God.

Mom had great difficulty concentrating though; her intellectual mind and exuberant energy kept playing tricks on her. Max, on the contrary, a musician at heart, easily took off and left the body to temporarily visit higher realms, to come back wiser, more loving and happier. Although he did not have "experiences" every time he meditated, he grew spiritually with the help of his Master. I think mom would have given up if it was not for dad, who was very devoted and kept encouraging her. Cecilia's spiritual practice was tied to Max's, ten years her senior, and his pupil in many ways. From time to time, there would be group retreats organized by the guru's disciples near the beach where unfortunately, dogs were not allowed.

"Ceci, I am going to a retreat next weekend. Do you want to come?"

"How many days, and who are you going with?"

"Starts at noon on Friday and we come back Sunday night. It is the usual crowd. The two Asian retired couples and Tara. You know younger people work or have other commitments. They are renting a van and we are going to take turns driving the nine-hour trip. We need to bring mosquito repellent and sunscreen. They say it is going to be hot."

"No thank you. It is too far and too long. Last time I went, one of the tires exploded in the middle of the road while I was driving and we were frying under the sun. We sat outdoors with the voracious mosquitoes and the stinky repellent does not let me concentrate. Besides, you guys meditate all night and I can't take it! You know I need a comfy bed and my A/C. I will be miserable and I don't want to spoil your retreat with my bad mood. Besides, I never hear, see or experience anything. I honestly think that God does not have pity on me."

"You always say this Ceci, but you know it is not true!"

"Then why does everybody have some sort of experience except me, or explain why their fascination for meditation? I really don't get it. I think they are a bunch of fanatics!"

"They probably have meditated in past lives; their souls have practiced before. No worries, your effort and sincerity count, you do your best. There is no need to have a thrilling experience to grow spiritually. Our Master has said that some of the best disciples don't even have experiences, or they have them but cannot recall them. Remember that the brain cannot register what happens in the superior levels of consciousness."

"Okay, but they see some progress. To be quite honest with you, I notice zero improvement in myself. I am still impatient, jealous and have many defects. I am sure my level is very low… after all these years of practice I am the same!"

"So, you think God loves everybody but you? Come on!"

"The truth is that I feel like he does not care. I have tried not to expect any type of experience if at least I become a better person, but this is not happening either!" Mom's tears were balancing on the rims of her eyes, shy and afraid to drop.

"Maybe it is the price you have to pay to be initiated. You don't know what your karma is, but the Master still is teaching you."

"But I am not progressing!" cried mom in total despair. "If I am a teacher and have one student who is slow, then I must teach her in a way she can learn. I think I am the disabled disciple or the spiritually-challenged student who needs special attention but is neglected and it makes me so sad! At the same time, I don't want to quit my practice because the Master promised to take us all to the next level of consciousness where there is no karma and save us from the wheel of reincarnation. Even if I don't get anything else out of my practice, I won't quit. The promise of never having to come back is good enough for me."

"God does not make mistakes. Accept it as the price for your deliverance," said dad who knew they could discuss the topic for hours without changing her mind.

Dad was to leave Friday morning and mom was already in a bad mood. "Daddy is abandoning us, Canela!" she said in front of him. "He loves his Master more than he loves us."

It was tough. The atmosphere of the house became somber and she clung to me like a hungry tick. I know she meant well, but sometimes it was too much, like her incessant hugs. I preferred her singing.

With my arrival, she remembered "My love is pure Canela, her sweetness belongs to meee, the honey of my lips I offer her and I give her aaall, aaall my heart…"[4] which was upbeat, executed when she was cheerful. Also "*Cielito lindo,*" a Mexican song adapted in my honor: "*De la sierra morena, Canela linda, vienen bajando, un par de orejas largas, Canela linda, de contrabando. ¡Aaay, ay, ay, aaay! ¡Ladra y no aúlles, porque*

[4] Aguilar, Homero. *Canela pura*. 1962.

ladrando se alegran, Canela linda, los corazones"[5] or "*Sœur Canela, sœur Canela, dormez-vous? dormez-vous? Sonnez les matines, sonnez les matines, ding dang dong, ding dang, dong…"*[6] when she wanted to practice her French. Better yet, "I belong to you, you belong to me, you're my sweet dooog!"[7] which she discomposed from a popular radio tune; another common one was, "You drive me crazy... oh, oh, like no one else, oh, oh, you drive me crazy and I can't heeelp myself,"[8] and whatever song she happened to be humming at the time, she changed the lyrics to accommodate my name. She had a talent for that.

Mom had an ample repertoire of songs, old, new, in Spanish, English or French, but Christmas songs were her specialty ("Canela the wet-nosed doggy" and many more), and she also came up with all sorts of nicknames for me. I really did not care, I only paid attention when she called me by my name, which, by the way, I love, and ignored the rest. Some of the most common were: "Madame Hairs," "The Hairy Maja" (inspired from Goya's the Nude Maja), and my favorite "Mi Chiquita" (nothing to do with bananas), which means "my little girl." The nicknames evolved during our lives and experiences, like this one she used when she was mad at me: "Yucky-eater" and absolutely, it was worth having my teeth brushed when we got home!

Anyway, I was in my usual state of contemplation while mom was busy moving things around the house and opening windows. She was going to turn on a deviled sucking

---

[5] Mendoza, Quirino. *Cielito lindo*. 1882.
[6] Rameau, Jean-Phillipe. *Frère Jaques*. XVII century.
[7] Schultz, Wesley; Fraites, Jeremy. *Ho Hey*. 2012.
[8] Gift, Roland; Steele, David. *She Drives Me Crazy*. 1988.

machine that made a painful and horrendous noise, when she caught me just as I was about to run for cover under their bed.

"It is futile to hide. You are a big girl now and you need to adapt to the noises of the house. In less than six months you have doubled your size, going from 20 to 40 pounds! Be a judicious girl and conduct yourself like the urban dog you are and not like a savage beast from the wild." I was not sure what she meant but she had me by the neck and I could not get out. Then she hugged me. Tighter and tighter... she was getting too close! I tried to move my leg but she immediately sat down next to me and held my back paw. "Don't run! Or are you going to leave me like daddy did? This is why I wanted a dog, to have company. If one wants to be alone then one gets a husband!" She put her nose on my nose and said in an agonizing voice, "Canela, you have the nicest wet nose in the whole world, and you feel sooo soooft…" I was trapped, but opportunely, the phone rang.

"Hi dear. How are you?...... Nothing much, Max went on a retreat and I am here cleaning the house with Canela …… Yes, we have been wanting to go to Italy for a long time. Your daughter's wedding would be the perfect opportunity to do so! ...... Wonderful! ...... Yes, of course …… I will let him know. Thank you, *ciao*!"

Mom turned back to me. "Love with paws, guess what...? We are going on vacation! Yes, you too! You will be going to Gaston's house. You'll be able to fully express your canine instincts there and play with his dogs in his backyard! Isn't it marvelous? Yeah!... and you will have a vacation from me!"

She held my front paws, moving them up and down at each sentence and talked for me. She had this weird custom learned from her mother-in-law to speak on my behalf, like a ventriloquist act:

"Hurray! Hurray! I will visit my doggy friends and I won't have to exercise! I will pee and poop immediately after Nena and Robocop and lie on the grass! I will get to enjoy the morning sun! And the best: I will have a break from the grabbing kisses from this crazy woman!"

The truth is that the kisses and hugs, although unnecessary, were an outlet to Cecilia's motherly love and a de-stressor for her. I put up with them the best I could! A break was okay, but vacations had its inconveniences too. I would also miss dad. He was the pillar of the house, my loyal companion, my meditation buddy, the disciplinarian, the one who fed me, and, of the two, the human with the highest spiritual level. Mom loved dad more than anyone in the world, to the point that dad worried what would happen if he were to die before her, making his wife promise she would marry again, if someone suitable came along.

By Sunday evening daddy came through the door and the light was made! We adored him!

"Hello, Canela! How are you? Did Ceci give you your sweet potatoes? I brought you a little something!"

My tail was wagging so hard it was hitting my eyes; he kneeled and I offered my tummy. He opened a plastic bag and gave me some bread. I took it and ran to my rug to savor it.

"Darling, I also have a surprise for you. We are going to Italy!"

There are moments in life one wishes could be put away in a drawer and have access to them limitlessly. One of these such moments was a simple and uneventful day when dad lay in the guestroom bed, hoping to take a nap and mom, joining him, sneaked me to her side.

"This is happiness! My Max on one side and my Canela on the other! I desire nothing more," sighed mom.

They planned to leave in the fall. They were enthusiastic about visiting Europe and seeing their friends and family there. I could not be happier. I thought they should feel the same, but sometimes they argued and it was unnerving. Unfortunately, those tantrums seemed to happen more often with time, but after taking a few days off, like going on vacation, things normalized. I think humans live under too much stress and some like mom want everything perfect and done right away (she should try some dog-chill pill).

After mom had left for work and dad was preparing to meditate, he summoned me with his habitual "Meditation time!" I was in the other room, busy with the important task of cleaning my paws.

He probably called a number of times, I don't know, but suddenly he showed up menacing, slipper in hand, which I dodged thanks to my quick reflexes and went straight to my place.

"Caneluska, let's meditate for mommy, so she is more patient with me and happier. Let's ask God to help me be faster, smarter and keep me healthy, so I never become a burden to her! You know, sometimes I feel so dumb…! I see how others do simple tasks with less effort but to me, everything is difficult. How I hated going to school, I did not understand much! I think that in my former life I could not be liberated because the intellect hindered my spiritual development and for this reason I chose not to be bright in the next one… but I went too far!"

Dad was indeed very spiritual. He would play some chants and repeat a mantra and in no time my soul would be going to higher levels of consciousness, even visiting or seeing other souls from my past or enjoying a blissful state of harmony and love. Dad was not always able to do so. I know his mind kept telling him to do this and do that, but he was very disciplined and prayed for his family and the world.

Days came and went like the breeze. I saw them packing their things and mine and a few days later they drove me to Gaston's. They had been telling me about my vacation for some time, so I would not feel abandoned, as they put it. They would pick me up as soon as they returned.

That was when I met Gaston's companions. Robocop was a handsome German shepherd, strong and smart. He was a misunderstood police officer and an amazing guard dog. Gaston had the good sense to adopt him when his trainer decided that his olfactory faculties did not measure up to expectations and offered it to him. He protected Gaston and his property by dispelling evil spirits and hungry ghosts which were attracted to the unhealthy habits of his human and his roommate. He was actually pretty busy, as Gaston's house was constantly filled with friends who sometimes brought with them "invisible visitors." Gaston was a very good person, noble and selfless but was vulnerable to the negative influences of these lower entities. Luckily, he also had Nena, the only female of the house, who helped by balancing with her feminine energy, the heavily charged atmosphere with her sole presence. She was a dalmatian mix and a hard snorer.

They dropped me off and left immediately. It took me some time to get used to my new surroundings, but since I had a special bond with Cecilia and Max, I could connect with them when they meditated, especially with daddy, whose concentration quality was better. Dad would take the time during his meditation to let me know they were fine and that I should be enjoying myself too and be a good girl. Less frequently, I would receive a message from mom, telling me to behave and sending me love.

Before the wedding, they wanted to tour the Roman Colosseum, a place with very strong vibes which nevertheless, were hardly ever detected by humans. Not for daddy! He started to feel like he was carrying an enormous weight, but he assumed it was due to the heat and said nothing.

A few steps ahead while heading towards the visitors' entrance, he suddenly felt dizzy and almost fainted.

"Darling, sit here, let me give you some water," said mom helping dad sit on the barrier's rough stones. "What happened?"

With difficulty, he responded, "I had a vision… I have been here before." Making an effort to get out of the spell, he continued, "I saw myself, as a boy, down there…" Mom stared at him with intrigued eyes.

Dad meant the arena, the actual ring where "battles" took place. "I was a boy, with a group of children around the same age, we must have been captured." He sobbed.

"They released violent dogs… I ran from one dog that looked me in the eyes… I wanted to climb the wall, but he reached me… It was horrible! I was killed by a dog!" Dad was still trembling from the memory and breathing heavily. The sunrays caressing his green eyes prevented him from completely opening them. He waved his hand in a fanning motion.

"My God! It is unbelievable, you actually remembered a former life? Wow! ...See everyone else, totally oblivious to the suffering that took place here, after all these years. I am sorry, darling, sorry!"

"I will be fine."

"Are you sure? Do you feel tired? Do you want to go back to the hotel and rest?" asked mom hoping to get dad good enough to take the guided tour.

"We already purchased the tickets and if you want to continue, it is fine with me… it has passed…" He held her hand and stood up. "This is why I was afraid of dogs, no wonder!"

"I can't believe you said it! First time you openly admit it. I don't blame you," said mom.

"Not necessarily. I had told you that a friend of mine was bitten by a dog on our way to school; I was with him, but I guess the dog did not like my chicken legs and chose him instead."

In his ensuing meditation, dad could not help but bring back the memory of this particular past life event to make peace with the soul of the animal, who took the opportunity (wisely) to ask him to forgive him. I also sent daddy a message saying how much I loved him and that I would always look after them.

Back at Gaston's house I waited for the sound of the car's squeaky tires to confirm their arrival, although my canine intuition usually kicked in long before they even started the engine. I had had enough chases, loud hard rock and cigarette puffs. I yielded to the temptation of trying some of Robocop's food which I thought exotic, to only throw up on the deck (unlike me, they were not vegetarian).

Although some amount of chaos can be fun, I missed my family and our routine. Besides, dad needed some additional training.

On the last night of their trip, I got the message that they were to pick me up from Gaston's the next morning after landing. Great! I would tell Gaston so he could start gathering my things.

Mom had her light chestnut hair in a ponytail and semicircular marks under her eyes. She saw me first and I ran from the back door to meet her at the side of the fence and jumped to give her a fleeting kiss. Then the others came. Gaston finally arrived with my leash, my blanket and a big bag.

"This is all. How was your trip?"

"It was wonderful," said daddy, opening the car's trunk.

"Was Canela a good girl?" inquired mom.

"Yeah, the dogs played outside a lot and slept in the bed. Canela loves her blanket. Everybody had a good time."

"Good! Canela, did you miss me?" she asked me.

"I am ready to go home. Your vacation alters my routine," I wanted to say but my excitement could not be contained when dad patted me on the head and my tail wagged out of control.

Then, in the car, mom commented,

"Max, haven't you noticed that Canela wags you the tail?"

"She does not wag me anything!" he said chuckling. "Perhaps it is because I give her her space; you are always smooching her, hugging her, touching her... you are constantly harassing her... poor Canela! Try ignoring her for a change."

"It would be too hard, especially if you are not around."

"You are just too much! You see, I don't pay so much attention to her and she comes to me voluntarily."

"And you are also the disciplinarian. She listens to you more than to me," she complained, while giving me a scolding look.

"That is right. She knows I am the boss!" responded dad sending me the familiar pair of green sentinels from under his rising brows.

"Canela, stinky doggy, you need a bath!" said mom opening her window. "You come back smoked. Like a smoked hot dog, stinky! I know it is not your fault Gaston is a smoker; at least you can go outside. You are lucky I don't have energy today, but start preparing yourself mentally and emotionally for a bath as soon as possible."

Inevitably, the next morning mom got in her undies and to the shower we went. I tried hopelessly to find an opening through the shunted door with my snout and moved in circles to every corner of the small space to escape the water. I tried jumping, but there was no use. The door almost reached the ceiling. Such torture seemed longer than ever! The worst were the ears. She stuck the towel in them, mercilessly and then rubbed my face in her characteristic harsh ways (hard to believe that dad was less rough than her). I cried out for daddy, but he was busy making breakfast.

She kept me captive in the bathroom until she finished her own shower. She finally opened the door.

Freedom! I ran through the entire house three or four times. I rolled around on the carpet in the bedroom to finish drying. Then mom appeared and tried to stop me and dry me some more with a towel, when my own method was better! Dad must have seen the anxiety in my eyes and brought me a warm tortilla saying,

"Good girl! You are shiny clean!"

"And fluffy too!" added mom while putting my blanket in the washer.

I slept nicely that night after all the stress and smelling my lovely fresh scented blanket.

The sun pierced the living room windows at the zenith of the morning. Of course, I would take advantage of its magnificent embrace to receive warm blessings and meditate better. Often, dad had the same idea.

"Caneluska, you beat me again! You got the best sunny spot in the house… share some! Don't be that way!" and asked me to move a little bit. Then, we would take off. I felt totally blessed to belong to this spiritual couple, who followed a guru like no other. One with such power that would lift us to higher realms purely by grace, and who could take me Home solely because I was his disciple's pet… words cannot explain my gratitude!

Life was good. Mom and dad loved the mountains and whenever they had a chance, they rented a cabin and we would be gone for a few days. I enjoyed the car ride. I had the entire back seat to myself (tried the front but was not comfortable there). We made stops to stretch, pee and drink some water. I would listen to music or lull to sleep by the movement of the car or the murmur of the wind. This was very much in contrast with mom's drastic turns and stops which frequently shook me in the city.

My ears flapped through the window. A variety of interesting smells surrounded us and a change in vibrational frequency relaxed everyone as we approached the mountains. These giants, one of many Mother Nature's majestic creations, pulsated in sync with the rivers and lakes nearby. Getting deep inside the woods could make someone think of being in a sacred place.

We never went to the same cabin twice, which was an inconvenience, as it took me some time to get used to a new place and by then, it was time to return home.

Dad had many talents, one of them was his ability with musical instruments. He could read and play classical music. He made me a song that he sang as a way of saying good morning: *"¡Caneeela, Caneliiita, Canela qué boniiita!"* The sound of his voice was divine to me and mom. We both enjoyed it infinitely, even when he was out of tune.

No wonder, Cecilia and Max had been together in other lifetimes. They made a pact to help each other and pursue spiritual growth until they could find liberation. They complemented each other well… and I was there for the ride and to offer some practical assistance.

One day they took me to their friend's house, a nice lady in her mid-60s, who loved art and collecting old things. I realized she shared the home with some type of pet. When I first met them, I noticed they had a similar acidic smell. Evelyn was Tarzan's human mom. He was a small, funny crossbreed of a mongrel with a stray mutt. His appearance was as wild as his name. To summarize: he had the eyes of a frog and the paws of a goose, rabbit's tail, elephant's ears, pig's nose, goat's beard, lion's mane and turkey's neck. He liked to lay in the sun like a lizard and was gentle as a butterfly, and to tie it all up, he was wise as an owl. His previous master had been a powerful Arab sorcerer, centuries ago, from whom he learned a lot.

"Hello, Canela. Do you want to play with Tarzan in the backyard?" said Evelyn with a big smile, opening the kitchen door while mom sat at her dinette table.

Tarzan seemed happy to have a canine visitor. He needed more exercise but with his mom not feeling well it had affected their routine. He was protective but friendly. We chased each other for a few minutes, but then we got hot and wanted to come in and sit next to our moms. They were partaking of a loaf of bread Cecilia baked the night before with some unappetizing fruit and tomatoes and were conversing lively, ignoring our noses on the window asking to come in.

Then a pale man, with protruding bones and no hair, came to the door. Immediately, Tarzan greeted him and introduced him as his dad. The man asked Tarzan to show some tricks he taught him. "I see, you have been trained to amuse people," I added. "My mom tried to teach me too, but she gave up quickly. Hey mister, can you teach my humans some tricks for me? Or better yet, tell me how to train them?"

All this uproar must have distracted the ladies from their conversation and Evelyn let us in. Tarzan and I lay under the table and the man sat with them.

"Puff! What causes that smell, Tarzan?" I asked referring to the bitter odor (never sensed before) coming from their side of the table.

"It comes from the guts. Mom's body is out of balance and it now reacts in a way that causes problems."

"Why is her body out of balance?"

"I am not sure. It could be because she has been unhappy despite my efforts to cheer her up, which only work momentarily. It could be that her body is tired of being afraid or perhaps she has been disconnected from her inner self for too long and it is finally demanding her attention… humans are complicated, you know," explained Tarzan licking at a section of Evelyn's calf peeping from her slacks.

"What is your mom afraid of?"

"So many things…! But it is nothing new, poor mommy! She has been afraid all her life, even from the womb."

"How come?"

"One day while we were taking a nap I saw her mother pregnant with her with a look of terror on her face. Her mom lived in Europe during time of war. She heard bombings constantly, there was a lot of destruction and death around her town in those days. Unfortunately, mom absorbed all this fear and everything scares her."

"I was scared too when I was little. In fact, my mom noticed me because I was afraid in a cage full of dogs and that is how she picked me (she also thought I would be submissive). It worked out for us!"

"Yes, but my mom lacks faith. She worries about what is going to happen after she dies. She struggles with herself. She has many doubts… she does not know whether to believe in God or not."

"It is going to be alright, our guru will help her," I said confidently remembering what my own mission was.

"Could your guru talk to my mom?"

"Our guru can do anything. He is mighty powerful. Of course!"

"That would be great! We try to help her but she is not very receptive. She blocks even her guardian angel from assisting her."

"Is this why you are here, to take upon yourself part of her disease? To ease her pain?"

"Yes. I would do anything to make her feel better."

"How do you do it?"

"In different ways. I try to dissipate her negativity. God has giving me the gift to help her by taking some of her karma on me, then I go through a process of transmutation in which I release it without too much harm to my own body. Unfortunately, I can only take up so much. If I were a Great Dane or a horse I could take more, but she would have never adopted such a large animal. Still, it does help her and her symptoms have not been too serious."

"But doesn't she acquire a karmic debt with you, which she will later have to pay?"

"That is what happens with human healers (it is different with veterinarians for humans, because they do not play with energies and do not interfere with their patient's karma). I have been granted permission to help her, it is in my contract and I do it with all my heart. Different animals help in different ways. I was given this gift, but there are many other gifts from other creatures."

"Yes, mom told me the other day about a dog whose mission was to help find a house for his homeless human. The dog, who was extremely obedient, motivated him to get ahead. Someone discovered them and that's how the animal became an actor and started making money for his dad. After he ascended, his human continued working with other dogs thus making a living by training them," I commented.

"Interesting, this time the dog got a home for the human. I am not surprised."

"How much of her sickness can you absorb?"

"I am not sure, but I take as much as my body and Heaven allow me. Only a portion of her illness can be transmuted. That is why daddy is also helping."

"What does he do?"

"He helps from another dimension. He sends an influx of high frequency vibrations to mom's astral body to help her stimulate her cells from their own spiritual plane to heal. Our power is limited though, but working together and focusing in her lower chakra we have been able to keep her alive."

"It will help her greatly if she changed her inner talk," I said referring to her negativity and apprehension.

"I know, here is where you and your mom would be a good influence. I saw your guru with you in the car when you pulled in the driveway. His exceptional body of light is like none I have ever seen before."

At that moment, Tarzan's dad raised from his chair with eyes opened widely and bowed reverently. The atmosphere became lighter and the fog covering the area cleared. A soft breeze of love filled the room with a fragrance similar to sandalwood. A rain of music like the sound of harps and a choir of angels was dispersed upon us. The Master appeared in the middle of the kitchen and his luminous aura permeated the whole house. He looked at the man and signaled the garden. Thus, they both went outside. The trees smiled and the flowers opened their petals to receive the blessing radiance emanating from his body. Even the insects and other garden creatures stood still, intoxicated with the aroma dispersed. The ladies, completely oblivious to the events which had been taking place under their noses during all this time, remained immutable, engulfed in their lively chat.

The night fell and soon after, they said goodbye. At the door, Evelyn exclaimed,

"Thank you for coming. I feel much better. You will have to come more often. *Ciao*!"

Since then, Cecilia and Max gradually increased their visits to Evelyn, who was becoming sicker. Occasionally, I communicated with Tarzan telepathically, to check on him and his mom. He told me that he was getting closer to completing his mission and that our guru continued visiting her while she slept. I kind of knew it, as mom and dad prayed for her during their meditation. Like me, Evelyn would have the assistance of a living Master and be given the choice to come back or be liberated by his grace.

Another day, weeks later, while we were having dinner at home, mom showed dad a series of pictures she had taken in Evelyn's house. In one of them Tarzan was doing one of his tricks. Mom put it in front of me.

"Canela, do you remember Tarzan? I wish he could teach you one of his tricks!"

"Ceci, do you notice something peculiar in the pictures?" said dad.

"No... let me see... that dog is skinny! I told Evelyn I would be glad to take Tarzan to the vet for her."

"No, that's not it. How little observant you are! I will give you a hint. What do all these photos have in common?"

"The obvious, the house, the occasion, the lighting... should I have used the flash?"

"Do you see the white shining sphere next to Evelyn and the dog?"

"Yes... I did not notice it before! You know, that time when I went to her house with Canela the dogs were barking a lot at something in the backyard, apparently the wall or the adjacent door, and Tarzan started doing tricks out of the blue! They were not even looking at us!" Cecilia had this quality of including me in her conversations with dad. She looked at me intrigued. I knew what she was thinking. "What did you see, Canela?" She added, "I will tell you one thing, darling; I would not be surprised if the dogs saw something paranormal. Evelyn told me that ever since her husband died, Tarzan has been behaving strangely, but lately more often."

"Only God knows... and perhaps the dogs! Have you shown her the pictures? I think she is agnostic, isn't she?"

"Yes, and that is what makes it so hard to console her. I try to tell her not to be afraid but nothing seems to comfort her. Besides, I don't think she is getting better. Still, it surprises me that she has been asking me about our Master. Maybe you should talk to her. Why don't you come next time? She is always inviting you."

It had probably been a year after my first visit to Evelyn's when we were invited by another of mom's friends to a big pool party at their country house. Mommy put a colorful doggy bathing suit on me and my fellow canines were forced to wear similar unnecessary pieces for the amusement of their parents. In their senseless world, we needed to use clothes to get into the water while they were removing theirs (to certain limits) to do the same. Plenty of interesting smells lingered in the air and the weather was perfect.

A poignant odor emanated from the dressing room area by the fence at the end of the lawn which a couple Labradors and I needed to investigate. The larger of the two opened the ajar door with his paw to reveal a little boy facing the toilet. Paper in hand, an unsuspecting mother was busy at work cleaning his son's behind with a wince.

"This one ate beef chili," clarified the owner of the brown twitching nose, in case there was any doubt about the little boy's diet.

That was no news. In the park I always encountered countless tracks of solid and liquid waste. What really surprised me was the messy buttocks.

"I had never seen such a smear in my life!" I exclaimed.

"I reckon you are not around mini humans. Ain't gonna poop clean! They dunno nothin better. Other animals have no problem. We drop it clean!" the Lab responded.

"The catch is their fleshy shape," intervened the black Lab. "Having a flat butt prevents filth. I am glad our design is more better."

"Yeah, and we also have more easy reach!" added the animal licking at the base of his white tail.

"It may also be related to their habits," explained the black quadruped. "I reckon that you are a vegetarian and particularly fond of sweet potatoes."

(I knew he went behind me to pee over, but I was not going to say anything. After all, this was his territory.)

"What a sharp nose! Mom says that daddy's sweat stinks less compared to meat-eaters," I concluded.

There was a large rectangular table covered with a checkered tablecloth close to the stone grill, full of goodies. Two hammocks were hanging from three lush trees with children playing on them. The grass was green and soft. The food was varied and the laughter loud. The lights started to reflect in the pool.

"The stars are swimming in the water. Look redhead, the fireflies are coming out!"

"Indeed," I said to the white quadruped next to me. "My name is Canela."

At that moment I sensed a subtle change of atmospheric pressure. I perked up my ears and I noticed dad became a marble statue.

The thin figure of our dear friend Evelyn came to the table. She was wearing a semitransparent dress and a sweet smile. She walked towards dad and mom, who were eating with the rest of the guests. She seemed to me wishing to join the party, but not finding an empty chair at the table she went inside the house, I thought to get one.

Then the kids jumped into the pool making a big splash and breaking the peace. Why do small humans have to be so loud? I don't know and I would rather not find out. I think it is better to avoid them.

The party was a success and nobody wanted to leave, but since people are slaves of the clock and we had a long drive, we left. The car lulled me on the journey home. I had skipped my usual nap and felt tired.

Once home, dad slept like a trunk, but mom kept tossing and turning in bed until she finally stood up and went straight for the phone.

"Hello, are you Evelyn's son-in-law? .... We were out of town and returned very late last night. I am calling to check on her… …… How…? …At - at what time? ...... I am so sorry! …… Please, do ...... If there is anything we can do please let us know …… Sure, of course...... I am really sorry! .... Thanks."

Mom searched for me and placed me at the edge of my comfy bed to make space for her, then she sat next to me on the floor. It took me a minute to realize she was just finding out about her friend. A few minutes later, dad came out, showered but unshaved.

"Good morning, Canela! Is mommy squeezing you already? Poor Caneluska!" He disapproved with his head and walked towards the kitchen. "Ceci, leave the dog alone and let's have some breakfast!"

Mom gave the news to dad and a sheet of sadness covered us all.

"Evelyn came to say goodbye. I saw her last night. She appeared at the party while we dined at the table. She saw me, you and some of the guests. She gave the impression of wanting to sit with us. She looked fine. I did not tell you anything because it was so sudden I was not sure it was real, but now I know she bade us farewell. It cannot be a coincidence. I was not even thinking about her, and it coincides with the time she left the body."

Certainly, Evelyn's ethereal body visited her beloved friends one last time, but mom did not see her and dad could not believe his eyes. Later, during meditation, they commended her soul to the Master. Their faith was great, because unable to see, hear or sense the spirit world, they believed their Master would fulfill his promise to liberate their friends and relatives, incarnated or not. He would even rescue souls from hell if the disciples kept the precepts and followed their spiritual practice diligently, overcoming the obstacles they might encounter.

I believed, but my third eye was a little bit more open than theirs and my memory was not as covered with the veil of oblivion which blinds all humans soon after birth. Even more, the guru would not prove his power to anyone whose third eye was shut or who could not remember experiences during the state of meditation. Mom in particular had a big mental block to hear, see or feel anything beyond her physical senses. Yet, she did not question the teachings and knew that dad would not lie to her or try to force her in any way to follow the Master.

This is what I admired most about mom. They had lost someone very close to their hearts and although they might always miss her, their faith would help them get over their sorrow and find solace as they continued meditating and hoping to see her again one day.

The customary arrangements were soon performed. After my humans came back home from the mass, mom put Evelyn's funeral program on the window sill, which showed a nice picture of Evelyn with her dog, who after the burial, moved in with the youngest daughter. When I saw it, I got a vision of Tarzan, exhausted, weak and sick. His little body did everything in his power to make her feel better and give her more time, which is what Evelyn wanted. He was there when she most needed company and that was priceless. Nobody ever suspected the valuable and unique role Tarzan played during the course of her illness; he would have died for his protégé many times over, but needed to live until the end. Tarzan was not as distressed as the others. He understood it was time to depart and witnessed Evelyn's transition into her real luminous self; he knew she would be all right. He courageously accomplished his mission and would join her soon.

Life continued like always. Dying is part of living in the material world. Individuals and events come and go, the only permanence is change.

Thus, at home, my humans were changing. Mom was more and more intolerant, desperate and impatient (especially with dad) and the worst was that she realized it and could not change, even though she prayed to God. Both had a hard time. Dad was an excellent person. He was so good he could have been a dog. He was adaptable, loyal and easy going. I loved the fact that he worked at home because it was less stressful on him and kept me company, but his spiritual practice was the most helpful, for body and soul. We had a masterful routine and, after his experience in Rome, he conquered his fear and became the best human-dad I ever had. He learned from mom how to love an animal, to speak to me and pampered me more than a real family member. Before, he did not care for dogs, but seeing mom, he improved greatly. Besides, he was my advocate, my friend and my meditation buddy. Not only did he become fond of me, he was able to extend his love to other dogs and all animals. One day, mom took a picture of us doing the unthinkable: lying next to each other on the bed (which was off limits to me, but she wanted to show the world how daddy had improved) and walking in the dog park, surrounded by a multitude of unleashed dogs of all sizes, many of whom went daringly straight to him to say hi. These pictures traveled the world to friends and relatives, especially to those who knew him best.

I also became "famous," everybody started sending me greetings and asking how I was doing each time they spoke. I was informed to have "cousins, uncles and aunts" everywhere. Olav, their nephew, was supposedly my human cousin so when they, by dad's initiative, gave him a keyboard for his birthday, I also "signed" the card with my little paw. They used to send out Christmas cards of us three wearing ridiculous hats and other weird practices; I let mom adorn me as she wished. It was totally worth seeing her smile and hearing her laugh. The only times I did appreciate clothing was in the winter and under heavy rain. Mom and I had matching yellow raincoats which made us the recipients of plentiful and continuous flattery.

Dad and mom were making big plans for their tenth wedding anniversary. Although they had been together longer than that, and beyond this life, they wanted to mark the occasion with a special trip to some exotic place. They were in need of some time off. They had been working very hard and were tired, not only from work or the routine, but from life itself. Especially dad, who, as time passed, had less and less material desires and more interest in the heavenly abode, particularly after a good meditation session. Sometimes I could see reflected on their faces a weariness for life and a despair before the impotence to help alleviate the suffering on Earth (notably after watching TV, but fortunately they opted to keep it at a minimum). Although, grateful for all the blessings bestowed upon us, deep inside, they were unsatisfied. They longed for a different type of life, for a place where love and peace reigned for all creatures, where all could be eternally happy. In the most recent years dad had visited such realms more and more often during his meditation and steadily grew spiritually, which in a way made it the more difficult to conform with worldly matters. This affected mom, who started to feel neglected and irritated for the shortcomings and slowness of her husband, which far from getting better, age accentuated.

Nevertheless, they loved each other dearly, although mom's reprimands and demands kept increasing. She thought she needed to keep dad on his toes to prevent him from relying unnecessarily on her for all the household needs and becoming useless. She always alleged, "That's why I did not want children." Dad compensated with silence and prayers, but he could never catch up with mom, and he worried he would become a burden to her in his senior years. The sole thought of it made him sad.

"Where are we going?" I thought when I saw dad placing his suitcase on the bed and packing his clothes. I kept sniffing for clues but all I could get was sand in my nose. "Achoo!"

"Bless you! Canela, you stay with mom and take care of her and the house. I will be back soon."

"I bet the Convention will be very boring. If you take me, we could do some sightseeing," intervened mom while holding their camera.

"Sorry Ceci, don't insist. Where is my electric razor?"

"It is in the drawer, right under your nose."

"I don't see it."

"Do I need to give it to you in your hand? It is practically poking your eyes!"

"Sorry, I can't see well with these glasses," replied dad in a lamenting, pitiful tone that prompted mom's explosion.

"I am sick and tired of hearing you complain about your sight! You have the appointment with the doctor to correct your vision. It is pointless to be moaning about it. Can you stop it?" retorted mom immediately, leaving dad speechless.

He took his cell phone and left the room, but not without an angry, reprimanding look first.

If humans could only see the ensuing effect of their thoughts in their aura and their immediate environment, they would probably wait a few seconds before voicing them or at least modify them a little!

Although by the next day they were talking again, there still was some tension in the air. Lately, I had seen the need to run to the farthest corner of the house to get away whenever their voices reached a certain harsh pitch, more and more often.

I discovered already that when mom or dad scolded me, all I had to do was to offer some sincere licking on their cheeks, tail between my hind legs and this soon stopped their anger and caused the opposite effect. Not wanting to give in, they tried not to laugh, so "I understood that such behavior was unacceptable." I kept teaching them this infallible technique, but they never learned. I am sure that if dad had started kissing mom in the middle of a discussion, she would have no choice but to acquiesce and calm down.

"Canela and I can drive you to the airport" offered mom as she saw dad ending his dinner.

"There is no need. I prefer to take a cab," said daddy, and he walked towards the door.

"As you wish," answered mom unfazed, finishing her drink at the table.

Mom, as usual, got busy with housework and took a shower. Hours later it occurred to her that dad should have already called her from the airport to confirm he made it on time. She grabbed the phone.

"Strange." She frowned her eyebrows. "Canela, daddy is not answering!" she informed me with a puzzled look. Dad was not the grudging type. "The flight should have landed already. It was a very short flight… I better check online," as if asking for my approval she sat in front on the computer.

The phone rang.

"Hello ...... Yes, sir ...... No, you don't understand, we have plans, you see... ...... Can I see him? ...... How… why, when…? ...... Yes, I know the hotel ...... Mm-hm ...... Okay. Yes. Bye."

Mom's face became hard as a rock, pale and her aura grayed. She searched for her keys and did not even care to change clothes, simply unwrapped the wet towel from her hair and threw on her gabardine. She said briefly to me,

"I will see you later. Pray, Canela."

I waited for her all night in my bed, next to the door. It was the first night I spent home alone. Although she had been late before, it was with daddy and usually for a pleasant occasion. I could not sleep or rest. I guess it was because I was uneasy and did not meditate that I could not connect with dad.

It was mid-morning when mom returned home. First thing she did was take me out and make sure I had enough water and food. Then she fell flat on the bed. She called me and signaled me to join her (she let me jump on the bed when dad was not around). I could sense she was tense and together we slept at least a couple hours.

Our ethereal bodies parted from our physical bodies and entered a cold room, full of machines attached to dad's body. It lasted but a second, enough to know that something went wrong. Fortunately, or not, mom's brain had not registered the vision, although she woke up fairly calm, considering the circumstances.

Mom, who was usually very talkative, did not tell me much. We ate and she left again. This time she took a lot of things in a big bag, including an image of the Master and a pillow.

The next two nights we went through a similar routine, but instead of sleeping on the bed, she arranged my bed next to dad's meditation chair and hers, then we meditated for about three hours. Scratching my tummy, she said,

"Let's meditate for daddy and for all the people involved in the accident."

Since mom's exhaustion was more mental than physical, she had no problem letting go of the mind, and we both had very good meditations.

The Master was busy at work with mom. He appeared to her subconscious continuously to help her and took her to higher realms, to show her other planes of existence and to impart spiritual teachings that would calm her mind and ease her spirit.

By the third day mom's sister, Olga, who threatened to come, would arrive from overseas.

Again, I spent one more night alone, but this time mom had other plans. The following morning, she opened the door as if she did not want to awaken me. Next, mom went straight to the kitchen to get a delicious yummy treat and put me on a leash while someone waited outside. She made me sit and let a lady, around the same age as her, with a pointed chin, plump rosy cheeks, wild oxygenated long messy hair, adorned with a colorful multitude of collars and bracelets, wearing a lengthy fluffy coat, soldier-type boots and dark circles under her brown eyes, come inside. Then, before I could bark, she gave the treat to her… what the heck? I could not unglue my eyes from it. My heart was pounding with greed.

"She loves this thing. Tell her to stay and give it to her."

The woman must not have understood the instructions, as she threw the treat far into the living room with an apprehensive look.

"She is big! Don't expect me to touch her, and don't leave me alone with her," the visitor grumbled.

"You will get used to each other." Mom, knowing perfectly well that I don't like to be disturbed while I am eating, addressed me pointing to the lady, "Canela, this is your Aunt Olga."

Olga stood behind a chair as mom continued. "She is a good girl like you, so you need to be nice to her at all times."

"Don't you have a place where they can watch her?"

I looked at her from a distance. She kind of resembled mom in size and features; she seemed like a different model of the same car that runs at a distinct speed.

"I am not sure; she is my 'dogther,' my pup-companion, my baby… but I do feel bad leaving her here so long."

"You see, I am right! Listen to me and take her to her sitter," adding with a begging tone, "Just while I am here!"

"It is not free, you know, and I don't even know how long she could stay. What is the date on your return airplane ticket?"

"It is in a week, but I will change it if necessary. I insist. I want to be with you until Max comes back home. If the problem is money, I will pay for Canela's stay."

"No, I can't let you do that. I know your economic situation is not the best. Save your money for now. Let me check with Gaston first. If he is not available Canela stays home, okay?"

She reached for the phone and within minutes it was all settled. The next day I would stay with him until Aunt Olga left. The siblings did not look happy, although I must admit that mom seemed a lot more cheerful with her sister. Mom went to the kitchen to cook my sweet potatoes and serve lunch to her guest.

"This is the last meal Max cooked, the day before the accident. I put it in the freezer for later. He makes the best eggplant casserole in the world! I saved some for you."

We all ate while they talked at the table.

"But how exactly did it happen?" inquired Aunt Olga.

"As I told you, nobody knows much, but I think they don't want to tell us yet. They are waiting for the black box to tell the story for them. All I know is that the plane never left the airport (it could have been worse. Imagine if the accident had happened ten minutes later!) Unfortunately, there was an explosion or something like that during takeoff and this is why the disaster was so massive. We are lucky, there are lots of fatalities. I could not see Max till the next day, after they rescued him from the wreckage and sent him to the hospital. They immediately operated on him… the doctor did not even ask me! Ever since, I have been at the hospital spending the nights with him. Thank God my boss has been amazing! And, I am on paid time off for at least another week."

"If you need to return to work sooner I may stay with Max a little longer," offered Aunt Olga, as she ate. "This is delicious! Can you pass the brown rice? I can buy prepared food for later at the supermarket while you take Canela to Gaston's house."

"Let's take a nap first. How do you feel?"

"I am starting to get sleepy. My jetlag helped me stay at the hospital last night, but you must be tired."

"And your neck?"

"That is the problem. If I don't lean against a flat surface the pain is going to get worse."

"That's it! I can't afford you getting sick. No more nights at the hospital! Starting today we are sleeping in the house. Besides, Max's condition seems stable and there is nothing we can really do for him there. In any case, the doctors and nurses all have my number and they promised to call with any news. I still want to be there when the doctors come to check on him (they don't tell you when it will be) and for anything else."

"I agree. The airline also assigned you a caseworker or something similar, right?" asked Aunt Olga.

"Yes, although I think she is pretty useless. I hear more on the radio than from her. I am avoiding television because I don't want to see any images of the wreck."

"I understand, the focus now is on Max and his recovery anyway."

"Maybe you should go back home sooner, Olga. I can handle it now. If Max requires extensive physical therapy, then is when I will need you the most, but if you take all your vacation time now you won't be able to return."

"We'll see… but I cannot go and leave you on tenterhooks. Go to sleep."

One would imagine they had not seen each other for a long time. Mom showed Aunt Olga a variety of pajamas to choose from with the proficiency of a sales person. She had only packed a bag with her medicines, underwear and one pair of deformed shoes that mom watched with horror. Her sister tried on some of mom's clothes and shoes and put her picks in the other closet. It was like two little girls playing dress up, combining belts, scarfs, hats and all kinds of accessories to adorn themselves. Staring intriguingly with her big almond eyes at the several jewelry boxes, Aunt Olga could not resist the temptation to peek inside. "*¡Qué guay!*" She smiled before a chunky ring. Mom placed the boxes on the bed, subtracting pieces filled with memories of places, events, people and of course, gifts from dad.

The two sisters slept together in the bed, leaving the guest room for the newcomer's recent acquisitions.

By mid-morning I was taken to Gaston's place. Cheerful Robocop and Nena came running, sniffing and curious to say hello.

"I learned about the accident on the TV. They are investigating if it could be attributed to negligence," observed Gaston who, as the rest of the country, had been informed of the situation but, accustomed to hearing terrible news, did not pay particular attention until mom mentioned it the day before.

"So many things can go wrong! I think it is going to take some time before they determine how this really happened."

"How is Max?" inquired Gaston while closing the fence's door.

"Same. He is still in a coma. As soon as they rescued him he went straight to the operation room. They had to release the pressure in the brain, the doctor said, and removed a big piece of his skull. The problem is that his brain has been in a continued seizure ever since," replied mom as if giving a medical report to a superior.

"At least he is not in pain..." ventured Gaston, who truly had no clue of what this sort of surgery entailed.

"That is what everybody thinks, but nobody knows for sure. The doctors tell me to keep talking to him, for it may be helpful. They do it too."

"Yeah, it is possible."

And with that, they said goodbye and I promised mommy to be a good girl, like always.

The following Sunday was group meditation, as they call the gathering of the guru's disciples to meditate together. On this occasion the meditation was dedicated to daddy, the other accident victims and to world peace, as usual. I connected with mom right at eight o'clock, like I did when they were in Rome.

"I went to see Max yesterday morning. Sorry I missed you." An Asian, middle-aged lady with tangled hair, dressed in pajamas-like clothing, holding a cushion, surprised mom. She caught mom on her way to her car, as she tried to escape questions or comments from the rest of the group still inside, gathering their things.

"Oh, thank you, sister. I saw your name on the visitor's list. I was on my way when you came."

The woman paused for a moment, and taking a deep breath added, "You know, your husband is not there. He came here to meditate, I sensed his presence among us."

Mom knew that some disciples had somewhat developed their third eye and was not totally surprised about her comment. She was rather sad for her, the wife, was incapable of perceiving any sign at all while an almost stranger, whom Max did not share a special bond with, did. Mom was beyond getting mad. By then she had given up hope of catching any extra sensorial cue or spiritual wisdom in her life. She tried to replace her frustration with resignation, thinking, "May be my karma." The reason why she meditated so diligently while dad was in the hospital was to manage stress and help her focus. She looked at her slanted eyes, big under the glasses, as if there were something written on them she was trying to read and kept quiet.

"At least he is not suffering. The Master is protecting him from pain."

Mom tried to fake a smile. She wondered if the sister had seen something more, but did not want to ask. Instead of walking to her car, she froze before her. The lady must have felt her internal battle and without malice, she added,

"Honey, you should let him go…"

"Sorry, it is getting late. Bye," Mom interrupted her and left.

Another week went by before mom picked me up from Gaston's house. During all this time the Master had been closer than ever, teaching her during meditation.

I will never forget that Saturday afternoon. The breeze was cold and it seeped through my bones, even though I was inside the house, lying down on my favorite blanket. Robocop and Nena were fast asleep in the next room. The birds and the squirrels outside were having a feast. It must have been two o'clock. The sun peeked from a big cloud and one of his rays came straight to me through the half open glass porch door as if aiming to illuminate an explicit spot.

"Hello, Canela. How are you, chiquita?"

I felt embraced by the light and a delicious warmth traveled from my nose to my tail. A familiar voice and profound sight pierced through my forehead, allowing me to sense the love and peace irradiating both ways. We met in the middle, connected in another realm, where the beam transformed into a human figure of sublime energy.

"Alma, I have to go. My mission has ended. I want to thank you for all you have done for me and for Ceci. Please be obedient and take care of her. Help her and make her happy as only you know. Our Master is with us all. He is taking me to a marvelous place, where there is only joy and eternal bliss. I will meet you both there when you are ready. You should be very happy for me. I love you."

The connection I felt was unparalleled. Max and I communicated on a higher level of existence, where the purest form of a being resides, away from the illusion of this material world, beyond time and space. It is magical when the soul comprehends that it is part of a whole, a whole which simultaneously can be manifested individually for the purpose of getting to know itself through the infinite possibilities of being. Now he knew I was Alma, not a physical body, but a soul who had chosen to perceive life in a particular form. I was neither a dog, nor a person, simply an artist acting in the theatre of life, where each one is the star of its own play. His was over, his character had to exit the scene. The rest of us actors have to continue the play, but in our case, at the end we will be retiring from our acting careers and returning Home.

For a moment it occurred to me to accompany him, to leave everything behind and go back Home. No loyalty is stronger than the desire to return to the Source. I did not want to come to Earth. This was supposed to be my last re-incarnation anyway! I knew that very likely my canine brain would not be able to retain the information from this divine level of consciousness, much less express whatever knowledge I could gain to share with Cecilia. I pleaded God for understanding beyond my physical shape and this is how the purest Alma essence had access to the information exposed next. Since I was still tethered to my body I had material besides spiritual questions, which I did not put in words but by the grace of our Enlightened Master through my third eye were answered, putting in place all the pieces of the latest events and giving me a better perspective of the laws of this universe.

Everything happens for a reason. No one is a victim of circumstances. At the end, there is justice, compassion and love for even the worst criminals. Each and every one aboard the failed flight that Max took had finished their current "contracts" (apart from two survivors). Moreover, each person had practiced leaving the body, to prevent the shock of such an unexpected end. The Master prepared Max who, by meditating diligently was familiar with the process which, per se, as the Enlightened Master put it, is like "dying every day." Even those least spiritual commended their souls to a higher power, bringing them some solace in the short final moments.

The ability to understand why a crisis happens greatly helps with the acceptance of the situation and brings immediate peace to face what otherwise may traumatize the individual. The "victims" were received with love on the other realm. They were actually very happy enjoying some kind of Heaven, above their life accumulated virtues. They were uplifted to their next level of consciousness by the grace of the Master. During the months prior to the accident, while asleep, they were taken by the power of God, away from their bodies to become familiar with the procedure. God had to make use of their sleeping hours since hardly anyone tried to connect with him while awake. Many did not pray or even acknowledge his existence. Most had spent their whole lives busy with mundane tasks, as if the only certain fact of life would never reach them.

I saw the plane and the passengers at takeoff. I watched the anguish before the pilot's impotence when for an instant, the events leading to this moment played on his mind. He verified the craft's weight and went over all the necessary checklists. He set throttle to stabilize, then increased it to takeoff. The V speeds were set while operating the flight management computer. With the 111 passengers and crew aboard, the plane taxied to the runway and he was cleared for takeoff. Within thirty seconds, the co-pilot called 100 knots, followed by V1.[9] Then, he noticed that the left front tire hit some metallic debris probably dropped by an earlier

[9] V1: Takeoff decision speed.

aircraft, throwing it into a spin. Almost simultaneously, one of the engines suffered a loss of thrust. When the alarm indicated an engine flameout, he attempted to shut it off... Could he, inadvertently, have turned off the second engine instead? Seconds later, the air traffic controller announced the presence of fire behind the airplane. The fire engine alarm beat hard in his head. The co-pilot informed him of failure to retract the landing gear. The runway was near the end and aborting was out of the question. As the plane lifted, it inverted and became uncontrollable.

It all happened so fast! The pilot was unconscious by the time the fuel leaking from the impacted aircraft's tank propagated the flames. There was a loud explosion. Within minutes, the firefighters, the police and rescue personnel were on the scene.

The majority of the passengers sustained severe injuries and died quickly. The most common causes were tearing of the aorta and consequent rupturing of the heart, many had broken their necks and suffered pelvic, leg and skull fractures when the plane turned; a few had a panic attack. Those not killed by the bodily trauma were asphyxiated by the smoke and the inhalation of toxic materials but not burned alive. No passengers were ejected from the aircraft. One survivor (a young flight attendant) had brain damage that rendered him physically and mentally incapacitated for life, but he would not be consciously aware of his condition.

The pilot survived the crash. The man should have retired already, his wife insisted on it, but he decided to continue working until the end of the year. He had chosen a tough life for his latest reincarnation. He wanted to progress quickly and pay up his karma. He suffered severe injuries, besides burns over 80% of his body. Cases like this require numerous surgeries, constant medication and prolonged physical and mental therapies. His quality of life took a turn for the worse. Yet, his emotional anguish and guilty feelings were the real torture. While other souls opt to pay their karma "in installments," that is, distributing it in multiple lifetimes, he wanted to accelerate the process, which proved agonizing. The risk of bearing so much pain in one lifetime is the temptation to commit suicide, which would sink him immediately to the lower levels of consciousness, from where it is very difficult to escape. Some souls miscalculate their strength when signing their contracts. Things seem so much straightforward from the other side!

Mister Daas was going to attend a high school reunion in the city where he grew up, some fifteen years ago. He bought the ticket at the last minute, after his business partner recovered from a minor surgery, allowing him to watch over the hair salon they owned together. He was able to schedule the operation on time so Mister Daas could make the trip. Mr. Daas' mission was to help his partner, who in a former life was his daughter, to open the salon. His then daughter took care of him during his last years and provided him loving care while he was sick. He wanted to repay her kindness and help her succeed. They had both agreed to meet again for a short period and continue their paths.

In the case of Mrs. Inok, a neighbor friend who worked for the airline, gave her the ticket. She was going home after taking her niece back to her brother's from a week's vacation in her house. She pretended to surprise her husband with an unexpected arrival. As it happens with courtesy tickets, she was on a waiting list, unsure of departing, but when a passenger did not show up for the flight, they assigned her her seat. Such passenger was Ms. Dupray, who was in a hurry to get to the airport. She overlooked her exit on the highway and took a long deviation as part of the road was under construction, making the traffic heavy and slow. Later, when Ms. Dupray learned about the accident, she thanked God for protecting her. In reality, she should have thanked her guardian angel, who had intentionally distracted her to miss her exit by whispering in the ear. Mrs. Inok paradoxically, was spared the suffering of finding her husband in bed with whom she thought was his best friend. One woman had completed her mission; the other had not yet fulfilled hers.

Liam was the only child on board. He was traveling with his parents to see a specialist who could help him with an incurable, rare genetic condition. Liam presented skeletal anomalies of the limbs, a deformed skull and face, and a lower intellect. The parents had suffered terribly going from doctor to doctor and seeking all kinds of treatments to manage the complications of the disorder. However, Liam, who had not been able to attend school, did not suffer. He was neither in pain nor did he realize he was different. As a matter of fact, he was a pampered child and enjoyed everything life had offered him: the perfume of mom's embrace, the splashing of water during a bath, the taste of fruits, the colors of all the objects that surrounded him and the caring voices of his parents.

Liam was a being from another planet, whose only interest was to visit and experience life on Earth for a little while. He found Earth an irresistible mystery because his planet was not material in nature. For this, he needed two souls who would agree to give birth to him. His parents had been brothers in a previous life who lacked compassion, tolerance and love towards others. As children, they used to bully other kids in school, behavior which did not improve as adults. When they died and realized all the pain and suffering they had caused, they sought the opportunity to cultivate those qualities and as a way of atonement. Having a child with great challenges put them in a perfect position to overcome their shortcomings, allowing them to advance in their spiritual path. There was no point for any of them to continue the exercise once the lesson was learned and the experience obtained.

There were lots of passengers on that flight, many of which agreed to this sort of death for financial reasons. Yes, a karmic debt can occasionally be paid with money. Among other reasons, Max had selected a type of death which could provide monetary benefits to his widow. Max wanted to make sure that in his absence, Cecilia would be taken care of and with enough money to do what she wanted. Also, he was aging and noticed his mental and physical abilities gradually diminishing. Although his wife loved him with all her heart, he feared he would end up being a burden in her life. Cecilia's demands started to become unreachable for him and her patience getting shorter and shorter.

Max considered that at this point she still had very good opportunities of finding a decent mate and restarting a new life. He was ten years older and Ceci looked even younger than that. Among her motives for not wanting to have kids was being free to move anywhere in the world (she once considered working with NGO to help people in need). If she had enough money, she could quit her job and volunteer anywhere she pleased. After all, this was an excellent way to use the languages she spoke. The most important one, was not seeing herself looking after a child indefinitely, since nothing guaranteed that he or she would be healthy, happy and independent in her absence. This is precisely what Max was afraid would happen as he aged. He had started taking medicine for hypertension and was showing signs of arthritis in his back and knees. His hearing and eyesight were worsening, and although those could be fixed, he knew that sooner or later Cecilia was going to turn into his nurse.

There are no mistakes, everyone who had to be there was, and everyone who did not, didn't fly that day.

Cecilia had no choice but to continue living. The next step was to get her "chiquita."

Almost one hour had passed since mom left Aunt Olga at the airport, yet the scent of hairspray and Chinese food, mixed with a whiff of Max's lavender lotion lingered in the fabric seats and carpet of the car. As always, mom was happy to see me and I was ready to go home. Gaston and company had been very accommodating and kind, but we have our attachments.

Mom seemed serene, played music on the radio, but did not sing. We stopped at the shopping center where she dropped off two big bags to a charity organization and I accompanied her to get a large package of food for me. Nothing seemed out of the ordinary.

The minute we got home, though, I realized things would never be the same. I drank some water mom poured in my dish and went straight for my long-awaited bed. Mom squatted and said solemnly, "Canela, daddy is not coming back. He got ahead of us and left us here; but we have each other, right?" She wiped away a tear.

Then she walked to her bedroom and carefully brought a box. She placed it in front of me. Her voice was beginning to break.

"I don't know if this can help you understand, but here is what remains of his body. Knowing Max, I think he already spoke or appeared to you or said goodbye somehow. Did you see him?"

Mom grabbed me by the collar and took me to the bedroom. She got a fresh clean blanket out of the closet and put it on her bed. Then she ordered me to jump up. I was hesitant. I knew dad would not approve, but before her insistence I gave in. She held me close, squeezing me. I lay down on one side. Mom copied me. I moved away carefully. She moved towards me. I turned my head away from her face towards the edge of the bed. She turned my head and placed it back in front of her. I stretched in the opposite direction. Mom snatched me from behind and positioned me facing her. We breathed each other's breath. I was suffocating. My tummy itched, I scratched it with my paw. Mom reached for my paw and put it down. She started to scratch my tummy. I waited for a pause. Swiftly, I stood up and went to the opposite side of the bed. I rearranged the blanket, made two or three turns and lay on my stomach. Mom reached for me, adjusted her position to face my nose and covered my back paws with the blanket. I tried to get up but she pushed me down. I waited. Soon she would fall asleep. She massaged my neck. I lifted my head to lick myself but she yelled, "Stop it!" I got quiet. She kissed my nose. I gathered all my strength and got up for the door as fast as I could.

This was the beginning of a bear relationship: loving, clinging and sticky, to which I did my best to adapt. I remembered daddy's words and was exceptionally obedient, at least for a few weeks or so.

The next morning mom got up extra early to take me outside, to "my tree" and visit "her ranch", according to her, before heading to work. She must have made special arrangements to her work schedule, so she could come home one hour early every day. Then we ate. Like me, mom ate only one dish, instead of the opulent variety of exquisite dishes Chef Max used to make. Afterwards, we went for our usual walk, although I am not a fan of exercise, I knew that if it was not for me, mom would have landed in bed for the rest of the day, like many sick humans do. Slowly, mom began to incorporate other activities, such as reading, painting and even tried to tackle playing the beautiful lustrous piano that Max loved so much. She thought she would never be as good as him, but she could learn. Besides she did not want to give it to his uncle, especially after his family, for reasons she did not bother to ask, did not even offer to come during his stay at the hospital or afterwards. In any case, Cecilia wanted Olav, who had expressed some interest in music, to inherit the piano. Aunt Olga was the only person who came (her father offered but she did not allow it due to mobility issues), even though Max had an excellent relationship with the entire family.

No doubt the house felt empty. The following weeks after dad's ascension to Heaven mom organized closets and drawers, rearranged the furniture and tried a new haircut. She even considered changing the car, because I was getting older and one day I would not want to climb to the back seat of the minivan and that it was too much car for the two of us. She would have put the condo on the market if it was not for the pending litigation about dad's case.

Mom had a lawyer and a support group that helped her navigate through the complex process of suing the airline and taking care of dad's affairs. She held long phone conversations where, accommodating me on her lap, she massaged me to sleep. During those conferences, I could see the mental images of her messages playing like a movie in my head. Mom kept lamenting being left behind in this world. She always spoke of dying together in an automobile accident or something quick, and later included me in the picture, so nobody would have to suffer anyone's absence by not leaving any survivor. Such was her plan.

Since dad had been self-employed, he had no benefits, but he had life insurance. The passengers' relatives sued the airline. Her lawyer, who, if winning, would retain a third of the total granted, would help her recover the maximum possible compensation, part of which would go to cover the costly medical expenses (including 13 days in intensive care) and funeral costs (a nominal sum in comparison because mom did not ask for any type of service or memorial, other than what the families of the other victims were planning as a group).

It turned out that the airline was going after the other airline responsible for unintentionally dropping the debris on the runway and this one, after the manufacturer of the piece. In short, soon everyone started suing whoever had anything to do with the flight. It seemed like people's favorite revenge was money. Though very few, including mom, were at peace, with pain and sorrows but with an acceptance which could only come from God.

She kept thinking of their last conversation, or lack of; of him packing and her yelling for a petty thing that grew out of her unchecked impatience; of arguing, often for trifles, which must have caused him undesirable sorrow. She was convinced she did not deserve him. God had taken him from her because he did not deserve such unjust treatment, which had gradually worsened over the last few years, as her demands had not abated despite the obvious slowdown in pace that comes with age. God took him right on time, before her volatile temper reached new heights, averting him of who knows what! He could have stayed longer, but she missed her chance to provide him a better environment and prove she was worthy of his company for another minute.

"As you wish." What kind of last words are these to the love of your life or lives, to be precise? I heard mom repeating in her head and in her little chats to concerned mutual friends. She did not even kiss him goodbye before going to the airport. She never had the opportunity to converse with him again. She would have been less demanding, if she only knew that their ten-year anniversary would never occur.

Mom never asked God or her Master to heal daddy, not even once. She did not pray or cry. She had wanted to prevent the seed of resentment from growing in her heart in hatred if her husband did not make it. This way she could not blame it on them for not listening, for not curing his injuries, for not granting her her most precious wish. She did not dare pray to Heaven for the life of her most treasured friend, confidant and life companion. Coping with the emptiness in her heart was so big that, paradoxically, it did not leave room for hating God or the Master. They could have prevented the accident if they wanted, why even go there?

Mom was very careful not to seem ungrateful. In spite of her pain she kept recognizing that we did not lack anything. We were healthy, she loved her job, had a nice home, a car and even enjoyed certain luxuries and was fortunate enough to go on vacation from time to time. We were privileged among millions of people. Who was she to say that these were not the direct result of their spiritual practice or her Master's blessings? Dad always voiced how incredibly lucky they were and called himself "pampered by God." He set an example for his wife of thanking God every day for their blessings, waking up with a simile singing, "Good morning joy, good morning sun, hello my dear, what a beautiful day!"

Still, I sensed the heavy weight in mom's heart, but I was not able to convey my experience with dad and tell her to be happy for him. I could, however, provide support, be there for her and dedicate the rest of my life to her. At least, mom got up each day because I needed her and I was able to provoke a smile with my "eccentricities" as she called them.

Mom's unconditional love found echo in mine and together we adapted to our new lives, to go on without the precious treasure of his being. I was grateful for the opportunity. No one better than me could relate to her, but sometimes I wanted to console her with words, which seemed to be so powerful among humans. I asked God for guidance and to show me how to help her, and that is how I reached the level of understanding exposed here.

Mom's witnessing her sister's suffering and consequent complete loss of faith was a living example of what she feared could happen if, like her, she turned to religion or God for help and did not receive the desired outcome. Olga was once a happy, positive and hopeful, Catholic girl whose life turned upside down with the condition of her son and the indifference of her husband.

Olga could never understand why, in spite of all her good actions (gifts to charity, attendance to church, moral conduct, noble deeds to people in need, love for her family and prayers) her husband started to treat her badly and the people she loved suffered. As much as she tried to improve the situation, there was little she could do to change it. Above all, the suffering of innocent children, like her son, who had to go through multiple surgeries and painful treatments when he was still a baby was an injustice they did not deserve (she did not believe in karma). However, she kept her faith for years although the situation gradually worsened. Olga was determined that her sorrows would soon end and both would be happy again. She doubled her efforts to find a solution. She investigated other religions, read scientific and metaphysical books, even consulted with gypsies and shamans to improve her fate and her son's health. After years of trial and error, visits to lawyers, doctors, psychologists, priests, fortune tellers, psychics, mediums and everything in between, Olga sensed falling into the limbo of the forgotten, the neglected individuals who no matter what they did, God would never show pity on them. Consequently, she rebelled.

Olga's family suffered with her silently from a distance from her crumbling life. Cecilia herself asked the Master for mercy on her sister, but nothing changed. Regrettably, perhaps influenced by her husband, Olga rejected the Master and did not want to have anything to do with him. Ceci was unable to offer any useful advice after her sister finally lost all faith in God. Cecilia considered she herself was not exactly an example of goodness or faith and could not tell her to follow her Master. "How would I suggest becoming his disciple when I know everything she tries fails? Then she will tell me that the guru is useless and I am a fanatic."

Actually, Cecilia totally justified and understood her sister's atheism and thought that if she had gone through the same travails, she may have very well become atheist as well, or even worse: resentful of God.

Nevertheless, Olga's heart was noble and strong and slowly her life improved, although dispensing with unnecessary beliefs (unproven scientifically) and dogmas. After years of suffering, thanks to her resilience, a few friends and "nothing else," she survived and her son's condition ameliorated, although they still struggled to get ahead.

Unlike her sister, Cecilia could not afford to lose faith, to throw away years of teachings and spiritual practice, so she opted for not resorting to God in her saddest moments. After all, her motto was "I follow the Master for the mere promise of not reincarnating, not to obtain material gains in this illusionary world." Curiously, not making God responsible for everything that happened was the key to her success, and although unconsciously, she obtained a level of understanding and resignation which could only be explained through her Master's teachings, imparted almost entirely during sleeping hours (including her "meditation" sessions).

On the other hand, everything related to her guru was connected to dad, therefore painful in his absence. Devoted as he was to his Master, dad had a hefty collection of videos, audios, photos and other objects he had acquired over the years, as well as mementos from several retreats he had been privileged to attend. Mom stayed away from them. As a matter of fact, the prior year, dad had the unique opportunity to see his Master in person, overseas, during a retreat. It was a last-minute notice and Cecilia arranged the trip for him while he was busy meeting deadlines and seeing clients. After an unexpected halt of visits to the ashram that forced all formerly accepted disciples to cancel their flights, dad was one of a selected few who made it. Cecilia had advised Max to let him lose his ticket due to the costly airline's cancellation fees, thus leaving open the last chance to see his Master in the flesh. They never suspected why, out of a myriad of fervent followers, he could not miss this opportunity.

It is interesting to see how, previous to his departure, everything fell into place, like a gigantic puzzle of events an invisible hand completed. Here are other events which Cecilia thought were not fortuitous:

• Three months before the crash, my humans attended a big family reunion to celebrate a beloved niece's wedding, overseas.

• Mom was assigned a new supervisor, a virtuous and loving lady, who supported her and facilitated all the time she needed during and after the accident.

• Dad's appointment for Lasik surgery was postponed for a later date, saving them the inconvenience and money they would have spent.

• Dad found the phone number of an old friend's daughter and they re-connected right away. The woman turned out to be a nice source of solace, fellowship and cheer for his widow.

Mom continued thanking God and her Master for all the blessings even during her stay at the hospital and the very same day dad expired. After all, it could have been worse: Max could have remained in a vegetative state indefinitely. He was under the best medical care possible in one of the best hospitals in the nation and she received support from the airline personnel, her coworkers and friends (not much to say about the family that only communicated via cell phone and half the time it was she who initiated the calls, to expose her husband to their familiar voices in hopes of generating a reaction from his coma).

Humans process things very slowly, both physically and emotionally. After a year of meetings, tons of documents, investigations, intrusion from the media, speculations, clamors and philosophical reflections, the negotiations to compensate the families of the victims were still pending.

To commemorate the one-year anniversary of the tragedy, a monument with the names of the victims was erected at the airport. Reporters and government officials gave speeches on site which only made mom and loved ones bring back sad memories, sorrows and regrets. Again, none of dad's relatives showed up, as expected (lack of money, time or visas were to blame). Mom told her godmother on the phone for this was a strategy to push for stricter safety regulations and to keep the issue in the public eye and that all really boiled down to obtaining the most money for the families (and their lawyers) and to pay as little as possible from the part of the airlines. The ubiquitous "Call me if you need to talk" was a bad idea. In her opinion, talking did not fix anything for her and even made her feel worse. In any case, where were they all those months later? It was after the initial shock and crisis when she may have accepted their offers. Not that she needed them, but to see who really cared for Max. Before, she was on autopilot, so to speak, and too busy to mourn. It is after life "normalizes" when everybody has forgotten the victims, when aid is most appreciated and she considered it sincerer.

In the meantime, mom had clasped to me as a tick to its host. Six months later our lives remained stuck.

As usual, at about three thirty, one windy weekday, the front door opened. Mom entered, hurriedly dropping her purse on the floor, removed her heels and ran up to me fast as a bolt. I waited serenely for her on the sofa, except for my tail, that seemed to have a mind of its own, I remained unfazed.

"Hello, my loving heart! How is the most wonderful, beautiful doggy in the whole wide world? Did you have a good morning, chiquita? Did you meditate and connect with daddy in Heaven?"

I kissed her hand gently, the reduced space on the sofa kept shrinking as she sat next to me and started leaning towards my side. "Why are you so pretty? My celestial chiquita! Are you my baby? Who loves you? You are so huggable!" She squeezed me. She continued in an agonizing tone, "Ohhh Canela. Thank you for being my Valentine! Thank you for being my puppy girl! You are my vitamin. Let me get my daily dose… Mmm… You are so soft…! Do you like being my precious?"

Sometimes it is good that I can't speak.

By now mom was down on the sofa facing me, one leg on my side, one hand on my head. Caressing me, she said in her traditional high-pitched voice, "So snuggly, give me another hug. Ohhh, how delicious! You are delightful…! I love your wet nose." Too bad I could not do anything about it. She touched it with her nose. We moved our necks in tandem as mine stretched to my back. "Why are you so beautiful? It is so good to see you! No, don't try to escape. You have been all morning home alone. You had your break, now it's time for mine. No! Stay! Don't leave! Canela...!"

Mom turned the TV on and went to her bedroom. I was safe under the dining room table. The neighbors were parking their cars in front of the building, I had to say something.

"What's the matter? Canela, it is futile for you to bark like this! As much as I love your sonorous voice, you scare the neighbors. I know, they are a nuisance, but they don't know you are wonderful. I am going to eat and serve you your sweet potatoes, okay?"

Then she entered the kitchen, where I was not allowed, and waited at the threshold. While preparing the food, she turned to me with a warm corn tortilla. I hesitated between taking and not taking it, swiftly moving my head back and forth to one side as mom stretched in and out her arm with the tortilla, until I decided to grab it. If too warm, I would run to my rug to rub it against my spine before eating it while mom rolled her eyes indulgently.

We ate and as soon as mom finished her plate, she went to the sofa, but not before bribing me next to her with a minuscule treat I could not resist. She started scratching my tummy while she watched the news. After that there came another boring program. There was no end in sight… and no relief from her…! Be careful what you wish for: I wanted a human who could never get enough of me, who tirelessly loved me, scratched, petted and caressed me... and now I can't take it anymore! Oh, God, what have I done! what have I done...!

Skillfully, I fled towards the door.

"Ungrateful doggy! Is it too much love for you? You are lucky you know. So many dogs out there, alone, hungry, suffering, or with owners who neglect them or don't treat them right!" I looked without understanding. "Wait, Canela. We'll go outside in a minute."

That always meant I better get comfortable. So I lay on the floor.

"Come, baby! What are you doing so far away?"

"Escaping from you, isn't it obvious?" It was ventriloquist mommy, right on the spot!

Before the sunset, we were outside. I found a cushy grassy pad and lay there. Mom did not find this amusing and forced me to get up. She stopped pulling the leash whenever a pedestrian came near. The struggle lasted a few minutes. I had already peed... there was no need to get tired! I finally succeeded in making her understand.

"Okay, Canela, go number two and then we'll go home."

Great! This time she was not as persistent. She pretended to hug me, prompting me to spring. I led in the opposite direction. A few steps later she threatened,

"Go one more block. If you don't do your business we'll walk all the way to the park."

I found a fragrant bush next to a building adjacent to ours. I pooped as high as I could but before I knew it mom had already picked it up. All that effort for nothing...! Fine, at least we were heading home!

"Why don't you like to walk? Don't be lazy! People must think I abuse you!" was the usual litany of complaints when I shortened our walk. I would walk if you let go of the leash…

Soon the sky lost its blue and the birds hid in their nests. Discreetly and stealthily I walked to the bedroom, where I waited for mom. It did not take her long to discover I had disappeared. She yelled my name a few times, but unless I saw the menacing slipper in hand, there was no need to worry. My human cannot stay too long away from me in the house, so any minute she would come through the door, wagging her ponytail and begging for kisses.

Could I help mom find a boyfriend or a needy puppy (I take it back, I like to be the only child)? Daddy would not mind... but mom may not be ready yet... but when? My time on Earth was limited and I did not want to leave her alone... On the other hand, my absence perhaps would push her to seek human company...

I heard the switching of lights and TV and her steps on the wood floor getting louder. The carpet in the bedroom crunched under her feet as she entered the room. Already in her pajamas, mom went to wash her teeth, then into the closet to prepare her clothes for the next day. Getting into bed she exclaimed, "Why are you so far away?" Mom changed her position to suit my anatomy. "Caneluska, you are a feast to my eyes, to my touch... why do I love you so much?"

Depending on her mood, she chose a different kiss modality. The multiple little smack was a series of six to ten instant kisses, sometimes in the air, sometimes on my cheek. Once she mentioned that her father gave her multiple little kisses on the forehead; she must have learned it from him. The other was the deafening thunder smooch. She had a weakness for the corners of the mouth, away from my whiskers. She protruded her lips and sucked the air in a singular way. The louder the better and more gratifying (for her) ...I suppose the neighbors must have wondered what kind of witch lived upstairs, particularly when we played hide and seek or chasing. She loved to hide behind a door or a wall and scare me with an unexpected jump coupled with a creepy shout imitating a malevolent creature from some horror movie. She always caught me off guard, which she found hilarious and caused some of her best laughs. Interestingly, it never worked the other way around, when I barked due to some activity outside the house. Unaware, mom also jumped but she did not appreciate it… humans can be very confusing at times!

The powerful clapping was a technique used to get me out of my comfort and moving. Her hands clapped louder than the ones of an experienced flamenco dancer. Dad used to complain, "Why do you have to make so much noise!" But now there was nobody to contain her… nor to defend me from her passionate embrace. It was only the two of us to the mercy of her resignation.

This time, mom was not yet sleepy… tolerance! She would read a book or watch a video on the computer. At least she was fairly considerate and, leaning on top of me to reach the drawer on my side of the bed, she grabbed the sleep mask and fastened it behind my ears, the best way she could. Finally, thank God, she turned the lamp off and sunk into the covers. Then, turning me around, placing her head facing me, she sang and wished me good night. "Night night, baby! Have sweet dreams! I love my baby girl!"

Little by little, mom was laughing more with me and she started to ponder what she was going to do with the rest of her life. Although nothing really excited her, she tried to find different ways to amuse herself, but in the end, none seemed fun without dad. She told me, before our meditation session, to intercede on her behalf in Heaven (she believed animals to be closer to God than humans) and begged for divine intervention because she was tired of driving the car of her life and wanted God to take over. She was not convinced that her prayers would be heard, but she had faith in me delivering the message (little did she know she was the answer to mine). In her opinion, her mission on Earth was over; she had received initiation from the most powerful Master of our times and the love of her life was gone. After all, isn't it to attain Nirvana and be one with God the ultimate goal of their spiritual practice? The only thing holding her to the world was me, and she was fine with that, yet as soon as I left the body she would want to follow suit.

A month before Christmas mom asked me:

"Madam Hairs, what do you want for Christmas?"

"I don't care." The ventriloquist soliloquy started.

"You'll know that since she left, my dear godmother is the closest to a mom." Sighted remembering her endearing mother, "but regretfully, I can't take you to her house and I don't like leaving you. Do you have a better idea?"

"Let's be useful and help others in need."

"You are right: 'He who does not live to serve, does not serve to live'."

"You need a change."

"I should listen to you. Why do I love you so much?"

"Because I am your doghter."

She was right about that!

Chimes coming from the phone interrupted her monologue.

"Hello Sir. How are you? ...... Fine, thanks …… Yes, perfect time …... I thought they would, now we don't need to go to trial ...... Okay ...... Yes, will you send me the letter? ...... Exactly, the medical costs alone are half a million ...... Yes, I know; other victim's families want to sue for more, but do you think that is realistic? ...... I see ...... I don't see how they will ever move on, if they keep dragging this issue for years ...... The support groups, personally I don't like to go. I perceive a sense of pity; but it may be helpful for some ...... Yeah ...... I think it is all about revenge ...... It is not that he is gone, it is that he left me here what's so hard... Yes, I know ...... Sure, thanks!"

"Canela, we are putting the condo on the market!"

And with this, mom searched for the card a realtor who was showing some properties to her clients had given her recently and scheduled an appointment.

"Did you hear that, Precious? What we need to do now is find a new place to live and move out of here, far away! But before, there is still a lot of work to do: pay the hospital, the lawyers..., hopefully Max's family won't come asking for money, because greed sometimes brings out the worst in people, you know?"

"I don't. I just wanna be comfy!"

"How about a house with a backyard?"

"Of course, I could sunbathe regularly on the grass!"

"How would you like to help find homes for other dogs? In a bigger place we could house animals for adoption."

"Okay, but don't bring me any cats."

"You must control your canine instincts! But I wish I were more like you and live only in the present. For me, every passing day is one less until I see daddy again."

"You need to keep busy, mom. That brain of yours is the problem."

"You know, Canela, maybe God dispatches our loved ones first, as a way of making dying sweet, giving us something to look forward to after this world. There is nothing I want more than being with Max again!"

During those days, Citlali, mom's new friend (the same person dad contacted mere weeks before the accident), was about to retire. They had some things in common, like their vegan diet and their love for animals (I liked her from the start). They shared an interest in learning the mysteries of life and the universe and mom felt comfortable expressing her spiritual views because Citlali did not follow a particular religion and had an open mind. Mom liked her positive outlook on life, in spite of having had a rough childhood and a chronic illness. Citlali had initiative, spunk and was a little bit obsessive when she wanted something. Her yellow straight hair teased her freckles under her expressive green eyes and her vibrant youthful voice gave her an air of a star singer of a musical band.

Citlali was the daughter of an old friend Max met on a previous job; a man that had traveled extensively during his youth and had had four wives and children with each one. He possessed a great sense of humor and loved to play board games. Dad became very fond of him, and invited him to his wedding, which he unfortunately could not attend due to poor health. The old man had a series of illnesses and died a few years later. Mom went with dad to his funeral and one of the daughter's phone number remained put away for several years. A few weeks before the accident, while checking a box full of postcards on the shelves, dad found it in a notebook, bringing back sweet memories, and decided to call her. Oddly enough, the lady had maintained the same number, although she had moved a couple times. Max invited her for dinner at their home. Citlali was divorced and had only one child, who emigrated to another country. The two women got along instantly and afterwards, started to visit or telephone each other frequently.

Not having much to do, other than guarding the door, I noticed mom colored her lips, signal #1, grabbed her purse, signal #2, and put on her shoes, definite final signal for the street. I immediately took a few bites from my plate, drank some water (one never knows when it will be available), made the mandatory leaps around the dining room table, grabbed a toy (I don't know why I get this sudden impulse to play) in preparation to sit by the door, and beg mom to take me with her.

"Let's go!" yelled mom holding the leash, waiting for me to finish my ritual, rolling her eyes. "How did you turn out to be so eccentric?"

"I am just like daddy."

"Hurry up, Canela! Why do you take so long?"

"Don't you see I am busy?"

"I don't like to be late. What am I going to tell Aunt Citlali: Canela had an eccentric attack and caused me to delay?"

(As we became closer, mom alluded to her friend as "my aunt.")

We picked up Aunt Citlali and drove to the park where there was a refreshing creek and lots of wonderful smells.

They brought food and put it on one of the tables. Mom got a mat and placed it on the ground, together with a book and some cushions. Aunt Citlali hung a hammock and the two ladies, big hats on, started swinging while I investigated the zone.

"Seriously, Ceci, you should come with me, consider it a business trip if you like (we can ignore your birthday, if you don't feel like celebrating), a search for a potential place to live. It will be fun!"

"Sure, if it is good enough for you, I would definitely consider it. Better to move where there is a friend. I will make arrangements. Are you meeting with a realtor or do you know someone there?" responded mom with a smile.

"I don't have a realtor, but I know someone who can recommend me one. The main thing is to see the area, what there is to do, who lives there and what kind of vibe you feel. You cannot get that from pictures alone."

"For me, being near the mountains is important. I think the closer to nature the better for the soul. If you can retire there, it means they have all the necessary services and is probably affordable enough. I hope they also have activities for younger and active people. In any case, I will just rent for now, I need to find the perfect house with a fenced backyard for Canela in a safe location."

"I know for sure that they are dog-friendly and big on outdoor activities. I think they have an artist community… you paint, it would be a way for you to meet people. There must be other cultural events going on, if not in town, in the capital, a few miles away."

"Sounds great. I am putting the condo on the market. If we find something we like, I can always move out and leave it to the agent to show while I am gone."

This time they nailed it. A couple of weeks later the women took off towards this novel place and did not seem interested in looking elsewhere. They both returned delighted and with lots of plans for the future. It turned out that they loved the town and located a community where they could rent neighboring homes while they acclimated to the area, which, by the way, was colder than our current place of residency, but much calmer and closer to nature.

Upon her return, as usual, mom went to pick me up from Gaston's after four days of exploration with her friend. I noticed right away that she was genuinely excited for the first time in months. I was so happy for her! Having an available backyard was nice, but was not as important to me. As long as we were together, any place would be fine. Mom could not wait to get home to give me the big news.

"Canela, guess what? I think I know where we will be moving. It is a place in the mountains, near lakes, rivers and is very different from here. Yes, they have nice dog parks and there is not so much traffic, the air is purer… I will go ahead and start packing. You and I are going to drive all the way there, crossing the country. I know you can handle it! You are such a good travel companion… almost as good as daddy! What do you think?"

She turned her head at the next red light to look at me. Sometimes I get the feeling that she actually expects me to speak. She would have a heart attack if I could voice an answer! I kept watching through the window.

Not long after, mom started to fill some huge boxes with stuff. She was making piles of things to keep, to donate and to throw away, and day after day, those continued growing. The next weekend, in the midst of her chore, she decided to take a break and call her sister.

I was focused on doing my "pawdicure" (a highly painstaking task of cleaning my little paws) when mom came to me, phone in hand. Her timing could not be worse, and on top of it, she got romantic. I tried to ignore it.

"Caneluska precious, look at me! Need any salt? No? I know you are exquisite, but you have all morning to yourself. Pay attention to me!" Her face was getting dangerously close to mine.

"You are so pretty! Don't you love me?" Her lips were tickling my whiskers. "Puppy girl, who is my chiquita?" Now she was whispering into my ears. "Canela, do you love me?"

A gentle growling should warn her off…

"I like your voice, but not necessarily growling at me!" She insisted. "Don't do that! I love you!"

Gwrrrrrr!

"Who loves you?"

We alternated growls and "love yous" for a few minutes. I could not make her understand!

"Too bad for you I like you even when you are mad!... It's okay pup. I get that you have to let me know the best way you know, what makes you unhappy. I should not be offended…"

Thank God! Why is it so hard to train this woman?

Anyway, she sat next to me but quit touching me. She should feel grateful she is one of the few humans I allow to pet me (she never gets tired! I know, I know… I asked for it!). What makes people think that we will always welcome strangers' touches? What if someone goes and starts randomly rubbing a person's head because it has nice hair, whenever he feels like it? …There would be war!

Finally, mom put on her earphones and dialed.

"Hi, Olga. How are you? ...... Here, packing with Canela. It is a lot of work! ...... No, but I am in no hurry. I have not made a commitment to rent yet and I won't sign any contract until I sell the condo …… Yes I could, but I may have to pay both, rent and the mortgage plus fees …… Thank you, I appreciate your kind offer but you know how the weather and the economic situation are where you live and quite frankly I think it will be hard to keep my job overseas; but if you ever consider moving with me, you will always have a place in my house …… Any minute now, my lawyer said that the airline already started extending the families of the victims a check. It is big enough to pay the medical bills and to cover other expenses …… I won't know till the lawyers get their share …… Yes, both airlines are paying, which is good .... And how is Olav? ...... Will you come visit me in the new place? ......"

How much compensation did we get from the crash? I could not tell, but dad had arranged it from Heaven for his widow and "dogther" to be taken care of because after mom was "compensated" and sold the condo, she pretty much was free to do whatever she wanted (she was also careful with money).

As Christmas faded, mom received an envelope with a sum that as she expressed, was dad's present to the two of us. She sat down with me on the bed and put a paper in front of my eyes. "See Canela, daddy is watching after us from Heaven!" She cried and sniffed. "I would rather have him!" Her tears were clouding her speech, but it did not matter, I was a good listener. "He always worked hard to provide for us, not only physically but also with moral support, advice, sacrifice, loyalty and unconditional love. He was a joy!" Unable to speak, she spoke to me with her mind, taking breaks to wipe her nose and pet me. "Those final moments must have been painful, but I am sure he thought it was worth it. I wish I had insisted and bought a ticket to accompany him… I know, Canela. I am being selfish..., poor you! Caneluska, it is so good to have you…! I thank God he did not leave me alone. Thank you for being my baby! Don't ever think about reincarnating as a human! I don't recommend it. Better go to another planet, more evolved. Better yet, stay in a realm above the physical. Don't ever, ever, get a human body, and please don't let me make the same mistake. I want to be with Max so much! If at least I could dream with him every night I would not miss him so terribly, you know?"

She went for a handkerchief and put the envelope on the nightstand.

"No money can pay for his life. How long do I have to live without him? Do you miss him too? He was perfect for me… and you know what, precious? He does not even miss me! Because in Heaven there is only happiness. He must not be allowed to look down here and watch the suffering of the world. Otherwise how could anyone rest in peace? Seeing your loved ones sad and all the mistakes we make… not being able to interfere. It would be terrible!"

I am not sure if mom ran out of tears or if she simply became exhausted. Her aura was subdued and her eyes red. She regained her voice. "How much longer before I see Max again? Do you know it, chiquita? Let's go to sleep, perhaps I'll dream of him."

And with this, she lay on her side, positioning me next to her, as usual. Not being able to breath, she sat down and closed her eyes. "Meditation time!" proclaimed mom in memory of dad. We did not get up until the next day.

Mom had written a note, really to herself, to commemorate their wedding anniversary. The following year, at the second anniversary of the tragedy, we visited the memorial one last time (my first and only) and met with the families of the deceased. She posted the note and my picture at the site, where relatives could share their thoughts.

It is well known that in the universe nothing is created
or destroyed, just transformed.
Where hence, does all the love go, that sweet energy,
when the beloved one abandons the body?
The soul, undoubtedly, departs to celestial dimensions
and continues its path;
the physical body that animated it cannot retain it.

Just as it does not take along any matter, it leaves behind
the professed love, like a letter returned to the sender whom,

stupefied and anxious, is unaware of a forwarding address.
Thus, he who stays in this plane remains stuck with all that love,
which unable to deliver it to the inert body,
falls with all the weight of its energy on the heart,
squeezing it and stepping on the throat.
Why does it not transform into heat, light or electricity?
If love does not vanish, can it be transported?

How to get rid of love?
Many worry about having love and others about
getting rid of it when it becomes a bothersome load.
Because love hurts, and as much as trying to ignore it,
hungry, it will continue to throb feeding from the hope
of a future encounter, for which it does not perish.
But love is not a gift, it never belongs to whom it is given.
The solution would be for me to keep its love
and for its soul to take mine.

That year we had a severe winter which extended all across the country, so mom decided to take the house off the market temporarily to avoid having to move in bad weather. Weeks later, as soon as the change of seasons, mom put the house back on the market and within days she accepted an offer on the condo and made arrangements to work remotely from the new place.

We made the trip in the van, the same she bought with dad and thought of exchanging. "We'll change it later, I am glad we kept it because it is roomy enough for the three of us," she explained while she placed dad's urn in the front seat, which was not a good idea. It made her cry, but she was not going to send the ashes with the rest of the furniture or by mail. "Canela, baby, do you need a step?" She must have also noticed that the car was growing higher and higher and the doors were heavier.

The journey was lengthy but charming. We stopped along the way in various cities and had a chance to see new and interesting places. We missed our bed and our food. Hotel vibes are usually low and stink of chemicals. Nonetheless, we managed; my sanctuary was my home and for now home was the van, where I had the best naps.

"This is the last stop before arriving to our new house, Canela. Aren't you excited?"

"I just wanna stretch my paws."

"We will be there in about four or five hours. Don't worry *mon amour*, everything is going to be alright. We'll have a nice backyard to play in and meditate. I think this is the change we need."

"Speak for yourself."

The van stopped at the end of a closed street, in front of a one level brick house with a carport on each side. There was a red sports car in one of them. Mom's first words were for dad, "Darling, this will be our new home for now."

As soon as I got out, I sniffed the air and peed on the grass, it needed some watering. The birds were singing. A familiar face appeared from a window. A few minutes later Aunt Citlali came out of one of the two front doors.

"Ceci, Canela! Welcome to your new house!"

"Hi, Citlali. We finally made it!"

Aunt Citlali came to pet me. She had been cooking with coconut oil. Mom opened the other front door and we all came in. The furniture was already there together with so many boxes all over the place that there was hardly any space to walk. Mom explored the house and said excitedly to me,

"Canela, do you want to see the backyard?"

A sliding door opened to a lovely fenced backyard which extended all the way to the next house. Freedom at last! There were several trees, flowers and a table with a blue umbrella and chairs on the deck to the right.

"Nice place for breakfast, if the weather is right."

"That's why I bought this patio set. You are free to use it anytime you want," noted Aunt Citlali.

"Thanks!"

"I hope you are hungry!" she added opening the other set of doors leading to her side of the house.

Mom got my dishes out of the van and filled them with water and food. I was so thirsty!

It was a blessing to see the two friends together again. God's perfect arrangements allowed for mom to move to an ideal location, precisely next door to a friend. Max would have been pleased.

After dinner Aunt Citlali gave mom some oatmeal and coffee for the next morning. Mom opened a big labeled box and got some objects out, took a shower and was relieved to discover that her friend had found the sheets and made the bed. She was tired!

"Come here beautiful! I am placing your blanket on this side for you to join me."

I vacillated at first. Although I recognized the things from the old house, everything else was new and strange. Mom clapped her hands signaling me to jump on so I did. No way I would have slept anywhere else in this unfamiliar house. I distinguished the cashew smell of Aunt Citlali on the other side of the wall. She locked the front door.

"This is home for now, I hope you adapt quickly. Tomorrow you will accompany me to get some groceries and of course, we cannot forget your sweet potatoes. Later we can walk around the neighborhood to explore some more. Do you agree?"

Then, mom went to the living room to bring the urn she had discreetly placed on the mantelpiece earlier and put it on a closet shelf, leaving the door open.

"Let's meditate before we fall asleep."

I tried, but I was uneasy. Oddly, I did not feel comfortable, as it happened in certain cases when there had been some disturbances in the ambience. I walked around the room and kept tossing and scratching. Mom did not seem to pick up on it and, although she had difficulty meditating, she attributed it to her fatigue. Accustomed as she was to a lousy concentration, she blamed it on not having her meditation chair available. She will get it tomorrow.

Poor mommy, she was completely clueless! But this time it was for the better. Sooner than later I would discover the reason for my lack of sleep, a condition highly unusual for my genus.

The next day was hectic and exciting. I really liked the town and the awesome view of the mountains. The yard was pretty good too, but once I marked the territory I was ready to explore other places. Mom planned to start working right away and threatened me with "I am all yours" not having to commute and staying home all morning, which would free up more time for kisses and hugs… I was not sure if she was joking.

Although retired, Aunt Citlali was always busy, either tending the garden or inside the house, decorating, sewing, playing the keyboard or doing yoga. She was also volunteering regularly at an animal refuge. Now that her cat companion had passed, she was seriously considering adopting a pink cockatoo which recently arrived at the shelter after the demise of its human "dad."

"Ceci, guess what? Last night I registered for an astronomy course to meet new people at the community college. They also offer ballroom dancing; I know you dance salsa and tango, so this would be a great way for you to meet guys. You said you wanted to get out of the house more. Your feet don't hurt like mine, otherwise I would join you."

"You can still come, you could sing to the music."

"By the way, were you playing music last night, or had the radio on?" asked the friend.

"No, I did not, and if I play anything too loud, please come and knock. I went to bed early. Canela got up constantly though, but I don't think you would have heard her."

Aunt Citlali was right. If she had been a little bit more psychic she could have detected a presence.

During the day I caught up on my sleep. Since we moved to this house I had not had an uninterrupted good night's sleep. It was taking longer than ever to adapt and I was not sure yet why. The next weekend there was a full moon. Aunt Citlali would go with her astronomy class to observe the sky somewhere far away.

In preparation to sleep, mom intoned a romantic ancient tune I had not heard before. "Sweetheart, I'm tempted to kiss…"

"Better whistle it!" replied mom as I ran for cover, but I returned due to her begging and before the menacing slipper.

I was in my place, next to mom, who had fallen asleep during a late movie night session when an old car parked on the vacant side carport. I heard someone breathing hastily, approaching the house. Upon kicking off her high heels, running towards our bedroom, a lady opened the door.

"Tania!" a male's voice exclaimed from the inside.

The lady found her grandfather on the bed with his eyes closed, her brother (stethoscope around his neck) by his side, touching his hand.

A big ball of fur snuggled at his feet. Tania bent over the nonagenarian and kissed his face, but he did not move. "Do you think he could hear me?" she asked fearfully.

From one of the walls she took an old violin. Placing it over her shoulder she carefully lifted the bow and inhaled deeply. The granddaughter, timidly at first, decided to rip out the violin's most beautiful chords still harbored in its entrails.

She closed her eyes and the rhythm became more vivid, matching the fire of her heart. The strings took turns of high and low in short, quick and slow sequences, making the violinist stretch and contract with passion. Her gasping for air made the atmosphere exhilarating. Gently, she opened her eyes a little, as if checking if her feet were grounded on the carpet and glanced towards the bed.

Her brother, still touching the elderly man's hand, perceived a fleeting tremor and a vain effort to speak. He signaled her to continue, without looking away from his face.

The instrument took over the situation. The delirious music increased in intensity. Tania was possessed by the bow, as if holding a note could also hold the man's life as long, her playing became even more feverish. A compassionate saltwater stream refreshed her face. The notes vibrated on the glass, on the walls and on everyone's souls. Even the cat was hypnotized by this power.

The end was near and it was unavoidable. The violin, in conspiracy with the music, had transferred away all of her energy and exhausted Tania was about to collapse when her trance was interrupted by a cacophonous sound.

Grandpa had stopped breathing.

The next morning the birds, singing cheerfully in the garden, woke up Aunt Citlali earlier than expected. Mom and I were having breakfast on the deck when she came out of her door, coffee mug in hand and wearing her robe.

"Good morning, Citlali. Did you discover a new star last night (I bet you named it Citlali[10])?"

---

[10] The name Citlali [seet-LAH-lee] means "star" in Nahuatl language.

"Good morning, Ceci! Good morning, Canela! No, we were actually studying the moon."

"How late did you go to sleep last night?" asked mom.

"I came back around two or three, but I could not get any sleep. I wished to stay in bed longer but I cannot. I don't think it was the excitement of the class, and I did not feel exhausted or had any pain. I am starting to worry…"

"I have been meaning to play the sacred chants from Max's collection. He said it helped him meditate. He claimed that it also cleans out the ambience from lower ethereal entities and that its higher vibration harmonizes the living and brings good energy. I put it on my nightstand, but I forgot to charge the device… I also have a cd. I think I know in which box to look. I will get it for you. I ought to play it all night sometimes."

"I hope it helps me."

"It will. Max often used these types of recordings and he swore they worked. I, for better or worse, am not sensitive enough to see or hear paranormal things like him or you, but I believe him. Besides, the Master's voice is very powerful and uplifts the surroundings expunging lower energies and negativity. You'll see."

Later that afternoon Aunt Citlali came rushing over with a big folder and anxiously knocked from the backyard door. I immediately went to greet her and fetched mom. She is coming!

"Hi, Ceci. I am back from the library. You would not believe what I discovered!" she said opening the folder over the kitchen table. "Read this."

"It is an obituary. Troy… who was this gentleman?"

"He was the previous owner of this house. He died here… probably in my bedroom!"

"Okay, I don't think this is terrible, except for his family… he is not buried here, I hope, right?" Mom replied nonchalantly.

"No, I got records from his funeral… he is in the local cemetery, but there is something weird about his death," commented Aunt Citlali, pointing to another document. "He was healthy and active, and in a few months, he got sick and died. His grandson was a doctor. No autopsy was done."

"It says here that he died of natural causes."

"Natural, my wig! I also went to check on the title of the house and the testament (they are public records). Incidentally, I found out that a few days before his death he changed his will, leaving the property to his grandson."

"And you think he forced him?"

"I think he killed him."

"Why?"

"It seems as if the old man wanted to leave everything to his granddaughter and that the doctor was the black sheep of the family, don't know why," informed Aunt Citlali.

"But the owner of the duplex is a woman. Who is she?"

"The landlord, Tania, was Troy's granddaughter. He died in this house before she converted it into a duplex."

"Why don't you talk to her? Ask her about the history of the house. There is nothing wrong with that, particularly if you are thinking of buying it from her," declared mom.

"I thought about it. I have to call her anyway because I need to tell her about the sprinklers…"

The rest of the day was uneventful. Mom and I went to the farmer's market and I got to meet some of the neighbors. The weather was nice, so we spent most of the day in the backyard. Mom liked to paint *en plein air*, so she started a new painting, finished an old book and we took a nap on the deck. Aunt Citlali partook in the grilled vegetables and I got two ears of corn and a spoonful of peanut butter. The ladies tried to feed me other kinds of strange vegetables, but I refused. I have a highly discerning palate and strict standards when it comes to food. Mom should know better!

We started to adapt to our new lives. Somehow, I knew that this was the last time we moved together. I didn't know how much longer I would accompany mom, but I was going to enjoy every minute.

The thin figure of Mr. Troy usually became visible (for those with psychic abilities) after midnight. His spirit would be in the kitchen sipping coffee or outside in the yard, or next to the front door in a rocking chair we did not have. He would roam the entire house, as in the past it was not divided, walking through the wall towards mom's bedroom (his bedroom) and would sit on the bed. I got the impression that he did not see any of us and thought he was still alive, stuck in his house, frozen in time.

As mom was getting ready for bed, she played the famous Buddhist chants continuously in her bedroom, barely audible. Aunt Citlali did the same and even made a copy of the cd.

Not long after the ladies fell asleep, I saw a beam of warm light coming from the ceiling. Then, I perceived an exquisite fragrance and the change in pressure. It made me feel lighter and peaceful. Troy was entering the room and looked at the ceiling. From it became distinguishable the face of a woman of similar features.

"My beloved Troy!"

The man must have recognized her as he smiled to her presence and extended both arms out to her, like a ship-wrecked survivor she was rescuing from a vessel below. Troy was lifted by an invisible power and in the process, he started to irradiate light from his heart.

It was stunning! In a second, the face, lovely and serene winked at me in a sign of complicity and then, faintly, it turned to a dim shaft whose other end opened to a higher dimension. Troy, the luminous face and the beam of light all vanished into the air. The sandalwood scent lingered in the room.

Just when I was starting to get used to the old man!

In the morning, I went straight to Aunt Citlali's back door and sniffed to my heart's content. I wanted to give her the good news and tell her that she would never hear strange steps in the night or the sound of a violin playing from the adjacent bedroom… but it was she who had news for us.

"Good morning, Canela! I am going to have breakfast out here while it is nice. Do you want to accompany me?" she exclaimed as she opened the door for me.

"Hi, Citlali. Did you sleep well last night?" asked mom joining us.

"Divinely! This cd is a jewel, I heard nothing and I did not get up all night!"

"I also slept fine, but I usually do, although not very deep. I am glad the cd worked for you. We should play it regularly, very low. You see the difference! Would you like some bread?" Mom had baked pumpernickel bread and its odorous trail was attracting all kinds of noses, physical noses, fortunately.

"Mmm yes! I should not, but only a tiny piece, the delicious smell has invaded the entire house and…"

Low and high tones from the soundtrack of a classic science fiction movie propagated from her phone.

"Hello? Hi, Tania. How are you? …... (It is the landlord)," she whispered to mom, while spreading something reddish on her bread; I went to check it out.

Mom put the whole jar in my face. I turned to the other side; Don't you have something good?

"No thank you mommy, you know I despise fruit."

"You are the pickiest doggy I have ever seen!"

Aunt Citlali was making faces and gesticulating to her friend.

"…… So, your brother was jealous of you! …… When he moved in with your grandfather he started to get sick …... Poison! ...... You could have his remains exhumed …… I see …… I am sorry, it must have been hard for you …... Yes, why don't you come for lunch next time you are in town? ……. Thank you for sending the plumber ...... Ceci, yes ...... Super! …… Of course, I will let you know. Thanks again."

"It was Tania. She said that the plumber will come to check the sprinklers this week. He is supposed to call me to confirm. Did you hear about the house?"

"Something about a poison?" inquired mom.

"I was right. I should be a police investigator! Tania mentioned that she suspected her brother was poisoning their grandfather with arsenic. She did not go into details... Though we can bring up the subject next time when she comes over for lunch with us. She asked about you and would like to meet you. What I infer from my own research and this conversation is that the brother somehow coerced the elderly man into not leaving the house to her, although she lived with him and apparently loved him very much. The brother moved in with them to supposedly help her take care of grandpa but it was a scheme," explained Aunt Citilali.

"So how come the house ended up under Tania's name?"

"Call it divine justice. The brother had a stroke soon after and became unable to speak or move below the neck… he was just in his thirties! He was not married and their parents had died long ago, but Tania was given a scholarship in Europe, so he had to be institutionalized. As his next of kin, she now handles his affairs."

"Oh my God! What a terrible story!"

"And this is not all. She says that if he had not had the stroke she would have sent him to jail for homicide."

"I don't know what is worse, to be incarcerated in jail for life or to be incarcerated in a body which does not function," added mom.

"Either way, his life is ruined. Tania says that given the circumstances of her brother, it would be in vain to exhume the body to confirm the cause of death…. No wonder the brother did not allow an autopsy!"

"If Mr. Troy indeed was murdered in this house, imagine the wickedness and rage these walls witnessed..."

"I hope Heaven helps his soul to finally find peace!"

"Maybe this is what you were hearing… think about it, we are living at the crime scene!" Mom said jokingly, confidant of being blind and deaf to the afterlife. "What kind of scholarship did she get? Did she mention it?"

"Music. She plays violin in a Chamber Orchestra and teaches at the Conservatory."

After that night, only the sound of the wind, the trees and the mountains could be heard in the dark, and only by having the "third ear" opened.

Winter came and went, but this time it stayed with us a bit longer. I was not expecting this. I thought the seasons would come as before, when daddy was with us. The fall was spectacular. I had seen the ochre, golden, reds and burgundy hues sparkled over the trees around our cabins during past vacations, but nothing this grandiose. The air seemed thinner and it filtered through the skin. There were different sorts and more abundance of wildlife. Soil and sky were richer to the senses, but the winter… mom lived to cuddle with me, yet I was not a lap dog and I struggled to be released from her well-intentioned embrace. Still, she could not help it. She said to me innumerable times that she missed her "dearest pillow" and that I would have to do. She both, apologized for my inconvenience and thanked me copiously for being there for her. It was when resting, eating and meditating when she missed dad the most.

However, I must admit that the presence of snow made the season all the more bearable. Not only was the scenery completely renovated, but the snow was tasty and fun to play with. On the contrary, ice was no fun! Aunt Citlali was particularly careful not to fall down and she wore paraphernalia almost as bizarre as Aunt Olga and other hippie humans. The boots and clothes alone must have weighed more than she… I wondered how she managed to move. Mom crocheted a lovely sweater for me and got me a waterproof jacket to play outside. I discovered the usefulness of a fireplace and the taste of chestnuts. Of course, she could not stop singing the Christmas carols to me (privately) until the last day.

Another year. I was surprised to notice how rapidly my body changed in twelve months. Mom was on reverse and seemed younger and more energized after the move, like the mountains suited her, although she was starting to cover some gray hair.

One day I was home alone with Sugar, the pink and gray cockatoo whom Aunt Citlali ended up adopting from the animal shelter. She had gone for a week to a conference-workshop on UFOs and ETs and had left mom in charge of the bird.

The cage was open and Sugar was standing by the door, deciding where to go next.

"Please don't land on my head," I warned. "My fur is thin and your claws would hurt my skull."

"Oooh poor dear! You have a thin skin? Hahaha! It may be precisely what you need, a little I scratch is always pleasurable."

"Not right now, thank you. I will let you know. Sugar, tell me, why do you like your cage so much? If they opened the door for me, I would go outside, at least to breathe some fresh air."

"I am used to my cage. It is my house, where I feel the safest. Outside one no-knows what can happen; one time I stepped on a ball, and that thing moved and oops! I almost felt to the floor. It no-is safe for a bird to be on the floor."

"If I ever see you on the floor I will come to your rescue."

"Thanks, Canela. It is good to have an animal friend, even of another species. No-get silly ideas... you are too hairy for my taste, no-offend you baby, hahaha!"

"I already have all the love I can take."

"Do you want to know something funny?"

"Yes, what?"

"That nanny thinks I am a female! She calls me 'missy' hahaha!"

"I noticed it when she first brought you home... I guess the people at the rescue center cannot tell the difference among birds."

"Right! It no-matters. Sugar is a sweet name either way."

"Your nanny may never know..."

"She'll know! Her boyfriend will reveal to her that I am a real boy."

"What boyfriend?"

"The one I am going to get for her."

"Are you going to find a boyfriend for your nanny? How are you going to achieve this?"

"Easily... you'll see!"

"Could you also get one for my mom?"

"Sorry, it is my gift to her; but you can help your mom too. Dogs are very popular among humans. I am sure you can attract a suitable mate. Does she kiss you too much... looking for a relay? Hahaha!"

"I am being serious, Sugar! I don't want her to feel lonely after I am gone. Sure, when we go out, people tend to feel attracted to me, but not to her. She noticed it too and even told me; 'Canela, if I were a fifth as popular as you are, I would have a line of admirers asking me out… glad you are not a human girl and I don't need to worry about you and besieging boys.'"

"Maybe this is the way it ought to be. At least you no-are relegated by human infatuation. Most humans limit the number of beings they want to love. By doing this they set themselves out for failure."

"Mom is the most loving woman I have ever met! You have not seen how much she loves me. I understand that for many people it is easier to love an animal than a person, but she has enough love in her heart to give away to an entire village… that's the thing!"

"She will do something with it. Keeping love to oneself no-is good for the soul. She will realize this."

That wise perceptive cockatoo, between joke and joke, threw out some indisputable truths.

As a matter of fact, not long after our lively chat, Aunt Citlali came home with a retired Army General whom she met through a friend. The man was a bird aficionado and wanted to see her winged pet. He was especially fond of cockatoos. Aunt Citlali was reluctant to bring in unknown male visitors, but being a bird, the easiest way for the general to meet Sugar was in her house.

At first sight, it did not seem like they had much in common, but by virtue of being there with Aunt Citlali, he perceived the peaceful ambiance and feminine touches of what makes a house, a home. A home he had not had in many years. Instinctively, he checked out the surroundings: a keyboard next to the window, a sewing machine in the living room, a large bookcase against the wall, no TV, fresh flowers on the table, pictures of relatives and the cosmos above the mantle, and a pyramid peeping out timidly from the back door. He learned more about the lady of the house this way than from a chit chat between them; and what he saw he liked. He was not seeking an adventure or escaping his solitude. He was genuinely comfortable with Aunt Citlali and perhaps would have never met her if it were not for Sugar.

The general, a widower, was an interesting man and a caretaker; he smelled of old bark and his voice was grave and deep. Clearly, he was the kind of person who inspired respect. He knew how to command others, but also how to obey orders, which was important for Aunt Citlali who was not about to domesticate any man of hers.

As it was my custom (unlike mom's), I passed freely from one side of the duplex to the other whenever I pleased. Both women liked to leave their back doors open to ventilate the rooms, which also allowed me to relieve myself as needed and to better guard the property. I was there the memorable day the general arrived.

"Hello Sugar. I wanted to meet you, my friend! Do you want to come out to say hi?" Sugar lifted the crest for the general to admire his plumage. "This is a gorgeous bird. How long have you had her?" inquired the general, as both humans stood in front of Sugar's dwelling.

"Not long. She is a great companion, and funny too!" Citlali put Sugar on her shoulder. "No missy, my earrings are off limits!" She pointed sternly and removed the pet from her ear.

The general observed the bird. "Well, Citlali, I have news for you: your companion happens to be a boy companion. I am certain of it."

"No way! How do you know?"

"His eyes, the color of his eyes. Maybe when he was a baby it was not clear, but now there is no doubt."

"Such must have been the case, because when he came to the animal shelter they said the name Sugar was meant for girls, and he responds to it... He'll stay Sugar. It suits him well anyway. Do you know a lot about birds?"

"Some, I belong to the "Amateur Ornithologists Club."

"Oooh! I would love to learn more about it. Would you like some coffee or tea? I also have carrot juice."

"Do you make your own carrot juice?"

"Yes, I can make some right now!"

"Oh no, I don't want to cause you any trouble. Water is fine."

"It is no trouble at all... we'll see if Sugar wants some carrots too!"

After that day, Aunt Citlali and the general became good friends. A few months later they started dating and by the following year their relationship became more serious.

The rescued bird not only rescued the general from his monotony, but he brought a new élan to Citlali's life so unexpectedly she considered it a present sent directly from above... In fact, by "winged intervention."

Mom was happy for her, but gradually saw less and less of her friend, who spent more time with the boyfriend. This prompted mom to socialize further and she opted for more steady company. The plan was to foster a couple of dogs until she could find permanent homes for them. She was unsure of how I would react and would take her chances with an adult dog (she knew I had limited tolerance for small breeds or playful puppies). She actually consulted with me about her idea.

"Canela, gorgeous, delightful, exquisite, *mon amour*, I need your opinion and your consent with something. How would you like to have some canine company? I know that you are the princess of the house, and you will continue being so, but perhaps you would like to share some of the many blessings God has bestowed upon us? Precious, remember where you came from. We need to help the less fortunate if we can, right?"

I was occupied doing my pawdicure and I must have seemed distracted to mom.

"Whatever." She continued. "Of course, we need the approval of the landlord, but since Aunt Citlali will most likely be the new owner, I think there would be no problem."

Indeed, Aunt Citlali was negotiating with Tania the purchase of the duplex, thinking this would be her last earthly abode. Mom wanted no troubles with ownership and would keep leasing. "Good thing we did not have to move again!" I thought... I was only partially correct.

Being a virtual instructor was not only the best way for mom to keep her job, but to maintain her mind less overcast with the clouds of dad. She got to know many people, but none of them in person, so she expanded her socialization field through her hobbies and began painting in public areas. This always draws a crowd.

The general had introduced mom to some of his friends, most of them fellows from his military career, many of them retired, none of them vegan. Needless to say, mom did not seem too inclined to date any of them. She would have preferred someone younger than her former husband (hoping that he would outlive her) and if not vegan, at least vegetarian; but she appreciated his good intentions. At the gym, everybody was connected to their electronic devices and did not remove their earphones even to say hi. Then she joined regular meetings with people interested in conversing and improving her favorite language: French. There she met only women (except for the organizer). Later on, she gave up her tango lessons when she was asked to learn to lead in order to help balance the class's male to female ratio. She switched to flamenco.

I was running out of time and a suitable candidate for mom was not in sight. Attracting men became a challenge, not for lack of beauty, but because I refused to take long walks as I got tired faster than mom. Actually, I was moving slower and started to use a ramp for climbing to bed. Also, mom had traded the van for a sedan after repeated battles between my refusal to get in and her impossibility of carrying me. She can be insistent, but I usually win.

During the holidays, Sugar told me, many people purchase baby pets to give as presents. The problem is that the animals (generally) age faster than people and some lose the initial enthusiasm of "owning"one, and if they do not know how to educate it or treat it, the human may be frustrated and want to dispose of him. This is why from January there is an increased volume of abandoned animals of all kinds and the work of volunteers to help them is absolutely crucial for their survival.

Mom knew it was time to act, for more than one reason.

"*Amorcito corazón*, you need to come with me. I want you to pick a doggy friend, whoever you prefer, to bring home until it is adopted. *D'accord*?"

"Okay."

"Please try to choose someone obedient, if possible."

"Okay. Can we go now?"

I got up and started my pre-going-outside routine.

Fifteen minutes later we were in the car. We parked in front of a stone house with a big fenced yard and a dog park aroma. A person came out and let us in the backyard. Six dogs immediately came to greet us. One of them, the boss, told me he was the supervisor and the other quadrupeds were temporarily there; that he was teaching them some various basic rules. He checked me out and asked me if I was also looking for a family.

"No," I told him. "I am here to choose one to do the same."

"Welcome! There are many dogs in here and not all of them are used to living in a pack. It is too much work for me and my mom."

"The lady of the fungi odor?" I inquired while the women talked.

"The same. She thinks she is in charge, but I am the one who organizes the ranking of the pack. Have you done this before?"

"First time. Mom wants me to select a good candidate for adoption. We do not have experience and she wants to make sure I get along well with him. I am not so convinced it is such a good idea, but we'll see... She relies on my judgement," I explained.

"Would you like a recommendation?" he politely offered, scratching his face.

"Why not! but I would prefer a calmed pooch..."

"Then don't take the sheepy odorous one. He is a little jumpy."

We spent a good while there. The women brought lemonade and started their conversation while mom did not take her eyes off me, trying to decipher which dog would be most compatible and with the highest chances for adoption.

Following a tail sniff inspection and an aura analysis, I found an adult Siberian husky that seemed tolerable. He did not express much interest in me so I thought he would not mind my own business, as humans say.

At first, mom seemed oblivious to my selection. I did not know how to make her understand my opinion. She was tempted to get a totally different dog, one more playful and sociable, exactly the opposite of what I wanted. On the other hand, the lady told her that the husky was good with people and this, added to the fact that he was apparently attractive by human standards, tipped the scale in his favor and he finally came home with us.

Timing could not have been better. Mom, loving as usual, started overwhelming the newcomer with crushing attention and pretty soon she realized her hugs and kisses were not always welcomed.

"Dandy" as he was named, was a good boy, but neither of us was interested in each other. He was curious at first, but not being potty trained sent him to a large cage and scheduled trips to the backyard. It took him several months to learn the three basic commands and become urbane (mom was not a "natural" provider of this type of education either).

Over the next weeks, mom attended adoption events at different locations. She normally invited me, but often left me home, so "people would not be tempted by my charms" to take me away from her. Yet I knew it was because I did not appreciate those small breeds (and mutts) usually hyper, high-pitched boisterous quadrupeds which get on everyone's nerves except their caretakers'.

Another summer, another fall… but who was counting? Mom and I only counted stars. We all would get in the car and drive to a remote location, especially during good weather and camp all night to watch the starry sky. The grass was a fragrant velvet, the wind new and innocent, the mountains whispered among themselves and the trees talked to their tenants. It was lovely. The view through the whimsical branches from below gave a whole new dimension to the forest. The rumor of the lake filled with swimming beings created a natural orchestra that played with the wind. Prideful, it shone during the day, mirroring the fluffy fickle clouds and winged spirits. Soil, air and water; there were living beings everywhere! Flying, floating, swimming, crawling, sprouting, running, walking, standing, there was not a void in such a vast space! And this was only considering the physical plane!

Mom was becoming a talented painter and a friend of a friend asked her about exhibiting some of her paintings in the art gallery downtown in the big city. She got so excited she started re-considering a project that had been hunting her for several years: painting her chiquita.

"I doubt I will be able to capture such a celestial beauty!" she said to me strongly holding my face in her hands (she never learned to be gentler). Passionate as always, she continued. "You are too beautiful! I need divine inspiration to embody such an ambitious endeavor. You know, I never, ever get tired of looking at you (sigh)! You are such a perfect, adorable thing! From your wet dark nose, to the last hair in your tail… I know! I have the perfect title for the painting: 'The Furry Maja' How do you like that?"

"I don't care!"

"You could become famous, like Goya's portraits. People would have the chance to admire your gorgeousness; you would be the definition of beauty!"

"Good Lord, mom!"

"Would you pose for me?"

"I sleep long enough!"

"No. I want you awake, to see your eyebrows, your ears, and your awesome bright eyes. You are such an expressive doggy! I prefer a vibrant model than to copy you from a picture. The best is the original, don't you think? Caneluska, why do I love you so much?"

I was supposed to be your daughter, I revealed to her mentally.

"Because I am your doghter!"

Satisfied, I licked her hand.

It did not matter. The important part is the essence of things. In any case, nobody saw me the way she saw me or the way she sensed me. I could not have been more loved. I simply cannot imagine it. I really doubt I had ever received more love in all of my incarnations, especially because she literally expected nothing in return. I cannot even recall her ever asking dad what she often asked me (which mom regretted), "What can I do to make you happier?" Only God loves us better.

Dandy and I spent long hours accompanying mom while she painted. She sketched me outside, following my gratifying grass-rubbing, on a spot where the morning sun's rays bathed me and my red coat emitted a myriad of hues, according to her. She tried a couple angles, finally deciding to face me directly, to "show off those ornaments on my head" arguing that if I were human, my ears would be the ponytails that gave me a mischievous air… Since I would not hold the ears in her desired position, she photographed my face more times than a paparazzi on assignment. I indulged her putting all sorts of props on me. "Adorable!" She glowed at the sight of me; it should be me the one painting her!

During one of those sessions, towards the last brushes of the painting, Dandy came to tell me goodbye.

"Congrats! Will you be going to your forever home?" I expressed carelessly, paying as little attention to him as possible, not to disturb my slumber. By then, I spent most of my time dozing and in spite of mom's insistence, ignoring everyone else.

"Dandy, come here! Madam Hairs is a little grouchy today. I want to show you the photograph of a little boy. He is looking for a special companion. He has some type of neurological condition, nothing dangerous, don't worry. He is not very interested in people, kind of Canela style, but in human terms. The family is traveling now but when they come back they want to meet you." Holding the picture from her cell phone, she followed Dandy's distracted eyes with it and tried to get his attention. Dandy kept moving his head and avoiding the artifact. She had him by the collar. If he could handle mom, he could handle the boy. I wished him luck.

We went to bed early that night. It was about to rain and it got dark earlier. I had no intention of moving but wanted to please mom. With difficulty, I got up and tumbled behind mom, whose countenance grayed with sorrow.

"Come here, Chiquita. Let me help you!" Mom could not carry me. She would have to put her arms around my chest lifting me to walk on my back paws. Standing up, I almost reached to her chin (not only because of my length), but both of us knew I did not like this at all, so I made an extra effort and followed her to bed.

Lying next to her, she positioned me, as usual, up towards the headboard and facing her. She placed a bedrest pillow behind her and pulled me with my blanket to her lap. She held me like a human baby.

"*Mon amour*, do you feel alright? The vet said that your svelte body is healthy, or did we miss something? Talk to me, Canela. What do you need? Is there anything I can do for you?" She kissed my cheeks and nose, "multiple kisses" mode.

I wanted to say, "You did all you could humanly do to make my life happy, healthy and comfortable. You and daddy were my world, and my world was full with your love. I will forever be grateful; but above all, I love you with all my soul."

My Soul! In an instant I recalled I was Alma, not a dog, that this was merely a body, one of the many I had had. Something popped up in my head and a hyper awareness involved me. The sensation of the silky blanket on my coat, those perfumed hands which fed me and scratched me tirelessly were more vivid than ever. The stars of her eyes that usually smiled before my reflection, suddenly clouded. I noticed their deep color, the black pupils and the red thin veins on the white outside, glassy like ice. I could almost count the nascent eyelashes on both eyelids, going from thick to thin, I felt the air as her lashes fanned upon me. It was magical! Then I glanced at the arch of her eyebrows, the little hairs aligned in one direction and going from vertical to horizontal, stopping towards the temples. Her lips were moving "Precious!" Some little wrinkles in her face became more pronounced, my body began making weird uncontrollable noises.

Mommy held me with adoration. She wanted to feel my breath on her chest, on her face; frowning, she squeezed me. I sensed her heart. Her eyes became watery and wet my nose. I noticed the temperature of my body slowly dropping from my paws. Mom's delicious fingers caressing my entire body made a quick pause to reach for her phone. She called someone and came back to my chest. She searched for my eyes, I was starting to fall asleep. Her voice was wandering off but, in my head, I repeated, "Is okay, is okay, please don't cry, please don't suffer, I love you so much! I want to be with you forever! I don't want to hurt you! Don't be sad! I love you, don't worry, is okay! Please, God, make her smile again! God, help me make her happy! I want to be with you forever! I love you! I love you! I love you! ..."

Part V

Following Cecilia's Tracks

I yearned to inhale her whole being inside mine to turn into one and be together for eternity! How painful, how distressing and impotent it is to leave loved ones behind! Why is it so difficult to let go? Why does love punish us with the chains of attachment?

At first, I wanted to remain in the heavenly abode with my guru and keep learning from there; I refused to go down. However, I was forced to do it and yet, when the hour to return arrived, I did not want to go up. My time was over. By then, I was so attached to Cecilia that I resisted abandoning her, primarily because my departure would cause her immense grief and suffering.

The illusion of the physical dimension is so incredibly tempting it finds a way to pull us deeper, even voluntarily! while knowing that we do not belong in the world.

There was no use, the expiration date arrived, not a minute late and no amendments to the contract were allowed.

Paradoxically, success means doom; remaining in the world postpones the ascension to higher abodes. Rebellious, I struggled to accept the facts, no matter how many lifetimes passed… am I stubborn? "What we love is what make us suffer." Is the alternative to suffering not to love? I envisaged the familiar bright light from Heaven, but I declined to embrace it. I would take care of Cecilia, as I promised Max, even as a ghost. If I could not stay in the flesh, I would accompany her in spirit, as entities stuck between worlds.

Albeit I had forgotten my goal of liberation, the guru had perfect memory. He came to rescue me from my own ignorance. Yet, I was ready to exercise my will and abstain from progressing to the next level, remaining as an ethereal chaperone or reincarnating anew to be with her. The choice was mine, but not without the opportunity to reflect.

The Master, in its infinite compassion, sent an ambassador I could not refuse. Out of nowhere, a nebulous mass started to take form. The first thing I noticed was a velvety complexion irradiating light. Slowly, there appeared the unforgettable features framed by bluish dark hair, a pair of loving emeralds contrasting with obsidian eyelashes which spoke so eloquently and a sweet smile I simply adored! My emotion was so intense I would have fainted had I blood circulating through my head. I always knew that life after life was better but having before me the proof of an enlightened loved one was truly powerful.

"M… M… MMM… Maaa… Maaax!"

My heart jumped out to him and I started crying uncontrollably. His body… I had not actually seen him after the day when he closed the door behind him. The last time he talked to me was to say goodbye. It was so wonderful to be with him again, I cannot describe it! All I knew was that I was Home once more.

"Alma, I am so happy to see you! We prepared a party in your honor. Today is a very special day. Welcome Home! It is so good to have you here; this time you won't have to leave if you don't want to. You are truly a free Alma!"

I was shown to a space elegantly decorated with golden columns raising to unfathomable heights, surrounded by translucent flowers which moved gracefully. Suspended above the area, there were small stars twinkling harmoniously which one seemed to be able to touch. Coming from the distance I noticed the murmur of waves that, as I paid more attention, became close enough as to get into the water; although the "water" did not wet. It was fresh but dry, soft and of changing colors, like a diamond caressed by the sun.

The place was full of friends and family from my past reincarnations. "Alma!" they exclaimed in unison. Everyone recognized me in spite of having seen each other an extremely long time ago. By fixing my sight on each candle as they appeared to me, I was able to identify and remember instantly who we were. It was the most amazing experience! What a reception! Like being in a hall full of people who meant the world not once, not twice, but hundreds of lifetimes: mothers, fathers, children, lovers, best friends, etcetera. I was captivated! I could not conceive a better fortune or a finer reception. This was the ultimate celebration and although Cecilia was not present, I suspected that she would be pleased and envious of my luck.

I even had a chance to talk to Ushmil! My beloved Hindu friend from my last human reincarnation who had already passed twice and I thanked her personally for her prayers. Without her, who knows how long it would have elapsed before meeting a spiritual teacher! As all actions have a reaction on Earth, my dear friend's good deeds and sincere desire were rewarded by allowing her to be reborn under auspicious circumstances. At a very early age, she learned about the Sovereign Master through her neighbors.

One day when she went there to play, she found a photo of the Master in one of the rooms. She insistently inquired about the enigmatic and majestic figure that, as she related to me, winked at her affectionately. Following this incident, she received initiation "telepathically" during a so called "dream" she had after reading one of his books. So powerful is the Master who recognizes his disciples and searches for them anywhere in the universe.

Fortunately, time does not exist beyond the physical dimension, which was very convenient, as I had no intention of leaving the party and wanted to converse with each one of those souls, so dear to me. Of course, both gurus were here: Sri Bawarta Laji and the Sovereign Master, who I met in my most recent life.

Max told me that he was chosen to be in charge of some sort of celestial temple, where he welcomed souls from all over the universe who wanted to come here to contemplate God and continue learning. Such learning is infinitum, as the aspects of God. He could not be happier. This was, at least for now, his new mission and he seemed absolutely elated. He invited me and said something Sri Bawarta Laji had mentioned before.

"We can meet anytime you please. All you have to do is think of me. We have countless ethereal bodies and can manifest them simultaneously anywhere in the universe."

"Do I have other bodies too?"

"Yes, all of us do, even on Earth, but there we cannot see them or manage them at will. You are still new and need to realize your wisdom, but eventually you will go to higher realms and could become your own master."

"Awesome! I am ready!"

"If this is your wish then you should ask the Sovereign Master if he would agree to give you initiation. Remember that your deliverance is through the connection with a disciple. He has paid your karmic debt with the Lord of Karma, therefore you need not to reincarnate. Nevertheless, if you aim to become your own master, further teaching is required. I suggest you keep learning from Sri Bawarta Laji until you receive initiation from the Sovereign Master." He smiled. "We will always be together; this time is forever. It is so wonderful to see you, Alma! I love you so much! You were my loyal companion in the world during my last reincarnation and you taught me a lot. Thank you, Alma!"

He had evolved above human... to a celestial being. His light, his smile, his wisdom, his loving energy; there was nothing ordinary of Max anymore, yet, it was a superior version of himself, a Maximilian Maximus as he was once called!

Being a family member of sincere practitioners like Max and Cecilia benefited me in more than one way. Not only had they provided me a great life (as is the case of many pampered pets), since they adhered to the five Buddhist precepts their guru demanded of all his disciples: to abstain from killing, lying, stealing, adultery and using intoxicants; by feeding me vegan food, I did not create the heavy karma of killing (though indirectly). Also, by the grace of the Master, I was raised to a higher realm than what by virtue I deserved.

The increased vibrational frequency of this plane of existence and the beings who resonated with it made one feel delighted and almost unable to perceive the suffering of anyone. Particularly because one understood the bigger picture and how everything was perfect; the lessons that needed to be learned and the spiritual progress towards God (in whichever given name).

However, I did not wish to be completely distanced from my beloved Cecilia, so I was determined to keep an eye on her. Max was right, I was still a neophyte and I would start by turning to Sri Bawarta Laji for assistance to check on her wellbeing and if possible, even send her a helping hand from Heaven.

"You are a nosy Alma!" said my guru after I expressed my intentions. "You can peek from here and also get in touch with her guardian angels. They are closer to her. This way you can send her a message, if permitted."

"More than one angel? Is it the norm?" I never noticed those guardians.

"She has three. All human beings are assigned one at birth, often two, depending on their accumulated actions, and the Master sends an additional special guardian angel to his followers. Also, he has an ethereal body linked to every disciple upon initiation (a true Master is omnipresent), so you need not worry," elaborated Sri Bawarta Laji.

"How wonderful! It is not that I am worried, I want to be near to learn too, I have tons of questions and there is a lot I still do not understand."

"Let's start! …what was left out…? You may want to skip your funeral. There is no reason to see the disposal of your canine body coupled with Cecilia's tears. Suffice you to know that she spent the night holding Canela until dawn."

"Nobody helped her?"

"Her friend Citlali had stayed overnight at her fiancé's. When she heard her message the next morning she came to her aid. Your ashes are adorned with Master's pictures in the same spot where Max's are."

"Ohhh... Can I see what she is doing now?" I asked, expectantly.

"You know what to do."

I concentrated and felt immediately transported to Cecilia's side, but with the realization that I could see simultaneously everything surrounding us, as well as the ideas and feelings of those around and how their thinking triggered certain actions (which will manifest in the future) and what the causes were of the effects of the present. Truly prodigious.

"Woof, woof!" It was Dandy greeting me, he recognized my energy. I did not think that anyone would see me. How exciting!

"Hi, Dandy. You are looking great! How are you doing?"

"Doing fine, Canela. Now that you are not here, I kinda miss you." He was still perceiving me as one of his canine brethren, which is how he knew me. I could let him see me as a human figure, but it would have been confusing. After all, we are not the body; neither human, animal or extraterrestrial.

"You were wise to say goodbye. I thought you were the one leaving," I responded. He was lying on my bed, licking his blanket.

"Not yet. I need to make sure Ceci is fine. She finds comfort in me, well, a little… she misses her husband and now she also misses you! I try to help her, but I am not you. She is in the raining room. See the fog coming in through the ajar door?"

"Do you think she'll keep you?"

"Why don't you ask her? Here she comes." Dandy's nose lifted to sniff at the fresh chamomile perfume with a twitch.

Like a cotton flower, wrapped in her white heavy cozy bathrobe (the same used by Max), Cecilia stepped into the bedroom, rosy and refreshed. She did not seem as stern as I saw her last, perhaps due to the warm shower. She took a pillow and put it under her chest, one hand on her chin and another on Dandy's ears. Facing him directly, she said,

"How are you doing, handsome? Ready for Morpheus' embrace? I too want to sleep and dream about Max and Canela. If you see them, please tell them I miss them and that they forgot to take me with them."

Dandy licked her hand. She continued.

"Look, I don't know what happened with the family of the boy interested in meeting you. I am not sure if they are back in town or what. In any case, your beautiful face is all over the internet for people interested in a lovely companion like you… Unless… you know what? I am not sure… what would YOU like? I'll tell you what: I am going to ask my Master for a sign. Of course, if you want to stay with me you need to let me know. Make sure you are pretty clear for a confused human who speaks no dog language, okay? Also, I hope my Master sends me an obvious clue. Let's say, if you don't get adopted by this child or someone you really like (and please, be clueless-proof for me, will you?) by the time my application to volunteer is answered, then we will continue as now. Nevertheless, if you make a really good connection with a family and I am accepted, it would mean that we have separate missions and we both will part our ways. D'*accord? Qu'est-ce que tu penses, mon cher ami?* I better meditate to see if God enlightens my understanding."

Cecilia kissed Dandy on the nose like when she kissed mine and went on the computer. She had downloaded an application for a nonprofit organization which sought volunteers to work in developing nations to help in various fields like health, environment, housing, education, etc. She wished to travel far and spend some time dedicated to others, specifically in education. She had previously filled out the application but was not ready for transmission. She reviewed it several times and made some minor changes, attached some documents and then closed her eyes, commending herself to her guardian angels and Master. "God, if it is your will and it is good for everyone involved, please show me the way." Next, she hit the send button.

I just stayed there and observed. Cecilia looked sad. Her face always lit up when she saw me. I wished she could see me now! I lay down adjacent to her until she fell asleep. Slowly, she slid down on her back and I accommodated my ethereal snout on her pillow, side by side, as we used to.

I had a few questions for my guru.

"Dear Sri Bawarta Laji, why is this happening to Cecilia? She certainly deserves to be happy."

"Happiness should not depend on the presence of others. Max could not stay any longer. He refused to become an old man. He was losing interest in the material world and was eager to return to the Source. Besides, both had agreed to their contracts beforehand. You too, but you almost backed out at the last minute, and if it was not for the divine intervention of the Sovereign Master you may have remained a ghost belonging neither to Earth nor to Heaven. If I remember correctly, at first you did not even want to live a long life! Even more, you made me promise that I would not let you forget your goal of liberation and warn you…"

"Yes, you are right! Thank you for saving me from myself. I certainly would be entangled in the physical world once again if I had not been rescued," I interrupted, knowing perfectly well that I would not have listened to him either, which is probably why Max came for me. "But at least, Cecilia could have been prepared for her husband's demise somehow. I don't know, perhaps a chronic ailment or something less brutal and unexpected."

"No, Max wanted to depart before his body malfunctioned; and you, my dear Alma, even put in your contract your unwillingness to die of any painful disease. The accident allowed Max to exit the scene quickly, while he was still whole and healthy. To help Cecilia accept the idea of his departure he lasted two weeks in intensive care. He chose not to die instantly (which would have been easier for Max) to give her some time to assess the situation, grant her some sense of control, as she faced the decision to let him continue being plugged into life support machines with no realistic hope for improvement, or to permit the nature of the injuries to take its course. During those days Cecilia received intense teachings and blessings from her Master and through her meditation she gained peace and clarity to do the things she needed to do. By the time they pulled the plug, she was convinced that this was better than having him home vegetating and thus honored her husband's wishes."

"Tell me guru, as a disciple of such a great Master, can you explain the pain and suffering Max had to endure and if the crash could have been avoided?"

"Everything occurred as planned. Perhaps, in a parallel universe, things could have been different. Max underwent a few minutes of suffering at the realization of the imminent catastrophe of the aircraft but he paid off whatever karma he had left in the world in order to ascend to a higher realm... You will know more when you learn from the Sovereign Master how he helps his spiritual practitioners ameliorate their karma. Besides, there existed the legal claim of those whose autopsies revealed the causes of death. According to human's laws, the individuals who did not die instantly, were granted an additional compensation for pain and suffering, which would help offset the economic portion of the loss, a burden many people had to bear on top of their sorrow."

"It makes sense...!" I stated, remembering those who left the body in that fatal accident. "Okay, can we see the future? What is going to happen to Cecilia? Will she find another man? How long before we meet again? Where..."

"Alma," intervened my guru, "Her fate is not set yet. It depends partially on the actions she takes today, but we can peek at her different options and see the outcome of each.

The only certain thing is that her Master will never abandon her until she reaches the Source and is reunited with her loved ones."

"Great! I want to know if she is going to find another mate."

"Really? Wouldn't you prefer to advance spiritually in this realm so you can move to the next?"

"Well… can I do both? Would I be allowed to assist her in some way?"

"You think that by knowing her future you may intervene positively; it is understandable, but such is the job of her guardian angels and the Master himself and quite honestly I doubt that your assistance would be required."

"Fine, but if I can be of service, as an instrument of God, I would like to be able to help. One way for me to know it is by following Cecilia's tracks. Is it prohibited?"

"Not at all. You must remember that she has her own free will and we may not intervene even for her own good. She has already made some decisions prior to her current incarnation and new ones will be considered according to her wisdom (for which she meditates). You ought to respect this."

I should have known better, but I still had a lot to learn. Living as Canela allowed me to meet the most powerful Master of the universe (thanks to whom I do not have to reincarnate anymore) but did not do much for my spiritual growth. As my guru explained previously, a human body is precious because it offers the soul the opportunity to progress more quickly. To know how to practice in order to reach full enlightenment I needed to obtain the Sovereign

Master's initiation. I was already liberated by his grace and my next goal would be to receive his teachings and become my own master.

Evidently, I was able to continue checking on Cecilia; nothing would prevent us from getting together at her ascending while gaining spiritual growth. Although progress without a fleshy body was not as fast, I had the guidance and support of my guru. Besides, I felt happier than ever before… well, since deciding to come down to the material world.

Being on this realm is nothing I can describe with words, but what I can describe is the rest of Cecilia's life and her experiences from a broader perspective. There are no space limitations where I am so, per Sir Bawarta Laji's instructions, she was never far from me.

The house was quiet, other than the sound of the electrical appliances, the only noises were coming from outside. Sugar was sunbathing in his cage in the backyard. He was absorbing the sun's rays with his eyes closed, thanking God for his love and the love of his nanny. A symphony of birds lulled him.

An aroma of freshly baked bread that inundated the air started to distract Dandy, who had been asleep on the deck. Citlali had gone back to bed after eating breakfast with Sugar. She felt tired and had no plans for the morning. Ceci was up, working on the computer.

That was the day a little boy named Gibran came to visit. A van, similar to which we had before, parked on the street. A bearded man of olive toned skin and pretty matching eyes stepped out and opened the door to a boy about six years old who seemed reluctant to move. The mother took his hand and led him to the front of the house. She was wearing a long blue skirt and flat shoes. Her face was framed with a purplish fabric going around the head, neck and down her torso. Her nose was long and her smile wide. She was unsure of what bell to ring, so she got out her cell phone and dialed up.

A minute later my beloved Cecilia appeared at the door, swathed in a blouse Max had bought her in Italy. After the usual introductions they went to the backyard where Dandy was waiting, looking neat after a bath.

Dandy got up and immediately looked for Gibran, who was behind his mother's skirt. The boy gently touched his head and smiled. "Gibran, this is Dandy," revealed the mother, delighted to see her son smile, which was not very common.

Although Dandy was not specifically trained for special needs people, he was obedient, intelligent and had a tender disposition. The husky, rescued from a puppy mill, was ready to become the best friend of a child who had none. Gibran was very headstrong and did not seem to care for just any dog. He had seen other animals before Dandy but never made eye contact with them or touched them (maybe they were too small). This was already a great start.

Ceci gave the mother Dandy's leash, who then attached it to a belt around the boy's waist. They walked around the backyard. When the boy sat, he sat next to him and when he ran, they ran together. Dandy did not seem to mind the peculiar mannerisms of the child or his unintelligible words. It was like he could read his mind.

"Did you train the dog?" asked the father, who had been silent most of the time.

"Not really, he was first with another volunteer, but she had too many dogs and I am starting with the organization, so she gave me an easy one. This lady is an expert. I am sure she trains all her puppies regularly. Those who get any of the dogs she hosts are really lucky."

"Is this your only dog now? Or may I say *was* your only dog," pronounced the woman trying to sound clever, but it made a stab in Ceci's heart, whose face paled.

"It depends. You are the last people to visit him. If not adopted today he is officially out of the market to remain with me," retorted Ceci with determination.

"Oh, wow...! We don't think that would be the case," continued the lady looking for the approval of the husband, who sat on a step and did not make a peep. "There is a pretty good connection between those two. I think they are a great match!"

"A match made in Heaven!" indicated Dandy licking the boy's face, whose giggly laugh resounded among the adults. "My brother, at last!"

Dandy was referring to his journey to care for Gibran. Searching his aura, I could see that this pair had a mission together: inspired by their relationship, the family would later open a pet adoption center for children with disabilities in their native country, where unfortunately, dogs were often neglected and mistreated.

After filling out some paperwork, the family took Dandy's few belongings and departed the same afternoon.

Despite all her efforts, Cecilia cried on saying goodbye to Dandy. After she closed the door she glanced at my portrait on the mantel and spoke to me.

"Canela, I love you so much! Why did you leave me behind, like daddy did? Why do you both keep ignoring me? I want to be with you…! Don't you too? I don't like it here anymore! God, please, I am not being ungrateful for all your blessings… I know that I am very lucky and have everything to be happy… but... life has lost its spark! I cannot wait to see my loves again… I miss them so, so, so much! I will never give up on them. Why do you keep me here? I fulfilled my mission, I received initiation, I have practiced within my limitations the best I could! I am done! I am ready to go Home!"

Citlali, who had watched the van disappear from her window was now knocking at her door. It was useless for Cecilia to pretend not to hear her, so she tried to cover her red eyes with her dark sunglasses and cleaned her nose.

"Ceci, how are you?"

"Fine… why do you ask?"

"I thought I saw people leaving… you told me that today was the appointment with the prospective family. How did it go?"

"For whom?" Ceci tried to avoid her, for her eyes were drowning behind her sunglasses. She turned away, pretending to straighten up one of her paintings on the wall to catch a fleeting tear with her finger.

"I am so sorry…!" exclaimed Citlali holding her friend, realizing that her suspicions were correct and Dandy had found his "forever home."

"It is okay… maybe I am not the right volunteer for this kind of endeavor. I could have kept him… but I was not sure… I asked for a sign, and he seemed delighted to go with them. Dandy started to bond with the boy right away. It was actually amazing to watch them together."

"Perhaps; but I think that Dandy also had a mission with you. He helped you through Canela… even if your pain isn't less, but it helped you cope, I think."

"You are right, and I believe it is time for me to learn that no one is forever. It's an ugly lesson, I'll tell you!"

Clueless me! I should have known! The presence of the husky in our house fulfilled another purpose. I could not comprehend why Ceci had to bring him home just to find him yet another home. If I had realized he was going to offer her emotional support during my transition, I would have been more welcoming. But Cecilia's transition to a new chapter in her life's book was far from over.

Not too long after Dandy's adoption Ceci received a second sign that her mission was still inconclusive.

"Tell me Citlali, now that you have purchased the duplex and your relationship with the general is cruising right along, are you considering living with him or perhaps renting out your unit?" asked Ceci, sipping her tea on the back deck, observing the small tubular pyramid the two friends and the general had recently finished building.

Citlali, unfailingly interested in alternative medicine, had researched about the healing power of pyramids and decided to make her own to meditate inside and improve her health. Since she had a boyfriend, she was more interested than ever in looking good and feeling better.

"I think I should move it closer to the pine," she thought out loud, unable to mask her lack of attention to her tenant's words. "Sorry, you were saying…?"

"I was wondering what your plans would be as the new homeowner."

"Umm… I would like to remodel the façade. I think it needs a facelift as much as me."

"Love having you as my neighbor and landlady, but I am afraid the general may take you away."

"As long as we do not set a date for the wedding, I am not worrying about living arrangements. Well, answering your question, most likely, I would prefer him to move in with me, rather than the opposite. God forbid things turn sour, he could not kick me out of my own house. He may keep his or sell it. We will definitely marry under separation of property regime."

"I am asking because I received an invitation into the health education program for one year of service in Vanuatu. You are the first to know."

"Congratulations, Ceci! I think it is going to be a very valuable experience for you! ...Have you mentioned it to your boss?"

"I have to, she gave me a terrific recommendation letter. We spoke about the application process timeline and I told her it would take months before I could get an interview. But time passes by and I will give her notice soon… I may even take one week's vacation to visit Olga and her family in Europe… now that I think of it they are halfway there! Quitting is going to be tough. I have enjoyed working remotely from home now and I have nothing but great things to say about my boss and the institution… I am really going to miss them! It has been many years already! I won't lie, it won't be easy to leave my job. I am already jealous of my replacement… can you believe it?"

"If they replace you. Nowadays the emerging technology is eliminating many jobs people used to do either with robots or with computer programs. In any case, it is time to move on."

"True, but I have had so many losses that it tempts me to keep my employment until I retire. On the other hand, this new assignment is an adventure. Of course I have considered it carefully; I am not the type who makes hurried decisions. Still, there is always a risk…"

Cecilia sat on one of the garden chairs and finished her cold tea, placing her elbows on the table.

"No worries, it may be exactly what you need! I am sure Max would be proud."

"Well, now finding myself deprived of strong emotional and physical ties, I think it may be the time to explore this interest I had before I met Max. Equally as bad things suddenly come, good things also arrive in life. Max used to say that God hand-picked me for him and considered my current employment the clear answer to my prayers (position which by the way, coincidentally opened up and has never been filled by anyone else). Similarly, I want to believe that God is showing me the way."

"It must be. In case doubts make you tremble, it is preferable to regret having done it than not having tried."

"I concur. So, I needed to ask you if you would not mind leaving my furniture with you during my absence. You can rent my unit furnished if you wish. I will order a tabletop pad for my dining room table and sew protective chair covers. My bedroom set, which was a wedding present from Max, should not be a problem. Those are the only two furnishings I plan to preserve. The rest is not a big deal and I'll box my personal belongings. We can discuss the details if you agree. You may also use the furniture if you wish."

It would be too much to ask Cecilia to also give up the relatively few material possessions with a sentimental value to her. Although she was perfectly conscious of her troublesome ties, she required time to gradually let go. More than once she moved to live in another country and started anew, but this time she wanted to find her things at the end of her journey, even if only temporarily.

While making preparations for her exciting trip, Cecilia continued painting. Previously, she had had a successful exhibition at the art gallery of the school she once attended and for the first time, she sold a painting. She was finally committed to finishing Max's portrait and put it in a safe place. Uncertain of being able to continue painting during the assignment, she would try at least to take lots of pictures to serve as inspiration upon her return. She was excited and also looking forward to putting her French to good use, serve others and learn as much as she possibly could.

From Heaven, I followed Ceci's steps throughout her life, although each time more sporadically, as new situations and people were less and less familiar to me and I became increasingly detached and advanced in my spiritual practice.

Cecilia assiduously recounted her rich experiences during her service in a notebook she carried with her. She thought it would be worth sharing her perspective of life with others in a totally different environment and all the people she met, especially those souls with whom she had affinity. Along with her job-related duties, she learned to cultivate vegetables, which helped her rely less on inconvenient trips to the city and make her vegan diet more self-sufficient (originally, the diets of many natives including the pre-Columbian, were predominantly vegan[11]) and of course, to be ecological.

The day Cecilia arrived at her destination was a day she would never forget. After the long trip with several layovers, Ceci landed in the capital, which she found covered with the ash of one of its active volcanoes, on the southeast of the island. At the airport, a local representative in charge of the new volunteers had the mission of accompanying her to her host, a lady who lived alone with her five children after her husband died of an infectious disease two years ago. On the way to their destination, a big earthquake occurred causing the boat they were traveling on to flip over. Fortunately, Ceci carried only one piece of luggage and had left important documents and money in a safe deposit box in a bank back in the city. After hours of uncertainty and prayers, they were rescued and taken to the village, which was also the castaways' destination.

Cecilia was very well received by the villagers. Her host provided her with custom made clothing that although was far flashier than what she would have picked, made her

---

[11] Super, J., & Vargas, L. *The Cambridge World History of Food: Mexico and Highland Central America.* Cambridge: Cambridge University Press, 2000. https://goo.gl/6gLJxY

more likable and helped her adapt to their culture more quickly. She felt like she belonged to a family for the first time since she lost Max and Canela.

Besides re-adapting to living with the bare minimum, she became more accepting of herself. She did not worry about her looks as she used to (leaving behind skin creams, hair conditioners and makeup). Also, by not having easy access to processed foods she did not worry about watching her weight and even improved her diet due to the organic growing practices of the villagers. She was very grateful for her past laser procedures that freed her from glasses and waxes. Meditation became deeper and less difficult near the sea, under the starred sky and she never had a sleepless night after her arrival.

The most important lessons were the ones imparted directly from the villagers: their sense of sharing, their easy and honest laughter, the aim to improve oneself and the hope to do it against all odds. She was finally able to feel useful again and to think of others before herself (and her dogs) and realized that by lacking material possessions, she could give more. She felt both, impotent before many sad situations, like death of children, scarcity of resources and social injustice, and extremely happy for sprouting seeds, clean water, a shared roof and above all, friendship.

Cecilia's life with her new family was challenging, especially at first. The five children were loud. She was not used to living with kids. Thankfully, the youngest was already three and all slept through the night and took naps. Cecilia liked to put them to sleep with fairy tales narrated in French and English, both languages used in the capital, which she wanted them to improve. In the meantime, she tried to learn theirs, although she thought she would never become fluent.

The days were full of activities, from taking turns to fetching water, assisting to tend the vegetable garden, cooking in the open, to fulfilling her job-related duties. Those included teaching others hygiene techniques, treatment and prevention of AIDS and sex education. The lack of electricity forced her to retire early and to concentrate on her work (no TV to distract her), cell phone coverage was not completely reliable and her communications were mainly through letters and email whenever she went to the city and could find an available computer at an internet cafe.

Months passed and she and her host became really close. Cecilia would have liked to take her to live with her, but she knew that her mission was to provide assistance to improve the living conditions of the people in their communities and offer them support from within. After all, the solution of all their problems could not be to abandon their country, which at least enjoyed peace and was beautiful.

December caught Ceci off guard when they offered the opportunity to take some time off and come back after New Year's, if she so desired. Therefore, she talked to Olga in Europe and bought her ticket to visit them for one week. She thought she should receive the New Year in the village. After all, they were also her family now.

She found Olav, her nephew, very grown up. He was attending the conservatory and becoming a great musician. With the compensation money Cecilia shared with her sister, Olga bought a daycare center and was on her path to becoming a very successful business owner. Her husband's company was downsizing and due to the soaring unemployment in the nation, he started considering working as an independent consultant. The first husband (Olav's father), was not doing so well. He moved in with an old woman, hoping to marry her to inherit her money. He was currently unemployed and with no friends. He was trying to persuade his son to move in with him and help him share the costs, but Olav had greater plans and living in the outskirts of the city, where rents were cheaper but life stagnant, was not one of them. However, this did not stop his father from trying to manipulate him, as he always did.

Taking advantage of his feeble character, he cried about spending Christmas alone (he did not want to join his girlfriend to visit her family) making the boy feel bad for "preferring mother" now that he was poor and sick (when in fact, he squandered his money foolishly spending the minimum on his son, besides, he had a troop of doctors watching every organ in his body since childhood). In short, the man was a whiner. In spite of Olga's best efforts, Olav did not have the guts to refuse his father's protests and spend Christmas with his only godmother, who crossed half the world to see him and his mom. Yet, blood is blood and karma is karma and Ceci always had to compete with his father for time.

The following year Citlali and the general decided to get married on an Alaskan cruise and invited their children and other family and friends who could afford the ticket. Cecilia could afford it but could not find anyone to go with her, even if she paid for the two. She asked her sister, her cousin, her aunt and like it always happened, nobody had either money, visas, time or their significant other would not allow it. Owww, how much she missed Max, her best travel companion! Since she was not sure she could take those days anyway, she did not try further. At the end of her assignment, she went back home. Luckily, the contract for Citlali's tenant was about to expire so she was able to occupy her side of the house next to her friend and her better half.

Unable to see the future, I asked my guru, with disappointment, if he thought that Cecilia's destiny was to be alone.

"Don't you think it is a waste of woman to have her living alone when she has so much love to give? I would have sworn that she would already have met a suitable companion by now!"

"I know, but there are tons of people like her… and those who you would think should not marry or procreate, do so. Such are the lessons they need to learn. Cecilia has been a parent and a spouse multiple times and made great efforts. Of course she does not remember, but regardless of how she feels about it, she has done her best under each situation and nobody is obliged to do more. I am not sure if she will find someone. Consider that she is not looking and that Max left very big shoes to fill."

"True, perhaps her spouse 'supply' has been depleted too or she may be better off single."

Meanwhile, Cecilia returned to painting. She had enough photos from the island and its people to keep her busy for life! She also resumed her other interests and started a new one: ecologically sustainable development and was particularly interested in animal biodiversity and conservation. She took some courses at the nearest college and online and after a two-year break, she set up to volunteer again, this time in Africa, to help with some organization working in this continent.

In her fifties Cecilia was young inside and out and living a life she never suspected. Widowed, renting but wealthy enough not to need to work to support herself modestly, free from binding contracts of any kind and more relaxed, she surrendered to her luck and finally felt happy.

One day she was looking for something in the boxes she had stored in the attic prior to her latest assignment when she found some pictures of Max. She took them to the living room committed to finally face doing something with her things. After all, she needed to downsize as much as possible and make room for her new paintings. She hoped she could eventually have an exhibition to raise funds for some of the humanitarian projects overseas.

Sugar was keeping her company while Citlali and her husband were out of town visiting their grandchildren.

"Look sweetie, Sugar. This is my husband… handsome for human standards, and so wonderful!" exclaimed Ceci while holding a picture of Max in front of the bird, who was standing on the flower pot next to the sofa. "You know what, ever since he left me he has not shown a trace of concern, love or even a hint of a message during my dreams, meditations or prayers. Don't you call me crazy!"

She threw a sharp glance to her feathered friend, looking intensely at his eyes and pointing with her index finger.

"I know you animals can sense things we humans cannot, but he was a good spiritual practitioner. Knowing me, he should have found the way to comfort me. It is pretty sad when you are living your life by default, hoping to make the best out of whatever you have left while waiting for Heaven to claim you… He did not wait for me… I know I did not deserve him, but he does not deserve my tears either." Her voice broke. "He is sooo happy without me he does not even try to reach out! Of course he is...! Sugar, would the ecstasy of God make you forget nanny?"

She pretended she was hearing an imperceptible response.

"You see! I am so tired of missing him! And the worst part is that I know this world is all a big illusion and I cannot wake up! I bet you Max does not think of me in Heaven. Well, you go ahead and tell him that he failed me, big time!"

The cockatoo flew to her shoulder and from there watched his caregiver take a last look at the pictures before placing them in the fireplace, where both spent the rest of the evening sharing fruit and watching memories become flames, then ashes.

I could not ignore Cecilia's laments and my thought went straight to Max guarding the temple's entrance. He heard my call while welcoming the souls coming in, and appeared to me with a peaceful smile.

"Hi, Alma. What brings me here? Have you been initiated by the Sovereign Master?"

"Not yet. I am here as a messenger."

"What is going on?"

"Ceci has been wondering why you don't communicate with her. She believes you have forgotten her."

"So you have been nosing around the physical world! The Master descended there to help lift it up, leave it to him!"

"Easy for you to say because you are in High Heaven, unaware of the suffering of the world. How could you forget so soon? Not long ago, you were part of the world and every little thing that happened there affected your life somehow, or at least the lives of most beings living there!"

Looking serenely, Max answered me:

"You are right, but I have a new mission here and I am not going to interfere with people's karma, even my wife's. That's the job of an Enlightened Master, and I am not one. You won't be able to get too far if you keep attached to the material realm. It is not real! And Ceci has to fulfill her contract. In no time she will be with us. Don't worry!"

"But the suffering is very real! Remember when you were sick or when you lost someone you loved. I cannot believe you could become insensitive!"

"Alma, first of all, I assure you that I still love Ceci, as much or more than when I was with her. Only my love has evolved. It is a different type of love, more universal, less selfish, less passionate. It may be good if she thinks I don't care, even to be angry at me; this could make it easier for her to move on. How in the world do you expect to live happily after someone is gone if the person keeps trying to have a relationship with the ghost? It is unhealthy! And people around her are going to think she is mentally ill. If I manifest to her on Earth she will be stuck and even regress in her spiritual practice as she may focus on me instead of God. Very few people are capable of truly communicating between worlds and not getting caught in dangerous games and feeding their ego. Cecilia could not deal with it, trust me. Besides, she has had many, many spouses through her lives. It is not fair to cry only for me! Don't you think some of the former husbands and wives were also deserving of her love and mourning? You should talk to her spouse from another life, but it is not possible! He chose to reincarnate as a little girl in a South American country. They used to love each other and now they are both reciprocally oblivious of their whereabouts. Each has his own path, but at the end, we all will be reunited and happy together as one!"

"Then go ahead and tell her to leave you alone! To let you 'rest in peace' as they say. Be cutting with her, if she takes offence, that may compel her to get over you once and for all!"

"It won't be necessary." Max closed his eyes for a second and paused. "She already burned my pictures… it would be better if you were in them too."

I dared not say a word. Ceci was also heartbroken about not having me in her life and I had not managed to console her. Given her plans, she could not commit to another pet and did not feel strong enough to host any more dogs for adoption as she did with Dandy. In any case, she had promised Citlali she would take care of Sugar if anything happened to her or the general.

Inquisitive as usual, I asked my guru for permission to check Cecilia's contract for my own sake. Albeit we will be together again, I calculated that I would be less nosy if I knew what it entailed. Before reincarnating as Canela, I had had access to her contract, to know how I fit in her life, but I did not go far enough as to see beyond my appearance on stage, as Sri Bawarta Laji put it.

Satisfied my need to know about my beloved Cecilia (a dog's loyalty goes truly beyond the world's limits), I decided to peek in a slightly different direction.

From above, there was nothing more than green, a huge fluffy cushion formed of a myriad of hues of green, occasionally spattered with crystalline eyes and white tails of water hitting hard at the end of their fall, morphing it into clouds of foam. The deafening conversation of insects, amphibians and larger fauna was only surpassed by the roar of a mechanical bird chasing away the dwellers of their penthouses below.

Descending into a clearing behind a long building, two hurried men came out of the helicopter carrying boxes and taking them inside. As the wind from the blades subdued, the animals resumed their activities.

The site was a mix of zoo, hospital and school. There were cages with a variety of creatures under observation, a large blackboard, chairs and a couple of desks with computers no one was using. A bed and an armoire were cornered next to a small bathroom.

A baby rhinoceros lay on a big table, a young native woman on one side and an athletic man with braided black hair on the other were immediately joined by the newcomers.

"Glad you are here, doctor. We have stabilized her and repaired the jaw, but she is going to need some reconstructive surgery."

"Don't worry, the graft we will be using should work for this baby. Nuru, please bring it!"

The helicopter pilot and conservation commissioner, a tall man around 50 wearing a white shirt that contrasted with his dark colored skin, delivered the box and said as he headed for the exit,

"I will be outside if you need me."

Three hours later the two doctors and the assistant came out. The look of their faces was promising. Dragging their feet, but smiling, they sat on the rocking chairs under the shade and let the soft breeze kiss their faces. Nuru was having a lively conversation to someone on the phone.

"Yes Sir, no problem. Dr. Bernard and I will make sure to welcome her tomorrow. I will let him know. Bye." When he saw the male veterinarian, he raised his eyebrows and offered him a drink. "Is she going to make it?"

"She will be fine. She is strong and I think that with the proper care, she should grow up to be an awesome rhino. Too bad we lost her mother… it is a real shame!"

There was a grieving silence. The four people shook their heads and fixed a blank stare at the horizon.

"We are getting a new volunteer tomorrow. This person will support us implementing a system to collect rainwater and solar generating power for the park and the village. She may also be able to educate us and the students in sustainable practices like organic gardening to protect the environment."

"Sounds too good to be truth," intervened the veterinarian woman who recently graduated from a local university, looking at her assistant, the vet technician in turn.

"She has spent one year in Vanuatu and two more studying animal biodiversity and nature conservation. The director of the park interviewed her and seemed very pleased. You can look at her resumé if you want. It is on my desk."

"It's okay. I just think that it is a lot of work. Good for you, Bernard! Perhaps she'll rescue you from your rice and papaya diet," joked the vet.

"Even the apes eat better than you. They like insects!" added the technician, showing his perfect teeth.

"Laugh all you like but you will be jealous of my vegetable garden when I start supplying my delicious harvest to the best restaurants in the capital."

The following day Nuru and Bernard went to the international airport, a two-hour drive from the park, to pick up the new volunteer.

Nuru dropped Bernard by the entrance; he had received an emergency call from the police. He needed to identify two alleged poachers in the nearby police station so they could keep them detained.

Bernard, confident in detecting the typical foreign, "deer in the headlights" looking volunteer coming from another continent, waited at the arrivals gate as the flight landing was announced. Nuru forgot to give him the piece of paper with her name or a physical description, but Bernard thought it was more fun this way, and carefully examined the disheveled travelers.

The passengers were a mix of colors and cultures. It was not tourist season and a few business people were traveling in and out of Africa. He knew they recently finished filming a movie and did not expect to find any actors or journalists around. He was surprised to see this big tall English producer he read about in the newspaper talking to his beautiful actress, wife, or colleague, both wearing elegant hats and dark sunglasses introducing her to a local who approached them. After a few minutes, they left without her.

At that moment, Bernard saw a pale woman wearing flip flops, wrinkled T-shirt, short pants and long tangled straight hair, searching for her cell phone with one hand in her big bag and chewing gum while carefully scrutinizing the faces of the people waiting.

"She must be her!" he thought. *"Excusez-moi madame, êtes-vous Cecilia*?" He did not know her last name.

The lady smiled with a puzzled look. "Sorry, I don't speak Italian, I am American."

"Sorry, I am waiting for someone with that name."

Then, Bernard felt a slight blush in his cheeks as he noticed the eyes of the actress upon him.

"Bonjour!" she said. He was not who she was expecting at the airport, but he seemed friendly enough, so she decided to make some inquiries. "Do you live here?"

"Yes... I do now... although I am French Canadian," he answered, noticing her velvety voice. Smiling with his deep blue eyes, he asked, "Are you here for business or for pleasure?"

"For both, I hope. I am actually waiting for a conservation commissioner to take me to my assigned post," she revealed wishing to get some valuable information from her interlocutor.

"Are you looking for Nuru, from the International Volunteer Organization, to take you to the National Ecological Reserve Park?"

"Yes, do you know him?"

"Of course, we work together! He had an emergency and had to leave, but I can take you to the Park."

"Okay... may I speak to him? Do you mind?"

"No, let me call him." Bernard dialed Nuru, who was still at the Police Station and unable to leave. "He wants to talk to you."

They talked briefly. Cecilia wanted to make sure he was legitimate before going with him. Nuru told them to get to the police station so they could all return together. Not long after they left the airport, a strong storm started, flooding the entire city within minutes.

The two of them found cover in a bakery, where they intended to wait out the storm. They talked for hours. Cecilia learned that he was spending his sabbatical year after having volunteered there before. He lived in Quebec and was divorced for so many years he could not remember. His love for animals made him a vegan and also to return to Africa. He had no children other than his students and he was fluent in two African dialects on top of the four languages he already spoke (French, English, German and Italian). He was 48, five years younger than Cecilia, fun and compatible according to the Chinese calendar. He had worked extensively with wildlife and was the only transplant surgeon specialist for large mammals in the American continent. He reminded her of a blond cowboy she once saw in a western. Intelligent and charming, Cecilia was having a hard time trying to figure out what was wrong with him. Certainly a man like him would have been pursued by women of all colors and nationalities.

The storm got worse with no end in sight. The employee of the establishment said he needed to close but they should not try to leave the city, as some roads would be shut down facing the risk of landslides. Nuru also called, telling them that the jeep was bogged down and he was going to spend the night at the station; they had comfortable sofas in some of the offices and he would be safe there. He urged them to find refuge somewhere immediately.

Not having many choices, Bernard contacted a couple of friends who lived in the city, hoping they could offer some help. They invited them into their homes, if they could get there. This was the tricky part. The city was swamped and some residents were climbing to their rooftops as the streets became little rivers. Bernard had never seen anything like it.

Fortunately, there was a two-story hotel near them. They went in, with the idea of finding some dry rooms vacant. The water had invaded the lobby and the employees were busy moving their guests to the upper rooms. When Cecilia and Bernard arrived, they were not sure how many available rooms they would have, if any.

By then, both of them were soaking wet and could not even see their feet under the water. The humidity and the heat had stirred up Bernard's golden curls and brushed his pink cheeks. Cecilia's thin blouse and skirt adhered to her skin, which she had to tie up to one side to prevent its hem from floating. Her hair was dripping under her hat, same as the rest of her belongings which she carried on her backpack, while Bernard had her suitcase on top of his head. They waited patiently for the guests and staff to get accommodated to realize that there were no more rooms left. Then, Cecilia asked the personnel if anyone would be willing to share a room, for one night. Seeing clearly that the two foreigners required more than a place to lay their heads, they made arrangements to offer them their more luxurious room, which had a private bathroom and shower.

After a relaxing indoor shower, Cecilia offered turns to share the only bed in the room, but Bernard courteously refused and sat on the corner chair. Secretly, they were checking each other out. Cecilia was able to find some relatively dry clothes in her suitcase and even offered a skirt with an elastic band for him to wear while his clothes dried. Bernard preferred to spend the night with a towel wrapped around his waist, until, quite unexpectedly, his towel fell on the floor while trying to reach a pillow from the top shelf against the wall.

By the end of the night they knew more about each other than most of their friends. Around four o'clock in the morning, when Cecilia got up to meditate until six thirty, she ceded the warm bed to her roommate. The chair finally persuaded Bernard to trade places. Within minutes, he was lost in the luscious sheets imbued with Cecilia's perfumed body.

Cecilia meditated on Bernard, although at the beginning she did try to concentrate on God. Bernard's presence in the room distracted her. "He seems such a great guy! Healthy and handsome too. He does not snore. A vegan veterinarian; it should be the norm! He is adventurous. I wonder what his ex-wife would say about him. I am glad he works in the same park! Will I see him often? I hope he likes to dance... What would he think about me? I bet all the women around are very nice to him! I cannot believe he is single!"

That year went by very fast for both of them. They became close friends and saw each other often. Bernard taught her the local dialect and Cecilia instructed him in yoga. Besides working together in the park, Bernard accompanied Cecilia to the neighboring villages to help her educate the locals about biodiversity and the environment. Once the vegetable garden started producing, they cooked together and shared meals with other employees and volunteers, who also contributed with their own recipes. Other than the times when people or animals were sick or died, their stay was pleasant and rewarding, especially after recognizing that they were there to learn, not to teach.

In spite of all the time they spent together and the closeness they achieved, they remained as friends. Bernard was not sure if after returning to their "normal" lives they would continue being so compatible or capable of seeing each other in person. He had a wonderful job back in his country and had been approved for a research grant to further his mammals transplant technique and Cecilia was living in a different country, doing whatever she wanted whenever she felt like. He was afraid she would be too set in her ways or too involved with her religion (or whatever that was). But above all, he believed he could not commit to a long-term relationship and he was not interested in fooling around. Cecilia naturally accepted her destiny.

So, at the end of his sabbatical, they said goodbye and he went back to Canada and to his new routine. Cecilia stayed another year on assignment. Their correspondence became less and less frequent, not because Cecilia wasn't an avid communicator, but because between the time change and the demanding schedule Bernard had, he took forever to respond. The Park welcomed another vet, an Australian lady that had never volunteered overseas, who was also interested in marine life and was a skillful scuba diver. The two women became good friends. During a break, Cecilia went to visit her in her native city and learned how to scuba dive with her help. The following year she packed up her things to go back "home" (though she was not sure any more where that was), not without first making a stop to visit Olga and company.

Given that the duplex was occupied (she had told Citlali the date of her return, but the tenant was a pregnant woman unable to move until after giving birth), Olga insisted on her moving in with her until she found a more permanent place in the same city or elsewhere. Cecilia, inspired by the latest affairs, was seriously considering building her own ecological, renewable and self-sufficient cabin, which would allow her to live almost free of utility and grocery bills. As an added bonus, she could teach people interested in learning these techniques and remain self-employed and useful to others at the same time. Not bad.

It had not been yet three months since her arrival in Europe when Bernard went to see her. He was going to attend a three-day international event about novel surgical techniques in Denmark and decided to arrive first in Madrid to visit his friend and meet her family. As soon as he saw her again, the inescapable Cupid's arrow charged with karma fell upon him. He could not resist Cecilia's warm welcome and beautiful presence anymore. In a second, he realized how much he really loved her and how much he missed her. He persuaded her to join him in Copenhagen, not before asking her to be his girlfriend. Cecilia accepted, not because she believed so much Bernard's words, but because she thought she was strong enough to overcome a disappointment. Their last day in the port, in front of *La petite sirène*, on his knee, he proposed.

They had a lovely small wedding back in Canada. Bernard's older sister, conveniently a former wedding planner, was crucial in helping the newcomer feel welcomed to the country and to the family. As usual, the only person on Cecilia's side to accompany her was Olga, who came with her husband. Olav was given a scholarship in London to continue his musical studies. The half-brother, although relatively close to Olga, was not invited.

My guru had explained how relatives, friends and enemies of the past usually came together in subsequent transmigrations, but Cecilia had never met Pelagio in previous lives. The latter was the product of an affair their father had with his secretary. In fact, father and child had been enemies of the past and in the current reincarnation they made each other miserable until the father forgave him. Pelagio held a lifelong grudge against his poor mother for not having "defended him and demanded what was rightfully his, as much as his half-sisters, to whom nothing lacked." Once Cecilia's parents divorced, and having moved with them, he told his mom that he never wanted to hear from her again. Then Cecilia went to college, so they were never close.

On the contrary, Bernard coincided in a past life with Cecilia, centuries ago. Cecilia was a Purepecha princess, of the territory that today is Mexico. She lived in a gorgeous palace with her family and servants. Bernard was a metalsmith, in charge of making precious jewelry pieces for the royal family. He was secretly in love with her. It was a platonic love because monarchs did not marry their subjects. Nevertheless, this did not prevent him from dreaming about the princess. He died young, as most people did in those days. He expired wishing he could have made her his wife.

The last thing Cecilia expected in life turned out to be great, "Heaven sent." Their loving relationship was an extension of their friendship. Cecilia had become a successful painter, and inspired by the pictures of her travels mounted a few exhibitions. My portrait though, occupied a special place in the house; my memory, a better place in her heart, next to Max. Somehow, she felt like she had lost a daughter. One day she would know the truth! The consorts continued volunteering whenever they could. When Bernard was offered an early retirement, they examined their options and decided to move back to their roots (karma always calls) and established residence in Mexico.

They bought a nice piece of land in the east region of the country, not too far from the state capital but distant enough from heavily populated areas, to a place near the Sierra Madre Oriental, where no public services were available. That was exactly what they wanted. They built their dream retirement home: an ecological construction of recycled materials powered by solar and wind energy with a self-sustaining organic garden watered through a rainwater collection system for self-consumption. They even built a separate cabin for guests specially designed with Olga in mind, who promised to visit them more often.

Bernard collaborated with state administrators for the Conservation of Ecosystems and Protection of Species, acting as a veterinary consultant, which included conducting emergency surgery for endangered pumas. Together with his wife, they opened a refuge for injured animals and provided free pet neutering to the community. Cecilia also offered seminars on ecological gardening and vegan cooking demonstrations.

So far so good.

Therein, I was invited to attend one of the welcoming receptions for a lower level couple arriving from Earth (souls came from many planets). Occasionally, a soul in the upper dimensions will want to descend to inferior realms, usually to visit a loved one down there. What is not possible, however, is to go higher up, unless by accumulated virtues or accompanied by an Enlightened Master that can take one there.

The newcomers were two middle aged lovers who were dispatched straight into a lower realm after a violent death, courtesy of their killer. Their ethereal bodies could still be seen (they shed as the soul progresses through higher dimensions). I found out that when some individual halts the life of another person, the karma associated to the victim's current life is automatically transferred to the killer.

"How horrible!" I exclaimed appalled to my guru. "No wonder certain souls spend life after life paying their debts!" I reasoned remembering that on Earth human judges sometimes condemned criminals to multiple life sentences as punishment, albeit they can only serve one.

"Of course, the victim's soul had a karmic debt which can no longer liquidate because its physical existence was truncated by the killer, so the latter has to settle it. Remember, it is irrelevant to the Lord of Karma who pays, and he has perfect memory," added Sri Bawarta Laji lovingly as always to my excitement.

"This is why it is crucial to get an Enlightened Master who can help the infractor and teach him how to stop creating more karma and making things worse." I concluded.

What I did not know was that this couple shared a connection with my dear Cecilia. Then when I discovered who the killer was, the spiritual consequences of such behavior, and the implications for the Master, I was in complete shock!

Part VI

We Meet Again
Reunion of the Souls

The laboratory was in penumbra, the growth media put away in the incubator, the centrifuges emptied and lyophilized genetic and tissue samples locked in the freezer. The autoclave was filled with a plethora of pipettes, test tubes and a variety of utensils. All microscopes and other electronic equipment were on standby. The classical smell of recently cooked liquid cultures and agar plates fled the kitchen. It ran through the different work stations all the way to the farthest corner of the building, to a small windowless office furnished with an old metal desk, a leather armchair and a large bookcase. A bunch of lab coats hung from the hook on the door.

Inside the office, two figures face to face discharged their frustrations, their anxieties and their tediousness. Expressing through rubbing, grabbing and squeezing their unpronounceable feelings. Suffocated in their own heat, drowning each other's moans with their tongues, they tried to release their long-chained emotions with an incandescent burst of uncontrollable repletion. The smaller of the two figures was sitting on the desk towards the door, her blouse and heels on the floor next to her. She was holding closely to a robust figure that concealed her chest. Her inflamed face on his shoulder was clearly noticeable in the semidarkness. A back, covered to his buttocks with his shirt, and pants on the floor hiding his feet, kept thrusting her vigorously through her legs from the edge of the desk and pulling her towards him with tenacity. Imaginative and ludic, the female turned and bellied down on the desk, allowing her partner to caress her glutes, but now the hard and cold desk was squashing her breast. So, after a few strikes she lay down on her back, the desk no longer cold. He took her legs and lifted them apart on his shoulders as he leaned forward. She, malleable as rubber. All these gymnastics on her part and her partner had not moved one inch from where he stood, as if nailed to the floor.

Their exchange was becoming even more rambunctious with guttural sounds of pleasure when the couple abruptly jumped at the sound of a beep which seemed louder than ordinary. They stared nervously by reflex towards the door. Undoubtedly, the autoclave alerted the end of its sterilization cycle. With the heart still pounding, she sat up; scarce long bangs felt down her eyes and brownish hair almost hid her shoulders. She embraced her lover, who was not sure if their hearts beat out of passion or fright under the excitement of their forbidden adventure.

The custodian did not have access to this section of the lab, where secretive eugenics research was taking place and the purposely illiterate cleaning lady had gone for the day. Other than the ubiquitous noises of the refrigerators and other sophisticated instruments currently running, there were no other sounds. That is why the female was so puzzled when the menacing silhouette of a person wearing a white lab coat materialized behind the door. She stared at the stranger without muttering a word, while her lover, oblivious of the visitor, continued totally engaged. Seconds, perhaps minutes of careful mutual scrutiny generated heaps of conjectures in their brains. This "imbecile" was trying to identify the individual, whose physiognomy was disguised under the brim of a hat, only partially glimpsed the gloved hands, tucked inside the wide pockets. Not their boss for sure, a coworker, perhaps? The obscure figure had something bulky in the right pocket, an electric current that traveled through the arm generated a shortcut to the trembling hand which held it and released it. The mysterious face reddened behind the glasses as its breathing accelerated, almost to match the rhythm of the copulating couple, but for very different reasons. Neither of the two observers could think of a proper thing to say. One had rehearsed mentally an entire discourse more than once, the other, scrambled for words. Pleasure turned into disgrace, satisfaction into punishment. Suddenly, the female's eyes, usually squinty, opened wider than her mind as she saw the hand seizing a small object and raise it to her head.

Two quick, infallible shots.

In the fraction of an instant, the woman tried to open her mouth and say something, but whatever it was, it never left her throat. A sharp bullet crossed her forehead and her upper body leaned to her lover for a final embrace. The guy did not have a chance to react. He was shot in the head and collapsed backwards on the floor under the other corpse that fell on top of him.

The perpetrator wanted to make sure she saw who did it and uncovering the face, moved the body to find her eyes still opened, barely alive, perhaps able to see, even fleetingly, the face of vengeance.

When they arrived at a lower Heaven they were sad and sorry for their love affair. Especially the woman, whose cheated spouse had long suspected something fishy and had been seeking the opportunity to catch them *in fraganti delicto* granting him, his wish, that scoundrel!

The scientist never thought her husband would be capable of murder, after their more than twenty years of marriage. The Chinese at least was single, although not free to take somebody else's wife.

"It was totally not worth it. I didn't even love her!" reflected the guy.

In a way, thanks to this relationship, their marriage lasted as long as it did. The husband, peevish and resentful was hard to please and a bore; if not for the refuge of peace and relief her lover provided her, she would have left him long ago... or prolonged the marriage indefinitely, given the dreadful divorce proceedings and its division of marital assets. The man would do the impossible to strip her clean and ruin her reputation, this, she knew.

In any case, it was too late for regrets and all the scientist could do now was to enjoy her stay here before she had to reincarnate again. This time she promised to herself never to cheat again "... Actually, it would be better if I don't like men... That's an idea! Life would be so much easier if I find them unattractive," she thought.

But what she regretted the most was to leave her research work unfinished. An entire life dedicated to discovering the secrets of the genetic code and how to manipulate it, to abruptly interrupt the experiments in the most interesting phase!

Graduated from the most prestigious universities, she worked in human genetics with top experts from all over the world. Due to certain ethical issues among the scientific community in the United States, she was forced to abandon her research, or her funding would be suspended. Thankfully, another donor decided to finance her work, although away from the public eye. The government of China welcomed her with a state-of-the-art laboratory and provided her and her spouse with everything they wanted. Her husband had for years brainwashed her into not having kids, making any major decision uncomplicated. He occupied himself to learning Chinese and studying its sign language, which he found simpler compared to pronouncing Chinese tones and required no writing from his part.

When I entered at the celestial reception I saw two dim lights surrounded by what I considered were former relatives and friends of their past. They were going to remain with them for a while, to rest and prepare for their new transmigration, as part of their spiritual evolution.

Knowing all this, in the most casual sense possible of the higher realms, I approached the geneticist.

"Hello, my name is Alma. I wanted to share with you that I was a dog in my previous terrestrial life because, like you, I did not want to get involved again with complex and mostly troublesome human relationships. Perhaps it has not occurred to you yet, but as an alternative, would you ponder reincarnating, instead of as an animal, incapable of conducting any type of scientific endeavor, as a homosexual person?

It is yet another experience in the physical world!" I continued as I saw her curious to hear more. "Why not be lesbian? It may be better than being a man, since my guru told me that the woman's body is the most refined form to which an earthling can aspire."

"How come? But still, women face a lot of discrimination and unequal rights."

"Times are changing. Besides having the potential to bring another being to Earth, they possess many desirable qualities. A feminine body can only be granted after many lives and virtues. What do you think?"

"I don't know... all I can tell you now for sure is that I don't want to be involved with any more men. My husband, for example, was divine at the beginning, but later he turned insufferable, although to be fair, it wasn't strictly to me, to his own family as well. He has a strange love-hate relationship with his father, and he despised his own mother, whom he bad-mouthed still after she died. To his half-sisters that did no wrong to him he is distant, for he hated their mom. He even stopped talking to one of them for no other reason than he disdained her husband. I actually liked the fellow when I met him! He was really nice to me; his name was Max…

That's it! That was the connection! Well, in reality we are all connected to each other. We are brothers and sisters, the humanity is a whole, even if we are not directly related; but this is something humans have yet to comprehend.

Knowing who the killer was, I could not help my curiosity to check on him. What would Pelagio be going through?

All I had to do was to concentrate.

I saw Pelagio inside an obscure cell, a sort of dungeon, in a huge rock building in a remote province, far from major cities, near a village farm. The prison housed all kinds of criminals, from murderers, drug traffickers, corrupt functionaries to political dissidents. Amid the horde, he was alone for whatever reason, maybe temporarily.

The men were forced to work under nefarious conditions, with a short 15 min. recess and two bathroom breaks for twelve hours plus of intense labor. Malnourished, with no medical care or enough water for their personal hygiene, they were punished if their job performance was below the minimum daily demand. Usually they assembled electronic devices destined for foreign markets.

The newest resident arrived after a quick trial, performed by the government in absence of a lawyer for the defendant or consular representation, without notification to the relatives (none were listed explicitly for him, other than the wife's family).

The double murder was a known fact by the scientific team members, but all kept complete silence. The entire operation was top secret and no one else knew about the eugenics research conducted in the building which, as a cover up, also housed minor governmental administrative functions.

The parents of the Chinese were notified the next day. They were informed that regretfully, he had been in a work-related accident during a dangerous operation in which his head exploded. They cut whatever was left of the skull, whose brains were blown out by the direct shot to the head and delivered the headless body to his parents for burial, which the government paid for.

The geneticist's parents were told a similar version and her ashes (by written instructions of the deceased) sent to them. Thanks to their advanced Alzheimer's disease, they were immune to the news. The siblings did not bother to investigate the issue any further after the hefty amount of money the Chinese government offered them.

Pelagio's mother had already reincarnated, and his father was kept in the dark once Olga learned of his disappearance. After several unsuccessful attempts to call China, Olga phoned Pelagio's sister-in-law, who asked her to meet her the next day. She explained what she knew without mentioning the "inheritance" she and her brothers received. She said she tried to reach out to Pelagio but could not get any responses. So, she gave Olga the Chinese Delegate's contact information and asked her to please share with her any news. The sister-in-law pretended to be worried about Pelagio, but in reality, no one cared. The scientist's siblings did not like him because they knew that deep inside, he did not have a good heart and did not make their sister happy.

Olga tried to get in touch with her half-brother using the provided information, but she had no luck. Then, she finally resorted to the Chinese authorities from his native country, to whom she spoke about the disappearance after what happened to his wife. They invited her to visit China and assured her that they would do everything possible to find him. Likewise, he was added to an international list of missing persons. Not having the minimal additional support from either country, Olga turned to Cecilia.

The latter had not had any contact with Pelagio since before his marriage to the geneticist and frankly, was not very inclined to look for a missing half-brother already missing from her life. Moreover, this all occurred while Ceci and Bernard were moving to Mexico. She could not offer much help, other than moral support to Olga and lending a compassionate ear to her father, whom they decided, would not perish knowing that his son was lost in a communist country, alone and thousands of miles away.

In any case, Cecilia offered to accompany Olga and her husband to China, but warned that without government cooperation, there was little they could do. At the end, Olga and her husband made the trip; Cecilia promised to join them if they needed her.

They arrived at their former apartment, still vacant, lavishly furnished but void of personal belongings. The authorities packed them in boxes and informed the family they were welcome to open them and take what they wanted, which Olga did. The government had already recycled all of the geneticist's possessions and confiscated her research documents and computers.

Unable to speak the language, Olga hung posters she ordered in Chinese with the missing brother's picture and her personal contact information everywhere. Her husband hired a local translator to help them navigate the town and see what they could find. Nevertheless, after ten days of zero success and without a single hint and no more money or time to remain in the country, they left.

The family never heard from Pelagio again.

Hence, I was looking inside this cell at this man whom I had never met, but somehow resembled my Ceci. Weird! He looked more like his half-sister than Olga herself.

The Chinese gave Pelagio a life sentence for the murder of the two scientists, which he served at the Guangzhou jail. Instead of playing back in his mind the last series of events leading to his incarceration, he focused on how he could get some help. Given his indirect involvement on eugenics research, the government was not interested in providing him with consular assistance of any kind, making him a missing person was a lot easier.

The penitentiary assigned interpreter was the typical Chinese bureaucrat that earned a pittance and had a work overload with the latest influx of drug and human trafficking criminals. He was pretty useless. After years of service, he had lost hope for most of the prisoners and had a very conformist attitude towards life. When Pelagio noticed a journalist snooping around to check on some foreigners, he asked for a chance to speak to him, or at least, to some of his fellow nationals serving time. He was then purposely distanced from anyone who could speak his language in a clear attempt to silence him. Following his superior's explicit orders, the jail director made sure there were no records of his case. Feeling outraged and violated of all basic human rights, he realized that officially, he did not exist.

Words cannot describe the desperation the man suffered as he slowly discovered that the worst possible outcome was now a reality. Losing his freedom may be similar to what his mother felt when losing him. Now he remembered…

Then is when he thought of escaping. Every morning, all the inmates were taken to a huge cell phone factory, practically next door, to work until dark. He knew the guards had cell phones. If he could steal one and call out, it would sow the seed of doubt about his whereabouts and fuel a search for him. The guards were not allowed to use their phones during work hours so, he felt confident that they would not try to use them until recess, if then.

One of the such guards was always smiling and looking at him indecently. It was pretty obvious to him that the guard was not indifferent to his charms. Under the circumstances, he could not imagine appearing attractive to any woman, but being attractive to a male jailer seemed repulsive (although perhaps convenient). Perhaps, an opportunity… if he could get close enough to him, to switch his cell phone for one of the ones he assembled at the factory to simulate its weight, he could send a quick message and return the device before the guard noticed the substitution.

During the following weeks Pelagio tried to gain the favor of the guard, smiling back at him and returning his furtive glances. He had to get close though, close enough to remove the device from his pants back pocket. Their silent communication had started to move in the right direction when the guard touched Pelagio's thigh while working on the assembling line. From then on, Pelagio tried to reciprocate with a gentle squeeze of his hand. A new line of communication suddenly opened! As much as possible, the prisoner practiced how to shift keyboards in Chinese characters and to find some key functions.

One day when feeling brave, Pelagio signaled the restroom, as he was taking advantage of his first toilet break. The guard followed him inside as the bathroom emptied. Hesitantly, Pelagio opened his arms in a clear invitation for an embrace. The warden fell in the trap and surprising himself, Pelagio skillfully squeezed the man's derrière with such strength that he did not notice his switching cell phones. The encounter was quick but effective. He went back to his place on the factory belt and during the next hours, with trembling fingers and sweating hands, he slowly managed to send a text message to his former language tutor, asking him to contact his country's consulate and be discreet by instructing him to not dare to reply. After transmission, he immediately deleted the message.

The second restroom break came sooner than expected. The guard seemed oblivious to the inmate's plan, who tricked him again for a second encounter, this time more intense, as the man returned the squeeze from the inside of his pants. "Disgusting!" he thought, but he had to reciprocate. "Wow, I seem to have a natural talent! … either I am a great actor, or he is dumb." In reality, the guard wasn't the brightest, but he imagined that playing with the pockets was part of the game. Later, when he did check his cell phone, he didn't notice anything unusual and of course, Pelagio's message was already erased.

Far from there, in an elegant and wealthy apartment, near where the geneticist and her husband used to live, Zhu was finishing up a Chinese class for an Indian businessman and his spouse. Zhu took his books, put them in his backpack and walked outside. Right when the couple closed the door, he got his cell phone out of his jacket to check for any messages before heading to his next private lesson. He found an unknown number and almost fell backwards when he read it:

Pel illegally imprisoned Guangzhou notify consulate NOT reply

The sender was undoubtedly "Pel" (as he called his vanished student). It was too late. The consulate had already closed for the day. In any case, he would have to take the train to get there, and the trip would be several hours. All Zhu knew was that the language school had abruptly discontinued his classes (which the government paid) and with no explanations or a chance to say goodbye, his student stopped answering his phone. He did not suspect anything strange then. He thought the wife either lost her job or was transferred, never of his student killing someone or going to prison.

It took Zhu a few days before he could find the opportunity to make the trip to the consulate and when he did, they did not pay much attention to him. He talked to an employee at the information desk who, after a long yawn, wrote something down. Zhu refused to give his name or admit he knew Pelagio. He limited himself to stating that someone he considered in serious trouble had sent the text asking for help.

What a terrible situation this was! And complicated! The two lovers the killer dispatched to Heaven were enjoying their stay and waiting for a new opportunity to return to Earth to fulfill their desires, while the criminal was steadily losing faith! Not that he had much faith to begin with; perhaps influenced by the scientific mentality of his spouse or on his own, he did not believe in God or anything which could not be rigorously analyzed, examined in a laboratory or demonstrated even if only mathematically.

I am not sure how many Earth days had passed, all I knew was that Pelagio was skinnier, paler and his eyes had sunk into their orbits and turned red. He had not spoken with anyone for some time and when I peeked, he presented a series of tics and erratic behavior in his cell. When I studied his aura, I understood that this was caused by lack of sleep, a common punishment for not producing the minimum quota of assembled cell phones, as demanded during the twelve hard workday hours.

Unfortunately, the circumstances worsened and the warden's advances grew increasingly daring. Pelagio wavered between refusing him altogether or leaving some room to play and not exasperate him in case he needed a favor, which he was unsure to get, enduring a price he could hardly bear. Life in the Chinese prison became a tangible hell.

I could not help feeling sorry for him; but what to do? I tried to get in touch with his guardian angel, but soon I discovered he had quit on him, or more precisely, Pelagio had kicked him out with his repeated taunts and misbehavior. Pelagio became so adept at ignoring his guardian angel's whispers, shutting down his ears and mind to his well-intentioned advice that sadly, he had no choice but to leave and follow another soul who allowed him to help. Like Olga, Pelagio did not believe in divine intervention of any kind and Cecilia was so emotionally detached from the man she almost forgot to pray for him. Even so, she prayed; and her prayer reached her Master.

When I asked my guru about this case, he said that I might contact Pelagio's former guardian angel to whom he referred to as "Sam." The angel was gorgeous and resembled one of those Renaissance paintings of blonde cherubs, with beautiful wide wings of crystalline feathers and perfect features. So perfect, it was arbitrary to determine a gender (duality only exists in the lower levels of the universe). When I questioned him (the human language obliges me to pick a gender), he told me he was recently summoned by a higher-celestial creature, the Angel Superior in charge of a certain class of guardian angels for human beings. Sam was already on a better assignment, hovering around an expectant mother whose child he would look after. I was surprised to discover that angels started their mission from the womb of their protégé. According to their "contract" they could assist a living human formerly under their care in an emergency situation, although without guarantee for success.

One of the aspects of the discarnate is possessing simultaneous vision, which I decided to exert.

Having obtained permission to follow Sam's intervention, I was able to observe the angel materialize at the information counter, where the consulate's clerk wrote the note with the scarce data Zhu had provided. The building was deserted and the lights of the computer

screens in the gloom gave the interior a ghostly ambiance. In front of him laid documents, trays and a notebook under a tea cup. His own being shed enough light to see the objects in front of him.

In a tiny cell, located in a secluded area, away from other inmates, were the individuals considered "dangerous" for what they knew. Isolated to prevent them from speaking to others and closely watched when working outside, they had their own wardens. A guard was dozing off at the far corner of the hall, awaiting the end of his shift. The moon illuminated a slice of the cell with a beam piercing through a window with iron bars, high on the wall near the ceiling. As if in a trance, Pelagio took his pants off.

The information desk was neatly organized, no loose papers, sticky notes or trash in the recycling bin or on the floor. Where else to look? When moving the chair, Sam noticed a long drawer… a possibility. He pulled, but it was locked. No key in sight. Sam emptied the pencil holder and removed the objects from the tray, but nothing. It was hardly a problem; his dematerialized hand allowed him to get into the drawer from above and search its contents.

Tearing the fabric of the pants was harder than expected… or perhaps he was so weak he could not gather enough strength for the task. Then, he remembered getting hooked with a screw or a nail or something with the table when leaving the factory's dining room

after a meal, he was not sure. It must have made a small hole in the fabric. Perfect! This surely will help tear those pants in rags.

Sam could not find what he was looking for. He knew where the office of the consul was; all he had to do was plant a clue for him to start a search for Pelagio, but with no evidence about his case, he would have to talk to the consul's own guardian angel to see what they could arrange. Sam was about to leave when he discovered a piece of paper on the floor, right behind the trash can. It was the note the clerk had taken from Zhu! He grabbed it and, like a magic trick, completed Pelagio's name… a little extra to boost the quest.

Slowly, trying to avoid suspecting noises and working as quietly as possible, with phony muffling coughs in between, Pelagio carefully produced a long and strong rag which he grasped with his right hand. He put whatever was left of his pants back on. Then, he started jumping in front of the little window, determined to test his cowboy lasso skills. Exhausted after a few unsuccessful barefooted jumps, Pelagio decided to take a short break. Although the night was still young, it had to be done tonight, or he may not have another chance... He paused briefly and continued.

The next morning the doors of the consulate opened. The consul, as usual, arrived at his office around nine with a coffee mug and placed it on the desk, next to the computer's mouse. Then was when he saw the note left by Sam. Without hesitation, as compelled by an invisible force, he searched on the database for names of compatriots residing in China which matched the one in his hand. "A very peculiar name," he thought. "I am sure it will be easy to find."

He soon discovered that the wife of his fellow citizen, another national, had been granted a work visa and had died in an accident. Pelagio was reported missing, but the authorities (of both countries) were doing nothing to find him. Immediately he contacted Ivan, his best lawyer, very knowledgeable about international laws, who specialized in China's legal system.

Within hours, Ivan was taking the next train with the assignment to pay a surprise visit to the prison mentioned on the note. Both men had keen suspicions about this missing person's case.

Back in Heaven, I was about to enter a lecture by a being from a higher realm regarding the influence of extraterrestrials in the development of ancient cults and mythologies on Earth when my dear guru Sri Bawarta Laji came to me.

"Hello, Alma! I did not know you were interested in Earth's ancient history."

"I did not either, but I think it will be fascinating to learn about this topic and to meet the lecturer." I added, "I see it piqued your curiosity as well!"

"Not quite, I actually came to see you."

"Great! It is good to see you too!" I replied with intense curiosity.

"You have been asking me a lot of questions about the lowest levels of consciousness and how a powerful Enlightened Master succors those souls that, due to their karma end up there, remember? Well, this is your chance to see the Sovereign Master in action. Now he will 'lift the veil' so to speak, to allow peeking into a salvation operation."

I nodded. "I would love to learn more about this abode and how to aid the souls in their confines."

"Alma, I must warn you, this is very dangerous and should only be attempted by an Enlightened Master of the highest level. If an unprepared soul descends to the lowest plane to bring one or more beings to a superior realm, such a soul risks becoming trapped there indefinitely."

For better or for worse, my curiosity led me to witness the horrifying dimension of hell, which, I am pleased to confess, had remained unexplored by me.

We got ready to witness the scene from the safety of our inner vision. A group of disciples and kindred spirits to the Sovereign Master reunited in a large space, something like a stadium, where each one was suspended as on a cloud in lieu of a seat around the Master. Everyone prepared to spiritually connect with him from the comfort of our brotherhood and under the protection of our beloved guide, who so kindly allowed us to share a little bit of his spiritual work for humanity. We adopted a state of contemplation.

Contrary to popular belief, hell was not hot, but cold, sharply cold, as there was no source of heat. I perceived what seemed a whining wind mixed with a foggy atmosphere, where the light of… the souls? was so dingy that it only enabled one to see so far. The air was heavy. It resembled being submerged under water, the deeper, the more pressure exercised upon the creatures at the bottom. The open space emitted a putrid scent akin to rotten eggs which gave the impresimpression of penetrating one's mouth and it extended over an arid surface where nothing grew.

I saw no mountains, no plants and nothing that resembled nature even on its worst condition. Could hell be located on some planet? "No physical planet," a mental message responded almost before posing my query. The sky… how to explain it? There was no sky! It was as if the horizon were incredibly high, again, like being inside a bottomless body of water, at a level where it became impossible to tell what was up and what was down. A plain repeat of the desolate panorama wherever the shadows persist.

Gradually, a figure wrapped in a white-robed garment became distinguishable. Similar to a Bedouin, he had a headcloth covering a great part of his face. Only the eyes were discernible, a pair of loving eyes I was familiar with. More than walking, the Master was gliding. Next, I saw a dungeon or something analogous for this realm. Surprisingly, there was no gate, no door or barrier which prevented its occupants from leaving… but where? if the whole place was itself a prison! There were a series of cavernous labyrinths simultaneously going in all directions, although this dimension had no cardinal points. I may describe it as being in outer space or a sidereal galaxy minus the stars, where there is not much oxygen. It gave the impression of having difficulty breathing… weird…

The dwellers were understandably depressed and some seemed to be crying. I could see souls being tortured by their own remorse or by hallucinations which only they could detect. Certain individuals behaved crazily, moving as if endless bugs were crawling all over them, scratching and massaging fervently. Perhaps they felt physical pain mixed with their emotional anguish. It was a horrifying scene! There was a plethora of sections in hell where various types of "treatments" as our Master put it, were applied to the "patients" who needed them. Hell, he explained, was a kind of hospital for these beings, a temporary stay until they recovered sufficiently to continue their path to evolution. Unfortunately, having descended to the lowest level, their journey had a brutal start: from the bottom up and it could take many transmigrations to reach the level attained prior to their fall into hell.

While Master was the only bright light in the shadows, few beings paid attention to his regal presence, so caught up as they were in their own misery. For me, it was totally incomprehensible to observe a Savior, capable of liberating in the blink of an eye the worst infractor of the law of karma, pass by unnoticed and ignored by everyone. Master approached a creature dressed in rags, with short hair and a mark on the neck, hunched forward with the head between the knees. He tapped on the shoulder to get its attention. The contrite was sobbing and it took a minute to react. Lifting its sight revealed the handsome and imposing figure. At first, the captive had to cover its eyes: they were not accustomed to seeing the refulgence irradiating from such a sweet glance. The magnificent figure offered his hand, which the penitent hesitantly took, albeit it did not seem to recognize the visitor. The Master pronounced the name of the Lord of this realm, and spoke the sacred language of the universe, known by him and few chosen enlightened beings.

As in "Ali Baba open sesame," a golden door appeared in front of them. It was widely opened and so sparkling and big that the residents turned to see the source of the luminescence emanating from the interior, from where it was impossible to distinguish a thing. The souls closest to them watched with curiosity and suspicion the slouched specter standing right next to the stranger approaching the door. The Master raised his hand in a friendly motion in a clear invitation to join them. Shockingly, no one moved, and although the pair remained at the threshold of freedom for a few moments, the bystanders returned to their grief while watching them cross towards an unknown dimension, with no signs of compunction. I took advantage of those moments to scrutinize the offender. Since this being possessed a grayish and forbidding aura, I concentrated on its third eye. It was unexpectedly closed and buried in its forehead, for which I needed an additional effort to penetrate.

How foolish! I should have known from the start! The emaciated penitent was no other than Pelagio, whom I last saw trying, I supposed, to escape from prison. So, what went wrong?

Sam, the guardian angel, had successfully launched a pursuit for Pelagio through the consul, who conceived a surprise visit by his most skillful lawyer to the Chinese jail the very next morning. I retraced Ivan's steps from the minute he arrived at the gate house of the enormous penitentiary entrance.

The lawyer extended a written permission to visit an inmate who expected another agent from his consulate; this was a trick to get him in, as there were no records of Pelagio's existence in the building.

Ivan possessed excellent people skills and maintained a good relationship with the penitentiary authorities, besides he had been working with the Chinese prison employees for a long time and his language skills were impeccable. They accompanied him to the convict who took him for a "gracious gift from God." Good for him! From this moment forward, Ivan personally took his case and later on he would be able to help reduce his sentence. At least, that went well!

After the interview he looked for excuses to snoop around and see if he could talk to anyone who had been in contact with the captive. He went to the restroom where he overheard two guards commenting that Xiong, the cousin of one of them, was sick but strangely enough, nobody had been assigned to cover his shift for him after the guard in turn had gone home the previous night. Knowing the rigor imposed to the vigilance of the convicts, he considered this so odd that it required further investigation. On his way out, he asked to see a different warden, one assigned to a separate section of the building, with whom he maintained some friendship. Not finding a good reason to refuse the lawyer's petition, he was allowed to see his friend at the small break room while in recess. As casually as he could, he mentioned he had this wonderful medicine which could help Xiong, who he heard needed something for his asthma; he happened to have it with him now (Ivan suffered of the condition and was carrying a brand-new inhaler he recently purchased in Germany). Luckily, Xiong was a popular man and his friend knew him among the dozens of guards working there.

Trying to please both friends, the sentinel agreed and personally walked with him down to the "special prisoners" area himself. As Ivan expected, no one was guarding the convicts. They entered through a narrow door at the end of a hallway. Located in the basement, the only light at this time of day was filtered by the small windows inside the cells. In front of them were heavy iron doors with a high horizontal opening. The inside was no bigger than six square meters and it was devoid of any furniture.

"He must be down the corner," exclaimed the guard. Without hesitation, as wanting to show off his ability to roam the building like a high-ranking functionary, he entered the hall, a little surprised that access had not been blocked. The lawyer followed.

Albeit accustomed to seeing the bad shape in which the men were maintained, Ivan felt his legs shake at the sight of the interior of a particular cell. He dropped his briefcase along with his jaw. Hardly ever speechless, Ivan's dizziness made him lean on the door and his breath steamed up his glasses, from where a devastating scene unfolded. A man, probably not as old as he looked, hung from his neck by the window's black bars with a rope, apparently of the same material as his pants, which had been torn. His expression, of desperation and agony, his hands closed in a claw alongside and his tongue out. The head fell slightly inclined towards the window, as if yearning to fly to the open sky.

Ivan readjusted his glasses and asked the guard to open the door. Nervously, he responded that he was not granted the authorization code to open individual doors and begged him to please quietly leave before anyone noticed. He proposed that if he did not say anything, he would also keep silent or both would be in big trouble. Ivan consented, and the men exited as covertly as they arrived. In a matter of minutes, they were outside, parting, not without inquiring first about the identity of the man. Ivan's friend did not wish to push his luck and ask about the deceased once officially discovered (because they weren't supposed to be there in the first place), but assured the lawyer that he would share the name if this information became available to him.

Sometimes I think we would be better off without our free will. Without it, Pelagio would not have taken his life. People commit suicide because they think death will bring them peace, but it is the opposite! This is the fastest way to hell, as logically, they sink at the consciousness level they were at that precise moment. When he was about to receive help, his impatience took the best of him. Sam was inconsolable… but when he learned that Pelagio had a relative who followed a powerful Master which would rescue him, he felt comforted. How lucky!

In his infinite compassion, the Sovereign Master did not let the truth reach the ears of Pelagio's family. The father would die soon, no need to accelerate his demise. Olga had a revelation during what she initially thought was a dream, which she shared with Cecilia. She had a vision of Pelagio looking healthy and young telling her goodbye, *"¡Adiós hermana!"* This brought closure to poor Olga as Cecilia made her realize that the shared karma with the half-brother had concluded.

It was not until Xiong's shift finished when the guard in turn discovered the body. The cover up continued until the end, and Pelagio's remains were discarded in a common grave without a word to anyone. The lawyer matched the image of the deceased, imprinted in his brain, with the description and photo on file and was certain it was the same. An investigation about Pelagio would involve delving into the death of the scientist, China's ongoing eugenics experimentation, and would trigger an international conflict the Chinese government high ranking functionaries wanted to avoid. Therefore, the consul was warned against pursuing further questioning if they wished to continue with their cooperation and visits to their compatriots in jail.

For me, my sojourn in Heaven was all one could dream. In fact, most souls never aspire to more; they cannot fathom higher, purer, nicer or more blissful existence. Since I was connected to a spiritual practitioner of the greatest Enlightened Master, I knew better, and needed to focus more on the spiritual and less on the physical to reach my true Home. So, after satiating my curiosity and learning the horrors of hell, I gradually detached from the matters of the lower dimensions. My only remaining interest was my beloved Ceci. Once she ascended, I wouldn't look down ever again.

Was she in her sixties? I guess, hard to tell as Cecilia had good genes and was in top health. Last time I checked on her, she and her husband were living happily in Mexico and fulfilling their dreams. It is important to fulfill dreams in order to prevent fruitless desires from pulling the soul back to the world and the risk of sabotaging the spiritual growth.

The higher the Heaven, the tougher it is to come down to the lower levels, the more preparation is needed to set forth on the trip and harder to endure its coarse vibration. I was contented with seeing Cecilia in my meditation, imagining her soft nose touching mine and her perfected technique for scratching my tummy. I still get thrilled when remembering her sonorous voice talking to me, with her big eyes that smiled purely for thinking of me. Those were celestial moments on Earth, like many others with Max. What a wonderful doggie life! I could still listen to Cecilia... sometimes she talked to my portrait or told one of her animals to communicate with me (as brethren that we were) and convey her message of love and express how much she still missed me.

It did not take me long to find a receptive soul in Bernard and Cecilia's house to whom I could talk. In the backyard, covered by a large mesh which extended through several trees, I found a feathered bossy creature helping recovering fellows heal their emotional injuries: it was none other than sweet old Sugar!

"Dear Sugar, how are you?"

"Is it you, Canela? I can hardly see you through this blinding splendor around you! What's up in Heaven?"

"Fantastic! How are things around here?"

"Busy... that mommy of yours keeps bringing all sorts of animals and Berny and I have to do all the hard work, you know, to help them get well. It is a good thing though, I have become a nurse-bird, hahaha!"

"And a very good one," I added. "You don't look a day older. Where is everybody?"

"Ceci should be here any minute now. She took her sister to the dentist (glad I no-have teeth). At this hour Berny is finishing up his last appointment in the free neutering clinic; it is the construction over there, the one with the rounded dome. Have you seen Nanny?"

I felt ashamed to say no, that it had not even occurred to me to check on her. Perhaps I would have known if she had ascended. A being who reaches a certain level can detect, at will, when a loved one is in deep trouble or prays for help. Citlalli was a cherished friend. I was not sure if Sugar was under Cecilia's care temporarily or not.

"I would be the first one to welcome her when she ascends. You probably know more than me."

"She misses me. Well, we communicate telepathically, although I no-know how much of it she can retain. She is old, weak, her husband is weaker, and they now require continuous assistance."

"So is life on Earth!" I said as I captured an image of the couple in a nursing home, a nice one, where they voluntarily entered to prevent becoming a burden to their children (who possibly would have put them in a cheaper one).

"If you see daddy, tell him I love him and that he I no-forget."

"Of course! ... Is there anything else I can do for you, Sugar?"

"Tell God thank you for all his blessings."

With this, I wondered who "Berny" was... it had to be Dr. Bernard! At that moment he was placing his latest patient, a collie mix, half asleep, on a cushion inside a large cage. It made me remember those days in the county pound. I followed him to the house. He started setting the table for three. A visitor, perhaps Olga? I sniffed around and greeted a very friendly gray feline which came to say hello.

As soon as Bernard placed the salad on the table two rascals came storming through the door, barking and thirsty, running straight to their water bowls. The room cheered up when the sisters entered, lively chatting, their spirits ageless, sempiternal. Olga, more tanned and blonder than before, with a full wavy fuzzy head floating from her forehead to her shoulders and two straws for legs covered tightly with jeans, surprised me looking like an upside-down mop; her broad cheeks smiled with her arched thread eyebrows. Ceci appeared jovial in her floral cotton dress, matching earrings and shoes, her hair in a silvery braid over her crown. Bernard, grey-haired, kissed them both and they sat at the table.

"What did the dentist do to you, Olga?"

"No torture this time, Bernard. A plain cleaning."

"Guess who called!" said Ceci to Bernard, raising her eyebrows.

"The President?"

"Better than that. Olav phoned from London! He says he is going to be touring America, starting from Argentina all the way up to Alaska… how about that, eh?" his godmother responded proudly.

"Man! He is leaving next week for Buenos Aires and by March he will arrive in Mexico City. He will be the *Orquesta Filarmónica de la Ciudad de México* guest conductor. I am so excited! My boy!" answered Olga protruding her lips in kissing mood.

"We'll have to save the date. Did he give you one? And also, we may coordinate to visit my sister in Canada! *Voilà!* Ask him if he will play in Quebec," said Bernard in a Frenchified Castilian.

"*Vale*. I hope he can visit us here too. He has not come since I moved in!"

Then is when I realized that Olga was a widow and was now permanently living with her family. She moved after losing her second husband to a rage which precipitated a heart attack. Per their prenuptial agreement, he left his flat to his rich sister. Olav became a nomadic orchestra director and his only permanent domicile was a PO box. Olga sold the daycare and had enough money to retire and live modestly though alone in Europe but decided otherwise. Olav's father never left Spain. He never married his girlfriend of twenty years (he hoped she would care for him during his old age), who one day broke up with him, kicked him out of her flat and replaced him with a younger lover. Fortunately, the health system had arranged for him a pension and a person to help him out twice a week. He was always sick, but under the care of good doctors and his own karma, he was kept alive for whatever mission he had yet to complete (he had not done anything for anyone). Actually, he outlived everybody, except Olav. What a waste of life, except for his three-minute cooperation to bring a terrific musician into the world!

My Ceci was fine! She felt happy and continued her spiritual practice although Max and I were not there to, as he used to say, "Give me a jump start" on her meditation. She had conditioned a cozy place in the privacy of the vegetable garden, hidden among leaves, fruit trees and corn stalks to meditate under the sky. When the quadrupeds were not with Bernard, they would congregate quietly on a rug and join her; the cat never missed a session.

Olav had a successful tour and scheduled a whole weekend to spend with his mom, uncle and aunt in their house. They followed him to Quebec and enjoyed a harmonious family reunion full of love and peace.

From time to time I liked to visit Cecilia at the family vegetable garden. Eventually it became its own ecosystem full of life. I enjoyed the aroma of fruit trees and flowers, throughout the year there was always something blooming. There were infinite interactions among plants, animals and microorganisms. Of course climate, soil, water and human presence affect the garden. All different forces work together to produce a crop. Absolutely remarkable!

The insects were particularly interesting to me. Observing the fervent teamwork of the tiniest creatures to survive and care for their kin was truly amazing. Since they did not use artificial fertilizers or pesticides in the garden, certain types of worms, for example, kept the plants healthy by feeding from their natural predators during growth; unfortunately, this meant the death of other creatures, but this is how less developed beings survive in the lower worlds of the universe. Too much violence, even at the microscopic level! I avoided watching their struggles.

What I liked to see was the survival skills and the intelligence of their behavior. Some plants had the added bonus of serving as defenders of crops. Anise, chilies and marigold, among others, repel insect pests and even mice. Fungi, bacteria, and yeasts are essential. They help plants utilize nutrients or suppress ailments, but they can also be harmful. There is a delicate balance among the entire ecosystem to produce a crop. Cecilia greatly benefited from the traditional pest control techniques of Africa and Oceania and successfully adapted them to her new habitat.

Whenever she took a fruit, she thanked the plant, mimicking the words of Max. In one occasion she saw him asking for permission of a rose bush to cut a flower and on another, showing his gratitude to an avocado tree for its delicious gift. Max taught her to talk to the houseplants, give them names, and to express love through voice, touch and good music.

For Cecilia, being a gardener made her conscious of how cultivating plants affected other creatures. She remembered her Master telling disciples about some spiritual practitioners who only consumed fruits. The purpose of the fruitarians, as they are called, is ethical: to respect sentient beings and avoid or cause the minimal possible suffering. Consuming the fruit that naturally detaches or falls from a plant does not destroy or harm it. In fact, when eaten, the fruits produced by plants can expand their seeds. A fruit is considered having the lowest suffering capability of any sentient being and is not actively living. From a broader perspective, I can see how unfortunate it can be for insects and other big and small creatures to compete for their food: they have a right to eat too! The Master did not follow a fruitarian diet because he did not want humans to see him as an unattainable ideal. He could have been breatharian (living without food) if he wished, but this would really turn him into a circus curiosity. After all, his aim was to liberate willing souls and the vegan diet was hard enough for many people, although a necessary requisite to avoid further karma in the present life. "If you think about it," he said, "every time we take a step, breath or wash our hands we are killing microscopic beings… what we want is to be compassionate and avoid causing unnecessary suffering to others."

At some point, Cecilia wanted to follow a raw food diet. She had shortly tried it the first time she volunteered while in Vanuatu, where vegan options were difficult to come by and it was easier to eat whatever the natives were growing. After learning to cook with the available resources (mostly on hot stones), she prepared dishes with coconut milk and indigenous herbs and spices. Having her own garden, she thought she would like to try again.

She soon realized that in order to feed her family with the gourmet foods they were accustomed to, she would have to sprout, ferment, germinate and dehydrate in large quantities and spend a lot of time in the kitchen. Cecilia incorporated some local raw foods like guacamole, salsas and replacing ingredients with local produce like mamey, sapote and jicama created meat free versions of other dishes, allowing them to keep a vegan organic diet which also included recipes from all the different countries where they had lived. But Olga was cooking-abhorrent, and Bernard did not want to give up his newly discovered local gastronomy: tamales, sopes, pozole, mole, nopales, and other traditional foods, all much tastier in the native country. This cuisine quickly became his favorite;

but when he learned that UNESCO had named Mexican culinary art an "intangible cultural heritage of humanity," he was determined to delve into the pre-Hispanic exotic flavors. He experimented with the region's original ingredients like vanilla, amaranth, cacao and, with the sisters' pleasure, took over the kitchen. He even made some memorable appearances contributing his own vegan French-Mexican inspired desserts into Cecilia's cooking lessons. More than once, someone took a video and posted it online.

Nature is magnanimous for when it gives, it gives generously. Fertile soil and water forge true miracles. Cecilia never ceased being amazed that practically from pure energy (in the form of sun and some minerals), bud such delicious delicacies. Although photosynthesis could explain the engendering of fruits, to her, it seemed practically magic. Whenever they praised her crops, she simply said, "I merely set the seed, water it and let nature act. It is the work of God and other invisible beings!" Such was the abundance of her harvest, she started to give away fruits and vegetables among the poor and to make regular deliveries at an orphanage, rendering their meals more nutritious.

One weekend, after returning from a trip to the Teotihuacan pyramids with some friends visiting from overseas, Cecilia felt a sudden intensifying pain in the abdomen which lasted for about an hour. She initially thought the pain was triggered by the effort of climbing the over 200 steps to the top of the Sun pyramid immediately after eating, but she decided to check with a doctor to make sure, as she was having some discomfort in the same area while doing yoga which did not seem to go away.

The two sisters went together to the appointment and the physician ordered a blood test and an ultrasound. The result came back the following week: high bilirubin and the presence of gallstones. The doctor recommended removing the gallbladder if the symptoms persisted, which is the safest operation, given the blockage of the bile duct, to prevent recurrence. Cecilia and Bernard considered her options and first tried some noninvasive treatments. After the third episode (more prolonged), she thought that there was no reason to risk enduring these pains for who knew how much longer; she was already following a healthy diet and exercising regularly, what else could she do? Never having had a bad medical experience or been hospitalized for anything (the closest was a routine colonoscopy years ago) boosted her confidence to face the procedure. Her excellent overall health granted her a prompt date for surgery. She would go back home the same day and take a very well-deserved vacation with her family.

Cecilia and Bernard arranged to meet Olga in the Yucatecan city of Mérida in two weekends, where the latter was sojourning. Olga was more outgoing than her sister and since childhood had a talent for making friends. Such was the case of Amalia, an old friend from school she recently reconnected with. She happened to own a house in Mérida, and not a plain house, but a gorgeous mansion in an exclusive residential zone.

Olga was not a vegetarian, but never really liked meat, and detested eggs and milk. Nevertheless, she hardly ever bothered to prepare a wholesome meal (not even when Olav was little). She used to suffer from migraines, palpitations, indigestion and a multiple variety of minor chronic problems. Luckily, she started to feel much better after moving with her sister and brother-in-law. The meals they prepared, gardening and exercising with them proved to be very beneficial to her health. She hoped to be a source of inspiration for Amalia, who shared many of the same troubles and complained of her drugs' side effects. Olga spoke of her family and the friend quickly invited them to join them. Amalia had moved to Mérida many years ago hoping that the weather and altitude would suit her. Olga had arrived in late-October and the plan was to celebrate together the Hanal Pixán, or Mayan festivities of the Day of the Dead in the peninsula.

This important annual holiday included visiting the cemetery to make offerings to the souls of loved ones who are believed to come back to join the living for this day. November first is reserved for the souls of deceased infants and children and the next, for those of the adults. The foods prepared are traditional of this region of Mexico and the souls are supposed to visit their graves and enjoy the aroma of their favorite dishes while alive. Altars are set in various locations and are beautifully decorated with cempasuchitl (vibrant orange colored flowers) beside fruits, food and water; photographs; candles; ornaments such as "calacas" (fun skeleton dolls to represent "The Death," which is considered feminine); traditional treats like sugar skulls called "calaveras;" copal (a type of incense) used for special ceremonies and cherished personal items which used to belong to the departed. This is a truly colorful and spectacular celebration mixing the beliefs of the Catholic religion with the ones of the indigenous people.

Amalia wanted to make an altar for her defunct baby, whom she lost many years ago. The infant actually was not born, as Amalia suffered a miscarriage before completing the third month of pregnancy. Even so, its memory saddened her still, and she thought that Olga, who had never made an altar, would enjoy helping her make one.

This brought up lots of questions not yet been completely clarified: when does a soul actually occupy the body? How true are the beliefs of ancient civilizations like the Mayan, the Egyptian or… what about Atlantis, did they really exist, and if so, were the Mayans their descendants? Do some souls actually come down on the Day of the Dead to accompany the incarnated loved ones who still remember them?

As usual, I resorted to my guru.

Sri Bawarta Laji was logically, always accessible, considering the manifold manifestation bodies he possesses. We met in a different corner of Heaven, so vast I don't think anyone knows it all! He was helping organize the reception of an influx of souls coming after "natural disasters" occurring on Earth. He was referring to two separate incidents in Asia and South America: an earthquake and a flood that together would expedite over 150,000 souls to lower Heavens.

"Is this preparation similar to the one for the victims of the accident where Max left the body?"

"Yes and no. We use additional resources, such as the spirits of the elements water, earth, wind and aether plus those drafted for special emergency works to welcome the souls, since this is massive. Like in that case, we try to prepare them spiritually in advance. The masses usually experience a collective shock and may be caught up in limbo, unaunable to transcend due to the traumatism at the time of their demise. Mr. Troy, for example, killed at home by his grandson with no one to guide him afterwards, became stuck. Unfortunately, events like this are occurring more and more frequently and we are busier than ever."

"Why is that?"

"Because humans are damaging the planet and their activities are increasing natural disasters at an accelerated pace. Climate change for example, has worsened the amount of rain and its frequency. The ensuing flooding kills thousands. World population keeps growing (few reach liberation), humans are covering the ground with waterproof materials, hindering water absorption and resulting in its quick accumulation in already dirty and clogged pipes. Indiscriminate logging to make room for animal grazing generates soil erosion, hyper urbanization often results in channeling rivers and construction of cheap dwellings. In the case of earthquakes, many human activities, like mining; geothermal drilling, gas and oil extraction; and injection of industrial liquid residues can trigger this type of catastrophes. Remember that the planet is a living being and it keeps being injured, it is in pain! The main culprit, however, is animal consumption because animal farming causes most of the greenhouse gases that disrupt the climate.[12]"

"Can disasters be avoided?"

---

[12] Steinfeld, Henning et al. *Livestock's Long Shadow: Environmental Issues and Options.* Rome: Food and Agriculture Organization of the United Nations, 2006.

"They can, but only if people change. The best and fastest solution is to adopt a vegan organic diet; if the entire world became vegan, global warming would stop and an atmosphere of peace and love would reign. The karma of killing would cease and with it the suffering of animals and humans alike.[13] A famous vegetarian, Einstein, said, 'Nothing will benefit health or increase chances of survival on Earth as the evolution to a vegetarian diet.'" My guru continued,

"Earth always provided for all its inhabitants, but what do they give her in return? There are fundamental factors which people urgently need to address: the majority of humans vibrate at a low frequency; the negativity of the entire world's population is too heavy and it densifies attracting undesirable consequences for them. Everything is energy, including thoughts, scientists have recognized this. Negative thoughts create negative words, behaviors and habits. Unfortunately, most people don't believe those manifest tangible consequences, but it is the universal law of cause and effect: as you sow, you will reap. It also applies to thinking. This is reflected in both the individual and the planet's health. Too many persons lead a life void of love and compassion, but full of violence, hate, envy and criticism, which lowers the vibrational frequency, contaminating their surroundings with this kind of energy. Physicians have associated these traits to health problems. Simply because nobody has yet proved in a laboratory that a world catastrophe can be the result of the collective negativity of the population, it

[13] *Supreme Master Television* | suprememastertv.com

does not mean that it is not happening now. Humanity needs to wake up!"

I thought of the dogs, cats, horses, birds, trees, plants and all other creatures entangled in the collective karma. I feel particularly sorry for the animal and vegetal kingdom, which are innocent victims of all this. At least I know they go straight to Heaven.

"You do a wonderful service for humanity with the preparations to receive their souls, like when humans prepare to receive a newborn child. I wish they knew it!" I declared.

"Some of them do," he said plainly. "Is this why you wanted to see me?" inquired my guru.

"Well, I don't want to bother you with my curiosity. I came to ask you some questions… they are too trivial…"

"Alma, it is okay. You are here to learn. Though the answers are inside you. You need to get enlightened. I think that pretty soon the Sovereign Master will be giving initiation to those who are ready… and you are first in line! In the meantime, meditate and enjoy. What would you like to know?"

"Are you familiar with the Hanal Pixán celebration in Mexico? I would like to see what happens at the spiritual level. They say the souls of loved ones return to be with their relatives, still incarnated, on a specific date once a year. I think it is good for humans to remember that there is life after life."

"Say no more, go ahead!"

Unsuspectedly, I set myself up for an unforgettable surprise, one which would mark the end of my current phase of existence in the least expected way.

Looking at the cemetery full of life with people festively dressed, smelling the aroma from appetizing foods and altars with copal and hearing the traditional music, made me want to show up even though I did not have my own grave.

Instead of simply opening a "window" to peek, I actually (with the help of my guru who constantly traveled between dimensions to assist his disciples) witnessed the event with my astral body, which is the kind of body that certain humans detect as ghosts. This way I would get the same experience of a returning departed.

A parade started at night with about 50,000 people. Some were singing, others were praying. Some families had spent all day in the cemetery "visiting their relatives" (or at least their tombs). As the night grew deeper, the temperature dropped and only the candle lights illuminated the persisting individuals who, very devotedly, talked to their loved ones and asked for help.

Not all the graves received the souls of the mortal remains they hosted. A number of graves received none; I supposed those death beings had already gone to other planes or were reincarnated. Several had souls that did not belong to the buried remains but decided to visit the vacant tombs to join the party (I think they are appropriately referred to as "hungry ghosts" by the Buddhists). Very few graves welcomed their genuine souls, in whose case they had recently passed and were still attached to their relatives, but unable to intercede for them in their mortal tribulations.

I remembered Sugar and looked inside, trying to discover where his human "daddy" was. I found him on a lower Heaven, enjoying his vacation. Briefly, I told him that Sugar, his cockatoo, loved him and still thought of him. He smiled and thanked me for the message. While at this, I searched for the soul of Amalia's baby but got the image of an empty womb. The soul had not yet descended to occupy its body when she lost it. I wished to tell her she did not need to mourn anymore.

It was getting late. I saw a family of Mayan lineage finish praying in their native language for the peace of their loved one getting ready to head home. Two spirits joined them as they walked past the exit of the graveyard and followed them to their dwelling. Other people also "picked up" entities floating around on their way out, either because the soul liked their light or because it had some affinity with them: they enjoyed drinking or smoking and being close to them provided them some satisfaction.

Unexpectedly, a thunder and a flash. The firmament opened from a crevice which gradually grew in diameter. The tiny stars that twinkled timidly in the distance started spiraling and forming a cone shape with increasing speed, like a black hole with wide and intense blue, yellow, orange, purple, pink, gold and green colors around it. A white refulgence from the inner ring appeared to come from behind like a silver tail of cosmic powder. I was hypnotized by its magnificence, when abruptly, the cone inverted and another beam of light emerged from its center. I glanced inside, the mass yielding to my will, opened like an immense tunnel leading to an infinite bottom as if a galaxy had gobbled all that existed there. I lost touch with my surroundings and magically, I became the sole spectator of a formidable view of the creation of a new universe or portal to one.

Emerging from its iridescent core, I saw a human figure leaving a body on a flattened surface flanked by three beautiful guardian angels in mid-air. From above, the benevolent face of the Sovereign Master, accompanied by Max, a man with a mustache and a pretty woman "a doll," also became visible. Then, I felt a sudden but gentle push, as a gulp by the divine breath of the Master summoning me from my witness stand while miraculously transporting me towards them. I sensed their loving eyes acknowledging my presence. When I noticed that I had to look up to see theirs, I realized I was transformed into my former image of Canela, young and cute. Then I was lifted up to their eye level and heard a celestial choir singing melodiously with a heavenly orchestra with the finest instruments and purest sound, the kind of music only God can inspire. I was elated. There was the expectation and joy of a prize being awarded to a contest champion. Master said to the being flying softly towards us,

"Dear Ceci, welcome Home!"

Part VII

Beyond the Universe

We Are One

The tension could be cut with a knife, the preoccupation of the anesthetist grew alarmingly when he first noted, towards the end of the procedure, an abrupt drop in oxygen and pulse of the patient. Just as the doctor was finishing up and about to call it a day. How unexpected! The clock was ticking. The surgeon tried to remember anything she could have missed… protocols, interview, pre-operative check-ups... nothing seemed out of the ordinary; another routine cholecystectomy to remove the gallstones blocking the bile duct. She had done it hundreds of times.

The surgeon looked at the screens above the operating table, then at the anesthetist, who was following the brain activity in another monitor, whose numbers were descending (the lower the number, the deeper the anesthesia), getting dangerously close to a state of coma…

Beep… beep…. beeeeep! Machines and medical personnel in high pursuit tried to regain the stability of the patient. Cardiac arrest!

"Prepare to resuscitate!" called the firm voice of the doctor; this was a rare threatening complication of her career.

"An embolism or a heart attack," thought the anesthetist, who could not believe his eyes.

An assistant removed the endotracheal intubation used for the general anesthesia and a vigorous massage was applied by a small thin nurse, on top of a bench facing the operating table. A command:

"200 Joules!"

Another massage. Another 200 joules. More massages. Exhausted, a replacement took over. The patient remained immutable, her countenance, in contrast with the doctor's, placid, almost smiling.

"300 Joules!"

Protocol indicated 40 minutes of strenuous labor to try to bring back the person. They performed it for an hour… there was no use… against all odds, she was gone!

With the same joyfulness and exhilaration her mother experienced when giving birth to Cecilia, she was with her on the other side, with open arms ready to receive her anew with infinite love and tenderness. Better than ever, looking young and radiant, unable to verbalize their delight, they embraced and kissed each other over and over. Cecilia awaited everyday of her life to see her again! Her father, whom the Master had temporarily lifted from a lower plane of consciousness to welcome his eldest daughter to Heaven, had chosen not to reincarnate and become his disciple in the spiritual path. Max, on the other hand, had already advanced to the highest level, where Enlightened Masters reside, expressed his satisfaction to having this family (including me) together at last. I knew what he meant. The concept of family immediately widens once one realizes of the many families one had throughout the incarnations, at the end, we are all siblings. Cecilia thanked the Master for reuniting us, forever if we so chose.

It was a glorious moment!

Cecilia looked at me and miraculously she confirmed her suspicions of being more to me than a dog. Instinctively, I shed my ethereal body and let her see through my Alma. We talked without words, it was beautiful! She realized I could have been her physical human daughter... but she preferred to avoid getting pregnant not only because she considered it impossible to guarantee that any child of hers would grow up healthy and happy; the mere thought of what would happen to her offspring if the child became an orphan was enough not to allow it. Besides, she saw no need to bring more children to the illusory world. Her own experience with a broken family and witnessing the suffering of her parents was enough for her. She kept apologizing, but it was in vain, I was immensely thankful to her for having selected me as her adopted "dogther" and for all her love.

"Remember you telling me, 'Canela, don't ever get a human body'? That was not truly my intention. You made my life worth living. Now, thanks to the Sovereign Master and to you we are finally free!"

Naturally, Cecilia wanted to know about the people and the animals who remained on Earth. Her adored companion, Bernard, was of course, shocked as everyone else about the outcome of the surgery. He told Olga over the phone when she called to ask how everything went, of unexpected complications and therefore they were not going to be able to make the trip. Olga, who coincidentally started to feel uneasy by the time the procedure started, had talked to her sister the same morning and concurred how they were going to have a wonderful time in Mérida and pointed out that she would pick her and Bernard up from the airport with Amalia.

Her conversation with Bernard worried Olga so much, she mentioned changing her ticket to be at their side. When Bernard did not oppose, she feared the worst, but she was too afraid to ask. She arrived before midnight. Cecilia was still at the hospital, an autopsy had to be done, but she was able to see her.

Bernard was holding on stoically, for now. He was very busy signing documents, texting and calling people, filling out papers, making arrangements, talking to medical personnel and acted rather mechanically. He had to do what he had to do. It wasn't until the funeral when the weight of the loss hit everyone, and Bernard was devastated, but with the support of Olga, his friends and the animals, he moved on; he had no choice.

Following her sister's wishes, Olga put Cecilia's ashes in the same urn with their mother and scattered them together in the Caribbean Sea, which Cecilia considered would have pleased their mom. To support the good work for humans, animals and the environment, Cecilia set aside money for several charities to become available after her beloved husband's demise. The house and the organic vegetable garden would become a vegan food kitchen for the disadvantaged.

During this time, Bernard had reflected on many aspects of his life with his wife, whom he cherished with all his heart. He remembered when they met back in Africa and how they transformed and enriched each other's lives. He thanked God for allowing him to share his existence with hers, unbeknownst that in the distant past such had been his very wish.

More than once, Cecilia had explained to him incidents when people, whilst briefly, experience how glorious the heavenly abode is, they stop clinging to this life as before and actually may be content to know their loved ones are enjoying true bliss and peace. She knew, due to her spiritual practice, that the only thing to fear was ignorance. She told Bernard that if she departed first, he should be happy for her and trust her Master would take care of him too. Bernard possessed an open and positive disposition and easily accepted everything which offered hope and welfare, so he sympathized with the Master and even expressed to his wife, "Tell your Master to take me with you, wherever you go, okay?" It was now a matter of time.

Olga was the most familiar with her sister's practice, and although she did not share her beliefs, she considered they helped her if not to die, at least to live. She consoled herself thinking this would be the closest to what she would have wished: dying fast and painlessly, leaving no dependents or outstanding issues (rancor, hate, worry or guilt). Olga remembered how much she missed their parents, Max, Canela, and all the other relatives and friends who went ahead of her. After Max's accident, her older sister conveyed that she would have preferred departing together. Ceci's words echoed in her head, "... this is the only good thing about accidents: entire families entering Heaven at the same time, what could be better than that?" But then, she would have never met Bernard and fulfilled her dreams… There was no logical explanation for her demise. To Olga, life was but a bunch of random events, good and bad; therefore, she learned to accept whatever came with resignation. Luckily, her network of friends and her wish to carry on Cecilia's service on behalf of the animals and the orphan kids kept her busy enough not to dwell on her pain. Within months, the owner of the art gallery where Cecilia used to exhibit her paintings became Olga's boyfriend. Bernard took refuge in his work.

Their "adopted children" knew about Cecilia's transition before anyone else. The day of the surgery Cecilia kissed all her pets as usual, but the feline wanted to accompany her. "Sorry cutie, but kitty cats are not allowed in the hospital. You would not like it anyway. I leave you in charge of the order of the house, deal?" The dogs, the cat and the bird all received messages from Ceci letting them know she went to Heaven, but they might communicate with her if they wished, as she was not abandoning them and to please help daddy and aunt Olga feel better and to be obedient.

Their patients and rescued animal friends were told they had "a direct line to Heaven" as the Master once said, and that he would help them heal and find a suitable home. Their human caretakers were not so adept in using this special "phone" and they had to be patient with them.

It did not take long for everyone to finally ascend. One by one, all souls awoke from their dream and returned to Heaven. As the poet and dramatist Calderón de la Barca wisely wrote:

"What is life? a tale is told;
What is life? a frenzy extreme,
A shadow of things that seem;
And the greatest good is but small,
That all life is a dream to all,
And that dreams themselves are a dream."

Some sleep longer than others, but at the end all will reunite and be one with God, the Source or whatever the name.

This sums up what I learned but, how did I arrive to this conclusion?

Enlightenment! The answer to all questions.

I had been studying Sri Bawarta Laji's teachings constantly until I was accepted for initiation imparted by the Sovereign Master, to continue my evolution towards the Source. At this point I had progressed to the upper levels of consciousness where karma has no reach. I gave thanks to my guru and headed for something which resembled a terrestrial mosque, an open space with an astonishing view of the breathtaking cosmos above. Max welcomed me from his post "guarding" the entrance, flanked by two golden columns, where the ceremony was going to take place. My beloved Ceci also accompanied me, the area was replete with spiritual beings yearning to know more of God. It was hard to believe that there existed something superior to the current level, a type of heavenly dimension which no ordinary beings attained on their own. After death, most people (if they were good) go to the astral or other realms and never imagine there could be anything higher.

From then on, the Sovereign Master took me under his wings. I could see Sri Bawarta Laji if I wanted, but now, having the most powerful guru in the universe, capable of taking me to the highest Heaven, there was no reason to continue being his disciple. It is like acquiring a more knowledgeable teacher once one advances to the next school grade.

The initiation itself is instantaneous and can only be given by an Enlightened Master. It is conducted in silence. A way to describe it is as if the Master activates a sort of internal button turning on the light and gradually, the soul remembers more and more of its real nature. Each one possesses the ability to connect with God, but we have forgotten how. It is like if the electrical current or vibrational frequency from God was severed, and each individual were an electric bulb unable to receive the electricity until it was re-connected by the Master's hand. This current is one and the same for all bulbs, no matter the size, color or shape. The problem is that we identify too much with the bulb, while the current is identical for everyone and it is our real self. We are not the bulb, we are the electricity (sound and vibration) and this is how we are all equal and one with the Source.

On Earth humans need to meditate to quiet the mind because when we pray we talk and talk and do not allow the answers to come. Then, first we should purify the vessel to receive the pure and high-quality teachings; a body which does not consume meat is better suited for the task. Also, the mind should be cleansed by observing positive and noble words, thoughts and actions. This is the reason for the precepts or commandments the religions mention. They consist of simple rules to live better and not harm others, "treat others as you wish to be treated."

A plant-based diet is prescribed because it has the lowest level of consciousness of all sentient beings that humans can consume and the karma to eat it is lower and can be eliminated during meditation.

The key is the inner power connection brought about by an Enlightened Master. Otherwise, the meditation does not have the quality to receive the heavenly teachings (which by nature, cannot be spoken), and all efforts would be spent fighting to appease mind and body.

As the spiritual teachings cannot be expressed orally and are transmitted by the sound, God appears to the individual as light. In reality, the body is a prison, the bulb that manifests the soul. It is necessary to turn inwards to know ourselves. This is why the meditation a true Master teaches consists of two parts: the inner light and sound. It is how the individual finds the Tao, or Kingdom of God within. It is the way to find responses to all of our questions and become wise. Enlightenment means to have light, to know oneself and to be consciously connected with God. It is a gift from him and cannot be earned by virtues or deeds. Anybody can and will be enlightened. The only way to stop the illusion is to realize that we are in all beings.

A means to verify the mirage the world really is, is understanding how other creatures who do not share the same five senses of human beings, or have developed them in different forms, perceive it. For instance, insects have a very fast vision, which allows them to escape quickly from some predators; bats orient themselves using echolocation (emission of sound and reception of echo); other animals, like reptiles, see infrared radiation. Colors in reality do not exist. What we distinguish is the image the brain creates when there is light (there are no colors in darkness) of different wavelengths corresponding to each color. It is our interpretation of how objects absorb or reflect those wavelengths what we call color. Each creature senses the world in a singular way. If we extrapolate this concept, we will realize that everything we perceive with the five physical senses is not what we believe.

It was nice to directly confirm the teachings from my guru, to have proof of his words. Before the end of my journey I was able to validate that God is the source of all, where everything which ever existed came from and where everything will finally return and like him, we are made of vibration, the great creative force of the cosmos. The Master is already one with the Source and can help human beings as long as he is in the world. He takes his disciples to the higher dimensions of consciousness, but in order to take their karma, he must still live in the world. The continued overpopulation and suffering of people prove that just believing in departed Masters (regardless of religion) is not enough. Once gone, they assume other missions and what is left are empty teachings, "theory." The Masters of the past have parted to new spheres of the universe and are helping other beings there. Nevertheless, God always sends Masters down to Earth for the sincere seekers of the truth and to whomever is ready to hear his message.

The incarnated Master saves his current disciples because they are under the same vibrational frequency of the planet at that moment and can take their karma or "pay for their sins" so they can progress. He only leaves the karma of the present life, otherwise they would die instantly: no karma, no anchor to the physical plane. However, if he or his disciple dies, the Master will continue to guide her until she reaches the highest abode. The commitment of the Master extends beyond the disciple's physical life, but when the Master abandons this plane, the power that accompanied him leaves, only the records of his oral teachings remaining, which lack the liberation power. It makes sense: if the Masters of the past could "cleanse forthcoming sins" of future disciples, the whole world would have been saved already (by Jesus, Krishna or Buddha, to name a few).

The teachings alone are helpful for the intellect but do little for the soul. It is like describing a caramel. We can read entire books describing what a caramel is, what it looks like, how it is made, how it tastes, etcetera. We may spend all our time and effort talking about the caramel, but unless we actually eat it ourselves, we really don't know. Like most invisible things in the world: love, joy, sadness, we need to taste to know what they are. The spiritual practice is the caramel. The oral instruction is for the inquiring mind anxious to know. During initiation a true Master lets us try the caramel and from then on, we will be capable of experiencing a taste each time we are in Samadhi, Nirvana, or the Kingdom of God. Then, we will truly understand the meaning of the scriptures and sacred books of every religion, since we will interpret them under an enlightened state.

In the world, the Master requires his physical body to pay the debts of his followers. He may get sick, be prosecuted and suffer physically, mentally and emotionally due to the wrong deeds of his disciples. Such is the universe, and the Master knows its laws: he is a consummate scientist.

Since Newton's era, the laws of movement ruling the physical universe have been recognized. We also know the bodies are masses and masses are compounded of particles which at the same time, are energy. The energy of thoughts and feelings set forth is going to obey these laws and we cannot avoid it. Under the first law, a moving body continues its motion unless a net force is applied on it. Therefore, when we place energies in movement, it should not be surprising that they behave the same way.

The third law indicates that all action triggers a reaction of equal magnitude and opposite direction back to the first object. If the energy we generated was of compassion, it is to be expected to return to us as compassion. Moreover, by the famous law of gravity, all objects attract each other with a force directly proportional to the product of their masses, which we know is energy. From here we should ponder what kind of energies we want to attract. Recently, the knowledge of quantum physics is permitting human beings to understand how the world of the invisible operates and, in some ways, explain the spiritual phenomena in this level of existence. There is already someone who has even calculated the "weight" in grams of a soul!

We constantly move energies, which come back like a boomerang to whom released them. Therefore, it is necessary to be very careful not to release energies of fear, anger, hate, etc., since those will return sooner or later; it is the law. The law is neither good nor bad, nor fair or unfair, it does not judge, it simply acts. This is the law of the universe, and everyone must adhere to it; as in a country, not even the president is above the law. In this case, the Master is the force interjecting between the effect and the cause of whom released it, hence the energy befalls upon the Master instead of the disciple, freeing her of the karma. It is as if someone throws a sharp boomerang on an open field. Then, the Master appears and intercepts the boomerang before it injures the disciple but wounding him. It seems too cruel to demand the sacrifice of a pure, living Master to save the beings in the physical plane, and that the Master is a victim of the disciples. Yet, he volunteered for this job and he agreed beforehand to obey the laws of the physical world to be able to free them.

There are many things which appear unnecessarily cruel in the world and I always complained that, as humans, we were incessantly cheated by the negative force and no matter how much we tried, we always lose. We cannot remember the lessons learned in previous lives, the illusion of the lower worlds is extremely strong and, unless a loving and innocent hero comes to rescue us from evil through his infinite, unconditional love and sacrifice, we could never be liberated and return to God.

Happily, there is the Law of Love, which supersedes all the other laws governing the universe because it is God in action.

If human beings are capable of forgiving, it is logical to think that, despite karma, someone with greater authority, who is beyond the laws of the physical universe, can get us out of the karmic mess in which we ourselves have been caught up into. The same way a ruler can grant pardon to a convict of capital punishment, moved by love, God, who is pure love, intercedes when we allow it. God, so to speak, splinters himself in the Master, who comes to save us. In some instances, the Master shields his disciples from some impending consequence of their acts, suffering the bulk of the karma himself, allowing only a small "fine" for the disciples to pay, as when a human judge lowers the sentence of a criminal under certain circumstances. Or he may, benevolently, let them suffer a very painful effect through a vivid dream, instead of in the flesh. Such is the love and protection the Master provides to assist his disciples in their spiritual journey.

So, our mind plays tricks on us. God forgives everything, but we are our own judge and the hardest thing is to forgive ourselves. The day of last judgement is when we abandon the physical realm and analyze our own actions. No one else is there to accuse us, it is us and our bare consciousness, that in such state is free from mental disorders and clear from the misconceptions with which we conducted our lives. This allows us to objectively see what we did right and wrong and seek a "corrective measure" which we also devise ourselves. God would not be so harsh with us as we are. He does not feel offended nor is he revengeful. He is all love and forgiveness.

The worst is when we do something detrimental to a person who did not deserve it or vice versa. Although karma governs most situations in the lower worlds, we can be the recipients of the corrupt free will of others. Such could be the case of a person that is, for instance, attacked by a random individual, possibly by someone the victim did not even know from a previous life. This is because evil exists, and it gets hold of a weak individual not highly spiritual or with few virtues and who does not follow a proper behavior or way of thinking.

We believe the world should be just and virtuous, but human beings have a longing for freedom and justice based on their individuality. Consequently, we will never be completely happy, regardless of wealth, fame or power. Once achieved, without a higher consciousness (which would not seek any of these), after the initial thrill, we will find ourselves unhappy. Nothing will satisfy us, we will want more.

Many advanced civilizations have gone to conquer other galaxies but, even if they could rule over the whole universe, happiness will be fleeting. We should go higher and more inwardly, beyond the physical realms to be one with the Source. Until then, we won't know what true bliss is.

We are all siblings, we are one with the animals, the plants, the mountains, the seas, the stars and the entire creation. Whatever harm we do to others we also do to ourselves. It is as simple as that!

Collectively, as Cecilia's father once told her, "Together, we know all, but among all." For the puzzle of the universe will not be complete until everyone, every being ever created, is reunited in harmony with the rest.

Altogether we'll come back to God at the end, without exception. We will end up evolving until unifying. It is only a matter of time and how we want to accomplish it.

My guru had explained that when Earth was formed, there were no living beings on it, for it took a long time for the planet to become inhabitable. As soon as Earth was ready to harbor life, beings from more developed worlds "seeded" it with creatures they brought from other planets, starting with the introduction of unicellular microorganisms, later dinosaurs and other animals which were gradually more evolved. Those capable of adapting to the changing conditions of the planet, survived. I have learned that in the beginning, animals did not eat or sexually reproduce. Those were modifications executed later by the beings who brought life to Earth in order to avoid having to replace them constantly upon death and to design specific foods for each one. Giving them the impulse to reproduce and to eat each other seemed easier. The violence started precisely when the need to eat and the urge for sex became part of the DNA, which triggered wars. Since then, multiple experiments have been taking place culminating with the development of the human race, granting it with free will. Likewise, open and direct interference from superior spheres of the universe was prohibited.

Human beings have devised several theories about the origin of mankind and they all have their own merits. Many cultures state that after numerous attempts, humanity was established thanks to the intervention of beings descending from the sky as related in their ancient scriptures (which are considered legends in the modern era). The life forms which populate the planet were animated with souls coming from superior realms (our true Home) but the physical bodies are a combination of Earth's species and genetic engineering performed by other physical beings from more scientifically advanced planets whose consciousness levels are not as high. Before the current civilization, Earth had housed far more advanced civilizations, such as those of Atlantis and Lemuria, which perished due to their ignorant behavior (the same happened to Mars and Venus). When a great deal of scientific and technological knowledge is attained but does not match their own spiritual development, it is like playing with fire. Because something can be done does not mean it should be done. It is very dangerous when a civilization where not everyone has the same high spiritual level, acquires skills and tools which (although initially intended for beneficial purposes) can be used to do harm. Also, it is not science fiction that artificial intelligence could turn against its makers, it is history. Lacking the wisdom to utilize their knowledge for the good of all, those civilizations succumbed to their own greed, selfishness, and negative forces and became extinct and virtually forgotten.

Furthermore, Earth has been visited since its inception from a variety of aliens. There are innumerable worlds full of life and some of their beings have intervened (without the earthlings' consent) throughout history to design and enslave creatures for their own benefit. The problem arises when people make them their gods.

Not all extraterrestrials are benevolent or spiritually advanced. Evil can take the form of extraterrestrials.

Some want to keep experimenting and improve their own races with advanced genetic engineering and others, of a superior spiritual development, wish to free its dwellers from their yoke.

From my current level of existence, I was able to see my beloved planet covered by some sort of shield or "electric fence," so to speak (there is no way to describe such technology yet), placed around the Earth to prevent the free transit of spiritual beings out of it. Some extraterrestrial totalitarian government has used Earth to exile unwanted elements from their civilization, to control the planet and its inhabitants physically and mentally by imprisoning them in different bodies. Many beings living on Earth come from diverse planets more scientifically and technologically advanced. They were sent there either because they opposed their regime's control or because they were rebels, free thinkers, revolutionaries, inventors, genius, artists (a few were criminals or perverts) hence, deemed too risky to keep on their original planets. (This explains the immense diversity among cultures, languages and belief systems which does not exist on other planets.) Once there, they do not allow their souls to be free or to remember where they came from. When they perish, they immediately capture their souls and later confine them in another body, perpetuating their exile. This ancient alien technology includes hidden traps that not only keeps them on the physical planet, but also forces them to reincarnate in the flesh of a person or an animal (for which they are doubly imprisoned) and erases their memory life after life, as when they die, a trap is activated which programs them to return to those traps each time and even orders them to forget again and again, to prevent them from knowing who they really are.[14] The souls cannot pass the low planes of consciousness where the instrument of karma obliges them to return.

Over time, failures of those machines have allowed certain souls to partially remember who they were and some of their past abilities, which accounts for their extraordinary talents and faculties. Much of the technology developing now on Earth is due to those people's awakened memories. Unfortunately, there are some individuals who feel uneasy and have a deep sense of not belonging facing problems adapting to life on this planet. Those whose memories of their former

---

[14] Spencer, Lawrence R. *Alien Interview.* United States of America: Self-published. 2008.

lives are coming back are exposed to ridicule or taken to be mentally unstable if they exteriorize their experiences.

Luckily, the Interplanetary Confederation reached an agreement to break this system. Recently, the machinery surrounding the planet has been dismantled with the help of the Gods, thanks to the intervention of the Sovereign Master.[15] At this stage of my own journey I get answers to all my questions and I was pleased to see that there is hope for the planet, because, besides the blessings of Enlightened Masters, there are other ascended beings helping raise the collective consciousness of Earth, not only from above, but literally, from inside.

Among the revelations which during my human life on Earth were considered fantasy, was the actual existence of highly developed creatures in the center of the planet. Long ago, the French author Jules Verne wrote a novel about what is at its core in his book, "A Journey to the Center of the Earth." These physical and spiritually superior individuals have been living under the Earth's crust, which is hollow and at the center contains a sun providing an adequate, comfortable and beautiful environment to thrive. They are tall, comely and can live very long. Some have made contact with receptive human beings through telepathic communications. They are getting ready to come out and help the planet on its ascension to a new era with all its inhabitants. They belong to the same human race but have evolved independently from those on the crust and are directly affected by their actions.

---

[15] *Supreme Master Television* | suprememastertv.com

Since Earth is part of the universe, its destruction would produce undesirable consequences on other planets and other galaxies. Human beings have developed technologies capable of destroying them, for which beings from other spiritually higher worlds are very interested in helping to prevent a catastrophe. Because they cannot interfere from outside, they interfere from within, in such a way that extra-terrestrials who have never being born on Earth have been incarnating there for decades. These "volunteers" are among the general population and have found it very difficult to remember their mission, since, when born, they forgot everything, as the rest of humans have. However, little by little they are awakening and are helping their brothers to develop and expand their consciousness to continue their evolution.

The secret space programs and the negotiations of countries with extraterrestrials will finally come out into the open and history will have to be re-written to correct all the deceptions and lies propagated to the masses. They will know about the suppression of free energies and scientific and technological advances, the fraud of the world bank system, the manipulation of food, communications, education, mass mental control programs and all types of coverups. Some worry humans won't be able to digest this information, so they are revealing it gradually, be it through physical means (audio and video transmitted electronically) or via receptive beings who transfer the knowledge by psychic channels and spread it to the public. Eventually, all will be known.

The change is occurring now. A cosmic era of 26,000 years ended in 2012. The Mayans called it the "time between" and it is a period in which the current paradigms are crumbling. "Natural" disasters will continue until the process is completed. Those are "cleansings" in which the souls will go and remain at their corresponding levels of consciousness. Consequently, there are constant world catastrophes and frequent rebellions against abusive and corrupt authorities.

Earth is increasing its vibration and shifting on its axis in order to ascend. Beings of low vibration will not tolerate the superior frequency of the planet and will not be able to stay. They will continue their evolution on less advanced planets and those who stay will pass from the third to the fourth and fifth dimension and will be in contact with other races of intelligent beings. Earth will change its position in the galaxy, as when it swapped its axis. In fact, in ancient times the axis of the planet was such that Antarctica had a moderate climate, vegetation and inhabitants.

Human beings should prepare and be happy for the events that will bring wellbeing, joy and positive changes. The emergence of movements for a variety of causes is already palpable: environmental defense, human and animal rights protection, even promotion of non-conventional spiritual (or metaphysical) practices be it meditation, reiki, yoga, charity, etc. There is a plethora of books, workshops, classes, seminars, radio programs, internet sites and movies aimed at awakening the human consciousness. Many human beings are being guided psychically and spiritually to help others elevate their conscience. Now they are going through a phase of purification after thousands of years of repression. There will be improvements in all aspects. Cosmic portals capable of changing the planet's vibration are opening, although not all realize it.

The planet will be reborn, the elements: water, earth and air will purify as well. The sun is sending pulses of energy like never before to assist in the evolution of Earth as being; it is a personal decision if the creatures which inhabit it evolve with her. The individuals will experience transformational waves by which it will become easier to eliminate their individual and collective negativity. They will be able to overcome their vices and adopt more loving behavioral changes, perform healings and recover and develop psychic powers that have been blocked.

A new human race will emerge able to realize their formerly inhibited abilities like telepathy, telekinesis, intuition and clairvoyance; therefore, no one will lie or act improperly. The world will renew itself and people will have time to spend in spiritual practice because they will no longer be oppressed by authoritarian governments or have the need to work to survive. Education will really be within everyone's reach and money will cease to be used. Nobody will lack anything.

Moreover, human DNA will evolve and self-repair, ending health problems. There will no longer be separate religions nor misinterpretations of doctrines or sacred texts because the wisdom to know God will come from within and the change of consciousness will unify all persons. There will be an open and positive communication with other civilizations. As all increase their vibration, people will refine their density until they will have no need to ingest food. Human beings will remember their divine origin, their past reincarnations, and will recover their befitting place as children of God.

The evolution of consciousness and the ascension phenomenon are predicted in sacred scriptures of the Hindus, the Zoroastrians, the Mayans, etc., and described by prophets. No one will be left behind. At the end, all will realize that we are one, this is the divine plan. These are exciting times to be incarnated on Earth and is one of the reasons it is closely being observed from inside and from outside and why many beings have descended at once on the planet. I am, nevertheless, very pleased to watch it from above.

Despite how wonderful Earth might become or that we could explore other extraordinary worlds, what concerns me is the evolution of the soul to the highest levels of consciousness, not to other material planes, which as technologically and scientifically developed as they may be, still belong to the lower levels of existence. Reincarnating on planets with superior technology has nothing to do with their spiritual progress. If they are within the material, as fine as the matter may be, they are still part of the low vibratory frequency dimensions and are governed by the rules explained before.

I want to jump, exist in the purity of God. I want to know what else is there for a soul who has reached the highest state of its creation, the top of the highest abode where a human soul can still exist. Will I be bored or curious again and wish to start experiencing more things? I hope not. Being wise and happy I have no more desires but to remain in the Source.

It will take millions of Earth years to ascend high enough to finally reach the source of my soul and return to my Creator. Yet, I had the privilege of being the Sovereign Master's disciple and knew that there was more. It is impossible to explain what it is like existing on this plane, but to put it in human terms, God splintered into individual manifestations to gain different experiences. Our universe is a shadow, an image of the real universe from the Almighty, The Original God who has always existed and is eternal. He resides in realms beyond those of the human soul where, unlike us, nothing was created because it just "is."

Since I was created, I could cease to exist. Still, if all there has always been is God, there is nowhere else to go back to, but to him. The realization of existing comes from an almost infinitesimal, but necessary amount of ego, which gives us individuality and allows us to form a being. If I lose my individuality, would I be reabsorbed by God and become, to put it in human terms, part of his body, like his hair or his skin?

There will be a point where the whole universe will stop expanding and start the inverse movement. The universe will contract itself by God's divine force and we will cease being. The big bang is nothing more than God's breathing where each time he exhales it creates new universes and each time he inhales it absorbs them.

A single breath of God forges and expands new universes and entire creations in what for us seems like an eternity. How awesome and infinite is God that all there is sprung from his sigh!... and he breathes endlessly and forever.

I remember wishing to be one with my Ceci and with Max, to be fused in their essence and become part of them. I did not want to get used to their absence because I knew I would see them again; and I did. How would this be different from being reabsorbed, dissolved within the "body" of God…? It can only be better.

www.ingramcontent.com/pod-product-compliance
Lightning Source LLC
LaVergne TN
LVHW010604100826
845148LV00014B/2842

9781733690010